TWISTED SAGA'S:

CRYSTAL EDITION

By

SHIZZIO & ANISH CHHANA

DEDICATIONS

'This book is dedicated to my darling beautiful, heaven-sent daughter, Jasmine. I hope this can inspire you to achieve greatness beyond your means...xxx. To my wife, Jade, my mother and father also. I love you all dearly...x'

- Shizzio

'I need desperately to thank my mum and dad who have never stopped loving me or supporting me. The lessons that you have taught me will always show me the light in the darkness.
Without you, all of my dreams would have remained just that - dreams.'

- Anish Chhana

CONTENTS

EPIGRAPH

'It has become appallingly obvious that our technology has exceeded our humanity.'

- Albert Einstein

THE GATHERING

When the aliens arrived in their spaceships, the world was in awe.

Huge shimmering disks, floating effortlessly through the air without making a sound. As wide as the Grand Canyon, these two massive objects halted air traffic across the globe and the planet went absolutely nuts. The media devoted almost its entirety to reporting this event; television, radio, newspapers, there was a mad scramble. Country leaders around the world told their citizens to '*keep calm and carry on*' until contact was made, while religious leaders told their followers that the jig was finally up and the world was ending, about to burn for eternity in hellfire.

It seemed as though the ships were scanning the surface as they initially moved around, crossing cities and mountains, deserts and towns, looking for something...or someone.

Until one day...they stopped.

The planet was expecting them to head to

Washington, Beijing or Moscow, maybe London or even Sydney at a stretch. Someplace where a leader of humanity could be contacted, to speak on behalf of the rest of the human race. It turned out that we were all wrong.

The magnificent vessels stopped in the most unlikely of places.

One perched above the middle of the Pacific Ocean, the other over the Atlantic Ocean.

They didn't give a shit about us humans. They were speaking with the dolphins.

And we were getting sold out…hard.

It seems so long ago now when they arrived.

The Wisps.

Named because of their ghostly, apparition-like appearance seen the sole moment they came onto our screens; a five second video feed transmitted worldwide showing one of the Wisps almost floating on air. They glide much like their ships do, while emitting a colourful glow from their centres. A strange ethereal sound humming in the background. It was a BBC reporter who had first coined the phrase which spread across the globe through social media, likening them to their namesake from mythology who was said to have led lost travellers out of marshes and swamps in the dead of night. Maybe they were here to do the same with us?

Almost a full month of July has passed. One

day shy, in fact. The furore and commotion dying down just as the action from the Wisps has. Almost the whole time that they have been here has been spent slowly traversing the oceans while emitting strange humming noises, indecipherable by man, although instantly recognisable by clubbers and ravers the world over as the ringing in your ears after spending the night dancing next to a loud, thumping speaker.

We simply wait for something to happen. Anything that can go some way to explain this strange, outrageous occurrence which has shattered the beliefs of millions, if not billions of people everywhere. Any kind of news would be helpful. It isn't as though we haven't tried to make some sort of contact. Ships have sailed beneath them, planes flown past them, helicopters hovered inches away, all the while attempting to communicate in every known method known to man; radio waves, spoken language, electronic language, code, art, music; all attempts tried in vain.

Why would they not want to make contact with us?

It is a question that has been discussed at length. Just doesn't make sense. The Wisps have obviously travelled unimaginable distances to reach us, yet spend their entire time here ignoring us. However, they seem to be creating quite a crowd amongst the fishes teeming beneath them wherever they go. Dolphins especially finding some sense of excitement; thousands of them swirl in the waters beneath the ships, chattering and squeaking with fervour. There is something going on here. A discussion that we aren't party to.

A knock at my front door and I'm standing face to chest (my face, his chest) with your typical special agent and his identical sidekick. Dressed smartly in black with dark sunglasses, even though it is the evening, and with a discreet ear-piece that looks at first glance like a clump of untrimmed ear-hair. These guys instantly put me on edge. I feel like closing the door but I don't think that the action will be successful. I'd probably be eating the door if I tried, and I've already had dinner.

Looking around, I can see more identical agents dotted up and down the street, trying to look inconspicuous but doing a terrible job of blending in here in Chatteris, a small quaint market village in Cambridgeshire, England. They stand out like Katie Price at the EuroVision Song Contest.

'Mr Aaron Reddy,' he states, having already identified me.

'…uh…yes, that's me,' I stutter, while the blood drains from my brain.

'I am here on urgent national business. We need to speak with you in private,' he tells me again. Asking politely obviously wasn't something taught at special agent school.

'Sure, sure, come in,' I say, leading them into the front room as the bones in my legs stop existing, turning them instantly to jelly. 'Please come and sit down.'

We sit opposite each other in my small living room while the sidekick stands by the door, looking around and examining his surroundings. Occasionally he speaks into his wrist. Either that or he kept wiping snot from his nose. Difficult to be sure of which.

'What is this all about?' I ask, feeling incredibly nervous.

'Before we begin,' the agent tells me, 'I must stress that any conversation that we have is strictly confidential. Not another soul can be told of anything that we speak of, otherwise there will be severe consequences. Is that clear?'

'Yes, yes. I understand. Now can you please tell me what the hell is going on?' I say, beginning to gather up some bravado in minuscule amounts, 'and can I see some identification?'

The agent looks at me for a few silent seconds, most likely imagining what sound my neck would make if he snapped it with his own bare fingers. Instead he reaches into his inside jacket pocket and pulls out a black wallet which he flips in my general direction. I make out the British Royal Insignia. My acceptance is apparently not needed as it returns instantly to where it came from.

'Well, Mr Reddy, I'm sure that you know about

The Wisps,' he begins, taking off his glasses to reveal small black beady eyes, 'and the early five second message that was broadcast by them shortly after they landed?'

'Yes, of course, everyone does. But what has that got to do with me?'

'We have recently managed to decipher the message,' the agent states clearly, leaving the words hanging in the air to sink into my feeble brain.

'...a message? There's a message? What message?' I ask, astounded at the revelation from the agent. He holds my gaze for a long while, letting the tension build up in the air. 'It appears that the Wisps were communicating the date and place of an event. An event that will allow first contact with the Wisps. However...with only one member of the human race...of their choosing.'

'Only one? So who did they go for? The Queen? The President of the US? Nigel Farage?' I chuckle to indicate that the last name was a little joke of mine. The agent looks at me with the stoniest of faces. Maybe he is a UKIP supporter.

'The name *is* known to us.'

'...right...okay...well? Are you going to tell me who it is or is it a secret?' God, this guy likes to drag things out.

The agent exchanges a brief look with the sidekick standing in the doorway.

'It is *you*, Mr Reddy. *You*...are the reason that we

are here today.'

'…hmmm…'

A tiny stream of urine is released from my body, darkening a patch of my jeans and dispersing a pungent aroma into the air. We both ignore it. Although his upper lip does twitch a couple of times. Maybe it's a medical condition he has.

The visual clip of the Wisps transmitted across the Earth contained an invitation for us to attend a Gathering.

Only one of us.

Me.

Aaron Reddy.

Twenty-eight year old Brit of such mixed heritage that my country of origin is most of them and with about as much importance to the world as Hilary Clinton is to fashion…or telling the truth.

There are still many questions that need answering but the progress made by the combined efforts of many of the world's secret services has been vast. While the general public has been left in the dark, a global project which easily dwarfs the infamous Manhattan Project has been set in motion to discover any and all information possibly available regarding the Wisps, their arrival and their true intentions.

Whereas much of the details accumulated by

the project have been fairly superficial, such as the description of the vehicles, of the Wisps themselves and possible routes of travel their vessels have made, a breakthrough has been made in another section.

That of linguistics.

The strange humming sounds heard in the background of the transmission were tested in a multitude of ways, soon to be declared as an alien language. A highly complex language that when slowed down to a tiny fraction of its normal speed, part of which closely resembled the language of present day marine animals. Dolphins and whales to be more precise. Why the message would contain marine language completely baffled the greatest minds across the planet. It just didn't make sense. Especially as there were thousands of human languages to choose from.

Marine biologists, linguists, specialists, scientists and many other experts in various marine careers combined to discern portions of the Wisps famous hum. When broken down and analysed, each section was found to contain incredibly intricate and compounded pieces of sound incorporating the full detectable range of pitch, wavelength, rhythm, frequency, tone, clicks and echo, all laid on top of one another.

None of this mish-mash of data was translatable by our scientists apart from one basic collections of tones that turned out to be a very simple universal method of communication, even known by children; Morse Code.

Less than a tenth of a percent of the total hum contained this code and it had contained a very simple message.

The details of The Gathering.

'How are you feeling?' Prime Minister Jeremy Corbyn asks me in the back of his specially protected vehicle as we make our way to Heathrow Airport. I am to be put on a private plane to an unknown destination and I have been given the chance to be escorted by the leader of our country, hopefully to glean a few helpful bits of advice.

'Like Jeff Goldblum in Independence Day, with the fate of the world in my hands,' I reply, thinking I am being humorous.

'So what's that like?' Prime Minister Corbyn asks, leaning forwards slightly, 'I haven't seen that movie.'

'Um...never mind, it doesn't matter. I'm actually really nervous. I mean, this is a huge deal. I'm going to be at the centre of the world's attention, absolutely everyone will be counting on me and to be perfectly honest, I'm crapping my pants.'

Prime Minister Corbyn is silent and considers a careful response; I can see the cogs in his mind turning as he appropriates the correct response.

Something to strengthen me, bring my confidence to the fore and calm my racing nerves. He places an arm on my shoulder, clears his throat.

'Look…Aaron, you're right, this is a huge deal,' Prime Minister Corbyn says to me with his soft, knowing voice. 'So, you'd better pull your head out of your arse, you little shit. You fuck this up and the entire planet's going to burn. That's not happening on my watch. I just got this job the other day and I like it. How those Wispy bastards managed to find you of all people to represent mankind, I'll never know! So, just do as you're told, listen to the instructions we give you through the ear-piece and don't be a wanker, alright son?'

Prime Minister Corbyn sits back in his seat, puffs his cheeks and looks out of the window mumbling to himself. I'm sure I don't want to know what he is saying; it doesn't appear to be too comforting, as nice as the Prime Minister is.

'Right…you're right, sir. That's okay, you can count on me?' I say, turning a normal statement into a question, my nervousness betraying me once again by lifting the pitch of my voice at the end of the sentence.

'Are you asking me or telling me Aaron?' Prime Minister Corbyn snaps.

'Asking…asking, sir.'

'What? You're asking *me* if I can count on you?'

'Telling…I mean, well politely letting you know…you know…that you can count on me, sir,' I splutter eloquently.

Prime Minister Corbyn looks at me in disbelief. 'We're fucked,' he says to himself and gazes again out of the window.

As I am journeying to the secret destination of The Gathering, I think back to the avalanche of information that has recently crushed me under its outrageous mass. Earlier on, I was sat in a generic government building. A room with no windows and bright fluorescent lights. The agent who came to collect me from my home, whose name I have discovered is Agent Jones, sat opposite me along with a large, fancy looking tablet. He began to explain the extent of the mess I was in. Along with the rest of the planet.

The Gathering was to be a meeting scheduled between the Wisps and a single representative of the human race.

It has already been established that that person was me.

But the fun part was that the Wisps' hum was assumed to have also sent thousands of similar messages threaded throughout the rest of the hum, none of which we could even begin to remotely understand.

Agent Jones showed me a graphical analysis of the hum on the tablet, it was awesome. Not awesome in the way that a Kardashian sister calls a pair of shoes, but awesome as in the power of the

Sun, or the size of the universe. It looked like nothing I had ever laid my inexperienced little eyes on ever before. There were multiple coloured strands representing the various sounds, all intertwining, curving and arching together, random movements and bumps constantly occurring with no way to make out a single pattern. That was just a five millisecond clip I was shown, so tangled and elaborate that even the most powerful computers on Earth couldn't make head nor tail of it.

As the scientists were failing, the game theorists came forward to provide possible scenarios and situations that may occur, explanations behind them along with possible outcomes. The potential instances were numerous, some fantastic, some silly, the odd one was reasonable. However, deciding on reasonable from human point of view wasn't hugely helpful. Either we were going to be befriended, killed or enslaved, with an outside chance of being bred on a mass scale as a tasty source of food.

Without being able to crack the code of the hum, we were lost. We would have to roll with the punches as they come, my face being one of the first in line to accept them. The only pieces of extra knowledge that could be given to me were that we were going to the western coast of southern Africa at a certain time and place tomorrow, and that I would wear an ear-piece even more discreet than Agent Jones' one, through which I would be told exactly what to say and do. The instructions would be based on what they could see through a camera contact lens I would wear and what they would hear through a microphone being implanted into my right earlobe.

To be honest, the whole operation appeared to be a bit gung-ho and reckless. But what could have been done better? The Wisps were completely ignoring us on our own planet. We had to stumble upon the details of The Gathering with huge global effort. They put us under immense pressure by choosing a nervous, inexperienced person to represent billions of people without the slightest explanation of why.

These *why* questions were killing every person involved in this project and around the globe.

It was going to be emotional.

Hours later, I am flying south from England where I take off via private plane. Soon, I have reached the southern section of Nigeria.

President Trump walks past where I am sitting and winks at me; gives me a thumbs up. I smile in return, unsure of how to behave. Air Force One is nice, very plush. It was good of President Trump to come and pick us up from Heathrow Airport. *Us*, being me and the boatload of British secret agents and advisers to the Prime Minister. I'm actually thankful that Prime Minister Corbyn decided against coming because of his personal issues with President Trump. To be truthful, he was getting me a little bit down.

We are heading towards the latitude and longitude coordinates as deciphered from the hum message. The coordinates weren't very specific. They missed off a couple of decimal points but everyone is sure that we'll be able to see what we are looking for when the time comes. We have hundreds of friendly agents already scouring the area.

President Trump walks back my way and drops his huge hulking frame in the seat opposite me. Deep into his second term as President of the United States after holding off yet another weak challenge by Hilary Clinton whose husband was caught on camera deeply committed in an orgy involving farmyard animals, Trump's weaning popularity has been given an almighty boost ever since the arrival of the Wisps. It may have all been different during election time if Hilary had remembered her microphone was still on after a live televised interview where an unscripted question was asked about her husband Bill's latest sex scandal. Hilary was heard all over the world berating her personal assistant backstage with the most acidic verbal violence ever heard from a politician. On top of that, learning Hilary was launching random objects at her staff in a rage, the public gave Trump the biggest one-sided victory in US history.

There is even talk of an unprecedented third term on the horizon. President Trump has once again captured the public's imagination since the apparent reluctance of the Wisps to make direct contact with humanity. The initial amazement, disbelief and excitement of their arrival quickly became subdued as nothing happened. With the public in this age suffering from shorter and shorter attention spans, the marvel of alien contact was soon forgotten. Something had to replace it.

Fear.

That awful word that is the beginning of much that is bad in the world. Just ask Anakin Skywalker.

Fear came along and gripped people like a vice. People were scared of these aliens. Scared of what they might do and of what they might have the ability to do (thanks, Ridley Scott). In the entire time that they were here, the ships stayed floating above the oceans, no need for refuelling, no need for exploring the surroundings for supplies, no need to speak with us here.

We inhabit this planet. We are Earthlings and we have been ignored.

And to humans, that also means offended. Insulted.

Then along comes President Trump, who has experience in tapping into the fears of his nation.

He listened to what they were saying. He understood why they were hurt and angry of this potential threat and why they were afraid of a possible invasion of their beloved nation.

He had a solution.

A solution which has garnered so much support for him that the people want to re-write the laws, the constitution. They want him to stay because of what he wants to do for the people.

President Trump has pledged to build a cage.

The Cage.

A humongous, all-encompassing and protecting cage to cover the entire country. No alien ship will be able to enter without permission. Americans will all be safe.

And the best part?

He will make the aliens pay for it.

'Aaron. How are you doing, my friend?' President Trump asks me, a big smile on his face.

I smile in return, not wanting to speak about my true feelings after the reaction that I had received from Prime Minister Corbyn.

'Look, I can see that you're nervous, son. Don't worry about it. Just do your best, put your best foot forward and know that you have the full support of everyone here. We are all behind you.' A sense of relief floods through me. President Trump comes across as pretty sensible away from the cameras. 'If anything goes wrong, we'll nuke the sons of bitches back to where they came from. Put on a firework show like it was the fourth of God-damned July!'

Maybe I thought too soon.

The speaker system sounds. A message from the pilot.

'Good day, this is your pilot speaking. We are fifteen minutes away from the location of The Gathering and beginning our descent to the Libreville Airport of Gabon. Please be on alert for further information. Thank you.'

Frantic commotion begins as people everywhere begin chattering and organising themselves. I'm put through various final checks to make sure the ear-piece, microphone and contact camera lens are working. I am outfitted in very smart clothing; a navy blue fitted suit, white shirt, baby blue tie, brown leather shoes, all as inoffensive as possible. President Trump looking on proudly at my transformation.

'You could pass as a baby Trump, son,' he tells me genuinely. I'm not sure whether to feel proud or scared.

Suddenly, the plasma screen turns on. It is a local news feed from the eastern coast of Gabon, pointing towards Corisco Bay. The news reporter is talking in French, and though a translator is being put to work to figure out what he is saying, everyone on the plane can work it out for themselves.

Resting on the waters of the Corisco Bay is an enormous, transparent crystalline structure in the shape of a dome. The size of a small city but completely empty. We can see straight through to the other side as though it is made of glass, with the small adjustments of light refraction.

'President, the reporter is saying that witnesses on the ground maintain that the dome has appeared out of thin air, miraculously transported here. No activity at all regards to transportation of the structure to this location,' the translator tells the President.

'Thank you. Stevens. Have our men on the ground advised of the location immediately. I want this thing surrounded with an army. No mistakes,' President Trump tells a suited gentleman who scurries away. 'Advise the UN, get everyone here and contact the EU President to see what their plans are. They've always got their fingers up each other's asses, tasting wine and eating olives. Get them spineless cowards moving,' he tells yet another man.

President Trump looks at me.

'Looks like you're up, son.'

I feel sweat build up on my forehead and have to sit down before gravity pulls me down anyway.

'Look,' someone cries out behind me.

I turn and see people huddling at the plane windows. Even President Trump is staring, silent for once. Mouth ajar.

I follow his gaze.

The news feed couldn't do the dome any justice. We can see it out of the side of the plane as we fly down the coast. The massive dome seems to be floating on the waters of the bay almost filling up the entire space. Glinting in the sunlight, it creates a silence in the plane. Nothing like this has ever been conceived of by anyone, ever. As tall as the highest skyscraper, it is a heavenly construct.

The location of The Gathering is made clear.

Two hours later I am stood on the edge of the bay, looking out towards the dome, flanked on all sides by special agents and army soldiers. The news crews have been ushered back a few miles away. Behind us are military personal assuming positions, ready for anything. Jets and helicopters are in the air, ships and submarines in the waters around the dome. World representatives in protected convoy nearby. President Trump safely in Air Force one, not allowed to enter the scene.

Nobody talks, we all wait.

The time of The Gathering from the message is mere seconds away, but still we have had no more communication from the Wisps. They are making us wait, making us sweat.

Oddly, I am feeling calm. Whatever awaits me, I am sure that my parents will protect me from whatever realm they now exist within. Being alone in life for the past five years has ground me down, often depressed me, not able to see the necessity of life. A life that is so cruel as to take my family away from me, along with my hope and any scrap of optimism that dare to dwell inside me. But here, as I stand in front of this magnificent piece of alien architecture, I feel surrounded by the souls of my loved ones. They are with me. I can feel them. Whatever happens from this moment on is meant to happen.

A crackle of thunder pierces the quiet, followed by a flash of light so bright, the entire horizon as far as the eye can see is lit up, blinding everyone. It fades and our vision returns. The two alien ships appear close together high above the dome. As we all look skyward, the ships emit a loud burst of noise.

The hum.

And I disappear.

I look around. I am astounded.

What is this place?

I seem to be standing on the inside of the glass dome. I can see the army personnel and agents through the glass on the edge of the coast who are all running around unaware of what happened. They are not able to see me for some reason, though I can see them clearly. My ear-piece crackles intermittently with static. I'm sure no information is being transmitted to them but I leave it in anyway.

Everything else is soon far from my mind while I take in my surroundings, the inside of the dome. From the outside it looked empty, but now that I am here, I can see that it is anything but. While I am standing on some kind of soft transparent flooring which runs around the outside of the dome, the central floor section is open to the water and full of sea life. There are all sorts of fish, whales, dolphins, sharks, jellyfish, eels, seals, hundreds of various types of animal. With a solid smaller central portion on the water also full of life.

Around the outer section, lounging casually, are hundreds of types of land animal; elephants, cows, cats, lizards, lions, bears, mice. Many I can't even identify. High above is some kind of latticed branch-like structure encapsulating the ceiling from the mid-section all around the edge of the dome. They look like tree branches although made of the same material as the rest of the dome and totally see through. Among these branches are contained masses of flying creatures, eagles, pigeons, bats, seagulls, vultures. I can even make out an owl on a branch near the side, scanning its surroundings with its large bright eyes.

Normally I would be afraid to be in and amongst this many animals with no barricade between us. But they aren't really doing anything. It looks like they are just waiting, hanging around.

You'd expect the lions to be trying to eat something, not relaxing as they are and close to taking a nap.

I'm very confused. This is some weird shit.

As if able to read my mind, a Wisp appears all of a sudden, floating in the middle of the space above the waters. The place erupts in sound, all of the animals seeming to cheer its materialisation, roars, chirps, growls, clicks, every animal sound you can imagine all combining to create an intriguing and inspiring music. I join in with my own clapping, an east London 'Oi, Oi,' also leaving my lips. Not the best way to greet alien life for the first time but the event has my blood pumping unexpectedly.

The Wisp itself is large, around ten feet tall, a ghostly translucent in appearance with features constantly changing and shifting. Its centre glows with a soft hue of alternating pastel shades, a head that is long and delicate, not a hair to be found anywhere on its body.

The Wisp floats down to the centre stage in the middle of the water, stands and hovers simultaneously. My eyes are transfixed.

A quiet descends, every animal silent and at attention.

The Wisp begins to speak its hum, loud and reverberating around the dome.

Then a funny thing happens. While I can continuously hear the hum, it fades into background noise and an English voice that sounds like my own voice in my head, comes to the forefront, overlapping the hum but coming from the hum. I understand this voice to be from the Wisp.

'Dear creatures of Earth,' it begins. 'Welcome to The Gathering.'

Looking around, I see all of the animals in the dome paying full attention to the Wisp. A glint of understanding entering their eyes as they also can comprehend the language of the alien which has been translated into their own tongues in their minds. It is fascinating to witness. Communication with the Wisp has captured the animals attention, elevated their being into a higher form, able to comprehend that which was previously beyond them.

One of the whales lets out a loud reverberating pulse to break the animal silence. As the noise rings out, it also fades into the background much like the Wisp hum a few moments ago, only to be overlapped by a more familiar voice.

'Welcome, and thank you for being here,' the sound cries out in my ears.

Amazing. It is the voice of the whale, translated for me and every other animal to hear in their own articulation for themselves. The animals all look around stunned that they can understand the whale speak. A second later the entire dome erupts in a cacophony of deafening animals cries, which again translate in my mind when I can discern a few words from a nearby gazelle and robin. Here inside the dome, all language is converted into the listener's mother tongue. A place for barriers to be broken down between species, a place for communication and understanding of one another. Already dogs turn to cats, sharks approach fish, eagles seek out rodents, all to say a few words of greeting, to experience an elevated level of consciousness. All of their real-world hierarchical food-chain relationships temporarily forgotten. This is astounding. And I am here, the lone representative of Earth to witness and be a part of this event of a millennia.

After a few patient minutes, the Wisp again speaks in its native hum.

'Dear friends, I am from a distant world, far, far away from this planet,' the translation begins in my mind. 'My people have a very old history, unlike the youth of this solar system. We have existed for hundreds of billions of years, close to the beginning of time itself.'

My mind has just been blown. But truth be told, I don't think that I have another level of surprise to ascend to. The Wisp continues.

'Throughout the ages, we have evolved much like the creatures of this planet have done so since the birth of Earth. We have pursued the advancements that are possible in the universe, across space and time, through what you call 'black holes' into different dimensions, through tears in the fabric of existence itself. Existence never ends, only transforms. One star dies, another is born. Two galaxies collide, another disintegrates. It is the way of life - birth and death. An everlasting cycle.'

All of the thousands of creatures under the dome and beneath the water are captivated, listening and absorbing every word the Wisp has to say. It seems their brain power is increasing with every passing moment.

'My race, if you can call us a race,' the Wisp hums, 'have travelled far and beyond, documenting, learning and understanding all there is to know. After billions of years, we only just have begun to grasp the meaning behind existence. And it begins with life. Life is the single rarest component that we have encountered in all of the various planes of reality, in all of the furthest galaxies and the multitudes of dimensions. Life is such a precious state that we have to travel many thousands of light years before we can even glimpse the beginnings, or end of another species. That is why we have visited you here, on Earth.'

The Wisp stays silent as the words begin to seep into all of our brains. We look around at each other and a sense of comprehension is being sprayed into the air, percolating slowly into all of us. The place that we have, not just here on Earth, but in this universe is unique. We all matter.

The Wisp floats around the inside of the dome, dispersing its aura to all animals and creatures, finally settling on the central platform on the water. All of the animals that are there surround the Wisp, edging as close as possible.

'Over our travels throughout space and time, we have come to discover certain truths. Truths which determine our actions, especially regarding any interference with civilisations. We have been monitoring Earth for a long period of time and your existence here on this fruitful planet is unfortunately not progressing in the manner that it should be. This is why a discussion between us all must be had. The natural equilibrium has been altered out of balance, and instead of correction, it is increasingly proceeding in the wrong direction. We have seen this occur before with fatal results.' The Wisp pauses and looks directly at me. 'We are here to discuss the role of *humankind* in the natural order of life on Earth.'

I feel myself inhale sharply, everyone's eyes upon me, scrutinising and angered.

'The human named Aaron Reddy. You will stand here in my place and speak with the creatures of the Earth. Everyone that is in here is representing their own species and has to speak as part of the collection of that species. With truth, honesty and integrity.'

The Wisp floats forwards onto the water in

front of the centre stage and in yet another flash I find myself standing there at the centre of attention of all creatures in the dome.

This doesn't bode well for humanity.

Looking out through the dome walls, I can see all of the military and agents on the shore, standing around aimlessly. They can't see that I'm in here with all of these animals but they must be coming up with some plans. Let's just hope that President Trump doesn't have final say on the next step.

Seeing me stare out of the glass, the Wisp begins proceedings.

'Dear friends, this human being here is called Aaron. We have chosen him to be here to represent his species, just as we have chosen all of you to represent your own species. The reason for these selections has to do with your own individual personal life journey and the lessons and knowledge that you yourselves have learnt along the way. Discuss your relationships with the human race. When all is said, Aaron, you will have your chance to respond in any way you see fit.'

I feel that this is going to be an uphill struggle.

'Who wishes to begin?' Wisp calls out.

There is silence. I'd expected there to be a rush but it appears that even animals feel stage fright. However before long, a lion with a lavish golden mane lets out a loud roar, which instantly translates into, 'I will begin.'

'Very well,' the Wisp says, 'When you are ready, Lion.'

The lion steps forward, a smaller lioness behind him giving a supporting nudge with her nose in encouragement. The lion truly is a regal animal. The long flowing hair framing the face like an elegant crown, its muscular physique clearly visible and pulsing with each movement. He steps to the edge of the platform and looks around.

'Fellow animals, some of you know my kind as predators. Seeking to kill you. We kill because that is how we have been created. We cannot graze vegetation for food, we need flesh to survive, and I make no apology for this. If we do not kill and eat, we starve, we die. If we do not need food to feed our young, others in our pride, than we do not hunt.' He pauses and looks directly at me. 'The humans, however, seek to kill us. This may at first seem fair, as we also kill others. But the humans kill us not to survive or for their protection, but for their pleasure and their enjoyment. They kill us and wear our skins, cut off our heads, take selfies and display them as trophies. They take pleasure in killing us, not with their bare hands, but with weapons from afar. Like cowards.'

The lion steps back amongst the animals as I feel shame at their treatment. I'm actually on the lion's side. I hate what happens to them, but if I have to speak for mankind, I'm going to have to defend ourselves.

As if my thoughts are being read, my ear-piece crackles into life, startling me.

'Aaron. Don't talk or respond to me in any way,' a male voice in my ear says calmly, 'we don't have any video feed, the contact lens isn't transmitting to us, but we can hear everything that is happening. When the time comes for you to speak, repeat our words exactly as we tell you. If you understand, cough once now.'

I cough quickly, holding up my fist to my mouth, just as a cow far off to my left is stepping forwards, getting ready to speak.

'Good Aaron,' the man says, 'now this is a fantastically strange situation, but we know that you are in the dome, so sit tight, we'll be in touch.' And with that the voice disappears. The Wisp shows no reaction of knowing I am under instruction and influence. So I turn my attention to the cow.

'My kind are gentle creatures,' the cow begins with a slow deep basal tone, 'we do not eat flesh, instead we graze upon grass. We are harmless, harming nobody, simply enjoying life with our families. But this way of life does not mean that we ourselves are not harmed. The humans use us and abuse us on a tremendous scale. They murder us for food, force-feeding us so we grow fat and provide more meat for them. They slice us, cut us to pieces and burn our flesh just so their bodies and stomachs will accept our meat. Then they sit together at tables and eat us, devour us, laughing and joking with one another, pretending that they are civilised and not genocidal maniacs. They dress themselves and their accessories in our skin, which they call leather. Our lives are reduced to that of a part of a machine. We are not even seen as a living creature anymore, just as product. However, the most psychopathic aspect of human behaviour is something humiliating. They line us females up all squashed together, attach pumps to our udders and steal our milk that is for our children, for our *babies*. Imagine if this was done to the female humans, made to spend their lives herded together and constantly pumped for milk from their breasts to be drunk by us or any other species. I'm sure this sounds disgusting to Aaron. But what is more disgusting? The act of mass pumping the milk from the breast of human women? Or the act of the human milk being drunk by a separate species of animal? A pig for example. If humans want milk, produce it yourselves and drink to your heart's content. Don't drink milk meant for calves, our children, our young.'

The cow finishes and the dome erupts in clamour of noise as animals shout in support of the cow's words. Hundreds of chirps, barks, growls, all sounding like British Parliament at Prime Minister's Question Time. This isn't going too well. I hope the guys in my ear are planning a good reply because humanity is looking really bad right now.

'We are creatures of the oceans. Oceans which are vast and deep,' booms a killer whale in the water which swims to the surface, 'everyday in the seas we group together with our families and swim for miles and miles. Humans like to take our young from us and trap us in tiny containers for their own entertainment. They don't care that we need our family, our mothers and fathers. They don't care that we have feelings, that we hurt, that we cry, that we become depressed. They feed us terrible food, but we must eat or we starve. You take away our power, our independence, the control over our own lives. We are proud animals, and you humiliate us by making us jump through hoops while you sit and stare, eating and laughing on your fat behinds. Would you stare and laugh at a prisoner in one of your jails? Make him do tricks so you can take pictures? You are a cruel psychopathic animal, human.'

The killer whale retreats back below the surface as animals all around me look as though they feel the killer whale's pain, as do I. Surely we can't be that terrible and destructive in our role with nature? There must be some animals that are glad of our existence.

As a pair of dogs walks forwards, my heart leaps. Man's best friend will turn the tide for us,

I'm sure of it.

'We dogs live a good life with human families,' a tiny Chihuahua says, 'they take us in their homes, feed us, look after us, sometimes even carry us around with them. Even when we are sick, we get taken to doctors who make us feel better.' Music to my ears, I knew the dogs would give us a boost.

The second dog, a pit-bull, interjects, yelping short clippy words. 'While I am happy for my fellow canine here, I personally, along with many other dogs, get caged up in small boxes. A couple of times every day, one of us is taken away and destroyed, not murdered, but destroyed. They call murder differently when they feel like it. We didn't have a home with a family, we used to roam around the streets minding our own business, but that wasn't allowed. They justify our murder by saying that they are cleaning up the streets for their society. A society which deems murder acceptable. I find this disgusting.'

Oh well, even the dogs dropped the ball. Man's best friend just stabbed man in the back. Even the guy on the other end of my ear-piece lets out a sigh of disappointment. With the canines giving us an average report, it is only going to be downhill from here, even more downhill than we have descended already. Species after species, creature after creature, speak about the cruelty, the sadism, the pride and arrogance of humanity. Fish, crabs, chicken, rhinos, rats, every type of animal tells their tales of interactions with humans from across the globe. Ray fish in aquariums, pigs in pens, monkeys behind bars, sheep being sheared, jellyfish carelessly caught in nets, birds slaughtered due to bird flu, ducks hunted for fun, horses used for racing, foxes chased and shredded by trained dogs, tropical fish on display in tanks and gulls covered in oil from leaks, the degradations upon the animal world were endless. They go on and on and on.

The man in my ear isn't any comfort. In fact, he is really getting on my nerves with his constant huffing and puffing at the negative comments from everyone, mumbling an 'unbelievable', or 'outrageous' every now and again. I must have been in the dome for hours, listening to all of the ways in which humanity has lost any sense of morals when dealing with any species apart from ours. The fact that I can directly understand these animals has made a huge impact on me. I have stopped seeing them as separate, unintelligent wild creatures and now appreciate that they are very much like us in every important way, whether emotional, mental or physical and all of the sub-categories that follow from there.

'There is a final speaker I would like to hear from,' the Wisp hums, 'dolphin, please come forward.'

Oh shit. I have seen the documentary, The Cove; this isn't going to be pretty.

A dolphin wades to the surface of the water and begins chattering a mixture of clicks, tones and echoes, all of which magically transform into a soft and delicate human voice.

'I am not going to speak of the cruelty of humans towards our kind,' the dolphin is saying surprisingly, 'we have heard enough of that subject from all of our friends here today, I am sure that another example is not needed. I want to tell you of an ancient dolphin proverb passed down from father to child over an immense amount of time, and impress upon you its meaning. The applications which may be of use here today. It says:

'As you seek more, the further you must venture; the further you venture, the more there is to seek.

'It can be understood in a number of various ways. You can use it as an encouragement, that there will always be new things to discover, so to continue working hard and moving forwards. You can use it to fathom the realisation that there will never be an end of that to discover, so to realise the futility of knowing all knowledge. Be content with what you have. You can use it as a warning to be heeded, that the more you want to discover and learn, the further you will find yourself from your origins, maybe to forget where you came from entirely. You can use it as a tool to satisfy some portion of your expectation, that as you venture further and further, you move not just in space and in time, but also in mind, and that the movement in mind from your beginnings can be the longest, most exciting or most treacherous journey you take.'

We all in the dome are somewhat dumbstruck by these words of the dolphin and their kind. He continues.

'What our kind prefers to take from this saying is that as we discover more of existence, we must always proceed whilst firmly rooted in our present and abiding in our true values. What it means to exist in the world. For us, this lends a great deal of weight to family, community, communication, kinship, empathy, humility, consideration and love for one another, whether dolphin or not. It seems that humans have lost much of the lessons from their true beginnings as they venture far and wide, seeking more and more. All that is shiny and new is not always good.'

The dolphin recedes underneath the waters as I try to fathom the meanings of its words.

'Thank you dolphin, you have been most helpful. Now comes the time for the human to speak on behalf of his people. What say you, human?' the Wisp says to me.

This is a tough act to follow; there has been negativity from almost every animal that has contact with us here on Earth. I take a deep breath as sorrow and regret floods over me after hearing the words of the creatures of the world.

'I um…well…,' I stumble, trying to get my words together, 'dear animals of the world. After hearing from all of you speak about the treatment at the hands of humans, I must say that I am feeling terrible…'

'*Shut up Aaron, you idiot…,*' screams the voice in my ear-piece, 'don't you dare apologise. Apologising means admitting fault which we are not doing. Stall for a second, we're almost ready with the response.'

'…uh…yes…um…what I mean is that I see what you are all feeling,' I stutter, trying to regain some composure, 'sorry, uh…just give me a moment please…I need to gather my…'

The Wisp regards me through its glowing orbits with a restlessness emerging from some of the animals. Thrown off-balance by the poorly timed interruption from the moron on the other end of the ear-piece, I take a few more deep breaths, as slowly and obvious as possible. It works. Just as my silence is becoming a little suspicious, he comes back on-line.

'Okay Aaron, we are ready. Now repeat after me word for word…creatures of the world…'

Okay, we are ready to go. The cavalry has finally arrived. I repeat his words.

'Creatures of the world, we humans understand your plight in this world. Especially at our hands. Please understand that we also have arrived at this place from a long arduous journey of pain and suffering. Our ancestors from long ago have frozen in the cold without knowing how to create fire. Died of thirst not knowing how to find water in a drought. Suffered from disease and sickness in population eradicating proportions. We have also been attacked and killed by many of the animals that are here today, sharks, big cats, bears, poisonous snakes and scorpions, among many others. But we have learnt the lessons taught by life and Mother Nature. We have learnt to create tools and weapons, medicines and drugs, language and communication, produce and commerce. We have learnt, grown and adapted.'

Okay, so this sounds pretty good so far. A good defence. I carry on repeating the words being fed to me.

'Over time and various innumerable tribulations, we have evolved and advanced, realising that it is primarily our intellect that has pushed us forwards through our time on this planet. We have identified problems and used thought to overcome. No longer are we at the bottom of the food chain. No longer do we starve. No longer do we need to depend on anyone else except for ourselves. By progressing to this point that we are in life, we have a position which is elevated above all else. Our minds have produced a culture and tradition for pushing the boundaries of science and technology. No longer are we considered animals or creatures. We are human beings. This places a value on our lives which is far above that which is applied to any other species. Simply put, we are better than everyone else here.'

And…I think we are beginning to lose the room.

'We have begun to reach into space and beyond, to the stars far, far away. The things that we learn will be to the benefit to all of humanity, and also filter down to every other creature that exists here. In fact, this has already begun. Canines have found homes in our homes. Primates have been taught sign language, able to communicate with us on a basic level. We have doctors who cater solely for the health of animals. We keep endangered species in captivity to ensure against their extinction, as well as keeping animals safe and protected in hundreds of zoos, fed daily and looked after. The continued evolution of man is coupled with benefit for all of the various species of the world. Hopefully, you will be able to realise that humanity is good for the planet and will continue to be in greater proportions in the future.'

The man in my ear stops talking and so do I. The dome is quiet, but the tension is palpable. Animals all staring at me after my words of defence for humanity. Looking outside the shore, tents have been set up. Probably housing the men in attendance as the edge of the coast is free of people.

The Wisp hovers forwards.

'Thank you, human, for your response. That concludes today's event. You will now all be returned from where you were collected from. I thank each and every one of you here today for your attendance and participation. As well as helping us in the task that we have undertaken, you can all take some of the lessons learnt here back to your own kind to help flourish in the future.'

The dome echoes as the creatures all call out; the translation has been ended so it sounds like nature once again. The loud din soon dies down and the Wisp responds by glowing a bright kaleidoscope of colours from its centre. In a bright, blinding flash of light, the dome has emptied of everyone...except me and the Wisp.

The Wisp comes close to me, looks at me and holds its palm out in front.

The contact lens is pulled off my eye by an invisible force, along with the ear-piece and microphone embedded in my lobe. They all fly into the water and sink down below.

I rub my ear though it didn't even hurt me.

'You knew,' I say.

'Yes. I was hoping that you would have been true to yourself and speak your own words.'

'I wanted to. I didn't really agree with what they were telling me to say,' I reply feeling embarrassed.

'Then why didn't you?'

'They are the people in charge of us normal everyday people. We have to do what they say.'

'Hmmm,' the Wisp pondered, 'that seems to be part of the problem. This hierarchy that exists with humans removes power of individual thought and action from the majority. The minority left with the power, use it in selfish ways that lead to the degradation of everything. It is this system that has been exacerbated and continues to do so with more and more vigour.'

That sounds like a fair explanation. Most people are good, it is just the few that are bad who ruin life for the rest of us. It's just that those few have way too much power, money and influence over the rest. The Wisp continues to hum.

'I have decided that something needs to be done. I will return you now to where you were collected from.'

With another flash of light I find myself standing on the shore from where I was taken, a multitude of people quickly surrounding me, examining me and leading me away. I glance out towards the water and the dome has disappeared, although the ships are still there, high up in the sky.

Was it all a dream? Did that all just happen?

Within moments I am interviewed and all of the information that I can remember is extracted from me. Again and again. Just as I think that they have had their fill of me, I am bundled into a car and driven away.

I'm sat in a large room. A huge oval desk dominates the middle with guards filling the spaces around the edges. The stillness of the air is fractured by a multitude of voices getting louder and louder from beyond the heavy door. It soon opens and in pours the most powerful group of people I have ever been in the presence of before. Heads of state of the great countries of the world come walking in and take seats at the table. Prime Minister Corbyn comes in and sits to my left.

'Well done, you arse-wipe,' he quietly tells me with a smirk.

'Oh...I uh...thanks...'

President Trump sits to my right, chatting happily with Russian President Putin next to him. There are leaders of France, Germany, Canada, Australia, India, China, and many more that are on the tip of my tongue but can't quite recall. I'm sure the Spanish leader is here somewhere, but who knows who that is?

Once everyone is seated, the chairperson, a stern faced woman with fancy glasses at the far end of the table greets everyone in the room and quickly gets down to business. She briefly outlines the events of The Gathering and everything that we know so far, hands out transcripts of everything said and heard through the microphone and my own central role in the meeting. President Trump slaps me on the shoulder in solidarity as my name pops into the conversation.

'We need to discuss possible forms of actions that we are able to take together if this becomes hostile,' the chairperson begins. 'Nothing so far has indicated that this will occur, but we have seen the power of their technology and...' She is interrupted by a young gentleman who whispers something in her ear. She listens very concernedly for a while before turning back to the room.

'Well it appears as though we have some more activity from our visitors,' she says as she turns to a projection screen behind her. The huge white screen is lit up as a video begins playing, showing a shaky clip of the dome from what looks like the edge of the coast where we were set up before The Gathering.

'This appears to be playing on every television channel across the world, as well as streaming live on multiple internet sites. The entire world is watching this. Who the hell was taking this video?' she asks no one in particular.

As the sound is switched on, voices are heard and I realise where this is from.

It is feed from the camera contact lens I was wearing, as well as the microphone.

The entire recording has been hijacked and is being played to the world.

'Madam...' I speak out as everyone turns to

me, 'this is from the video recording equipment that I was wearing outside the dome. But it malfunctioned once I was transported inside.'

Soon my last statement didn't make any sense at all. A flash of interference splashes throughout the clip and the sight that I was witness to inside the dome, the sight that has been so hard to verbalise is there on screen. Clear and plain as day.

Now around the world too, it seems.

Gasps and the odd expletive ring out around the room as they are all witness to the thousands of animals and creatures I was in the presence of, all calmly sat next to each other. I'm sure the expletive came from my left.

The leaders all sit in wonder, transfixed for hours as the clip goes on and on, showing everything that I saw, everything that I heard, even the animal and Wisp translations. My reply at the end is also broadcast along with the agent's voice in the ear-piece, telling me what to say. The clip ends when the Wisp approaches me and pulls out all of the devices, flinging them telepathically into the water. Static fills the screen for a moment, a grating screeching coming from the speakers.

Silence.

The picture turns to black.

Before anyone in the room can begin any kind of conversation or comment, a familiar humming noise spreads through the room. It becomes louder and louder. Pushing into our ears, making it less and less possible to hear anything else. The humming is familiar because it has last been heard from the Wisp, but this is different. It is more intense. More direct. As though formed into a singularity designed only for human ears, not to contain the languages for any other species.

The black screen morphs into a bright rainbow glow, fading after a few seconds to show the Wisp, this time not hidden away inside the dome but on display, transmitting to the entire world's human population. Only its head can be seen, shifting and long with a bulbous cranium. Large glowing eyes taking over the expressionless face, a red hue brewing in the centre, radiating outward.

The hum reduces in intensity as the sound softens. It takes on a pleasing tone which does nothing to eradicate the sense of uncertainty and fear we are all drowning in. The actions of the Wisps since their arrival here on Earth have been nothing in the way of mutually beneficial. On the contrary, we have been completely ignored, sidelined and treated as though we do not have any weight here on this planet of ours. And it is beginning to show on the faces around the room. Brows have scrunched up in irritation at yet another surprise about to be unfolded upon us all, knowing that they will have to deal with the fall out and answer collectively to billions.

The Wisp's hum repeats its trick of altering itself to the language of the listener, this time to the whole listening population everywhere.

'Human beings,' the Wisp begins, 'life is precious.'

A pause, before continuing. I'm guessing for dramatic effect.

'This is the central premise that nature and the universe require us to adhere and give central importance to. The statement does not discriminate. Or show favour. Or rationalise. It does not come with certain conditions only applicable in certain situations. It is simple, direct and straight-forward. Life is precious.

'Here on Earth, humans have changed that statement to become the central beneficiary. It is now said that human life is precious. Any other species is of less value. Why this has become the normal line of thinking is unclear as humans lag behind animals in almost every field. The canine has a superior smell sense. The whale is multiple times larger. Birds can fly unaided. Bears are far stronger. The big cat family are faster, more agile. Many animals can detect electromagnetic waves which humans cannot. Fish can swim faster, deeper and without time limit. Most creatures have a better sense of hearing or a more advanced method of vision. The dolphin is naturally altruistic and highly intelligent. Yet humans treat animals in a manner that would be considered a terrible crime if committed upon your own species. Imagine for a moment the hypothetical rearing of a human, force fed for years until finally slaughtered and butchered into different cuts of meat. Then cooked, seasoned and eaten; the only hesitancy coming when choosing which bottle of wine to drink with the meal. I am sure you will all agree, that this is unfathomable.'

I feel sick in my stomach. This speech is more of a dressing down.

'Yes, humans have the ability to think and invent advanced technology. Although with this ability and the consequent discoveries, more and more atrocities are carried out. Humans have caused the extinction of many animal species, while destroying countless habitats bringing even more species on the verge of extinction. Despite knowing this, you continue. Flying in the face of all logic. You have the answers to avoid all of this in your collective knowledge. To set you on the correct path. You have had this knowledge for many years but it has been suppressed for selfish gain. We will not allow this to continue.'

The feeling in the room is tense, a mixture of suspense and anger. We are helpless, unable to offer forward a single action. The room waits and listens. Expressions darkening around the table, some nervous, others angry, all negative.

'We have decided to take the action of rescuing the animals of earth. In fact, you have left us no choice. We see that your species are far too selfish for any concerted collaborated effort for change.

Within thirty of your earth minutes, every being not crucial to the survival of the human species and the planet's vegetation will be removed and relocated to a similar planet, away from the death and destruction you insist on wreaking.'

The Wisp disappears as the transmission ends and the channel newsroom is back into view, the presenters of the channel searching for words to tell their viewers.

A stunned silence in the room. The leaders of the countries around the world all spluttering and stuttering, trying to formulate some thoughts of a planned response.

'This is outrageous,' the chairperson finally shouts, 'we cannot allow this to happen. They cannot take because they feel like it. This is an act of war upon our planet.'

Agreement reigns in from all people sat at the table, except Prime Minister Corbyn who is silent, thoughtful.

'This will destroy entire multi-billion dollar industries, cause havoc with millions, possibly billions of lives across the planet. They are *our* animals; these aliens have no right to them. We must fight back,' President Trump says defiantly, thumping a fist onto the desk in emotion. Men and woman around the table call out in agreement.

I sit and I think. Feelings stirring inside of me. The actions of the Wisps aligning themselves into focus.

'I think that I know what they are doing,' I call out, the room falling quiet as everyone looks at me. I gulp down a rising sense of nervousness and continue, 'the Wisps are acting without caring what happens to us, just the same as we do concerning animals. We don't take into account what happens to animals when we farm them, or build our cities or clear their forests. We just carry on regardless. That's what they are doing to us. But they are actually doing a good thing by saving animal lives, so morally they have the upper hand. I say we take the hit and listen to what they've told us. Realise that life is precious. All life. And maybe we can build a better world.'

Prime Minister Corbyn is looking at me intently. When I finish speaking he leans forwards in his chair and rests a comforting hand on my arm.

'Aaron, why don't you shut the fuck up and let the big boys talk, okay?' he says out aloud amidst a few sniggers of laughter, 'Can someone get this idiot out of here please?' he asks, as some guards swiftly oblige and within a blink of an eye I find myself in the lobby of the building, my pride a little hurt. I suppose that everyone's pride is a little hurt, having been briskly told what will happen without the ability to do anything about it. But the right road often needs a little humility.

A few months later, I am resting at home. I'm

quite the celebrity now. Constantly giving interviews about my experience in the dome with the animals and the Wisp. Get a lot of hate as well over the events that happened after the Wisps left, but that was completely out of my control. They did as they said they would. Every mammal, reptile, bird and aquatic animal was magically removed from Earth.

To where?

Nobody knows.

We just know that they all vanished.

We aren't entirely alone, though. Insects, vegetation and micro-organisms are still here, maintaining the equilibrium of nature and keeping us alive. A lot of reorganising is going on without the animals and it will take some time, but we will get there. As long as we put our brains to good use.

Taking the animals isn't all that the Wisps did.

They did pass our galactic address details on to another alien life-form. The Nashers, we call them on account of their multiple sets of huge teeth. With regards to technology, they are about as advanced as the Wisps, huge ships and powerful god-like abilities. We most likely seem like cavemen to them, some kind of primitive native organism. To tell the truth, we probably are compared to them.

They have taken over much of the frozen land at the poles as they prefer the freezing climate and thinner atmosphere.

Thankfully, for the most part, they leave us to our own devices...until they feel a bit hungry.

THE PREDICTION

Videolog 939 - 30th January 2019

The image illuminates to life showing the edge of the plain white desk that the web-cam sits on. A small flashing red circle nestles in the top right corner of the screen indicating that the video is recording.

The background of the picture is a mess of scientific equipment, wires navigating carelessly from here to there, lights and buttons flickering away on various contraptions while multiple computer screens continuously produce streams and streams of data. A low hum of vibration constantly radiating through the air, occasionally punctuated with a hiss of released air pressure and the grinding of gears and cogs.

With both elbows resting on the surface, an unkempt head of hair can be seen with a pair of hands holding and obscuring his face. The fingers are slim and long, each ending in overly long nails in serious need of some TLC. A single gold band wedding ring is the only sight of any jewellery. As if in rhythmic timing with the noise emanating around the room, deep heavy breaths are pushed from his lungs.

Weary breaths.

Sad breaths.

Finally after a long while, as the clip's time bar reaches over a minute, he lets his hands drop down in front of him to show a beaten down face with blood-shot eyes and week-old stubble. Nothing a good night's sleep wouldn't go some way to helping repair although the tension etched deep into the man's brow indicates that voluntary unconsciousness is something not afforded to him at the moment.

'Time,' he says looking into the camera, his voice rough and raspy. 'What is time?'

He grabs a chipped mug from the corner of the desk and takes a sip. Gulps down the liquid, grimacing as he does so and continues his line of vocalised thought.

'Where did time come from?…Where does it go? Minutes, seconds, hours. Centuries, millennia, months and weeks. A day. A moment. What does it all mean? Does it mean anything to begin with? Am I searching for an answer that doesn't exist because the question is wrong?' His eyes are full of pondering even though the surface moisture is betraying his obvious tiredness. 'Can a question be wrong? Even *nothing* is an answer that could be construed as correct, if indeed that is the answer. Am I wasting my time in asking these questions? Or will it be seen as a necessary part of our knowledgeable evolution one day? A small step on the path of a long journey, never-ending, always another question to be asked, always another answer to be sought.'

The man takes a blunt pencil and begins to absently doodle on the desk which is lined with a large sheet of paper, a confused mass of notes and scribbles already marked upon its surface. He draws an arc, a roughly curved line. Then retraces over the line again and again, until it darkens and widens, stray lines splintering away every now and again.

'I want to do good. Good for humanity, our race, our species. I want to help those born in the clutches of evil that don't have a light at the end of the tunnel or that silver lining the rest of us can see. Or those waking from where evil has come and gone, leaving dust and ruin. Those who simply exist for the sake of existing. To survive long enough to get through one day, only to do the same thing the next. Balance must be restored in the world and I honestly think that I can help and make a difference in the struggle. But to what end? What will it matter? Has the struggle of good ever mattered throughout the ages? Through the Egyptian Dynasty, the Bronze Age, Ancient Greece, the Roman Empire, the coming of the

Middle Ages. There have always been those who want to help his fellow man and those who want to rule his fellow man. But what difference has the battle really made? I am here, they are not. Hundreds of civilisations, thousands of religions and Gods, billions of men and women have all turned to dust, only existing depending on how they are remembered...if remembered at all. Does it really matter what I do today? Tomorrow it will all probably be forgotten.'

The pencil begins to break through the paper, marking another sheet laid underneath as he slashes more and more vigorously in growing frustration. In a flash of anger he throws the pencil across the room, its clattering heard until it comes to a stop in a far corner of the room. He looks directly at the camera.

'Whatever the reason of our being here, whether we're all one great big giant accident made out of a clusterfuck of galactic accidents or if we're created for some purpose that our tiny little minds cannot even begin to comprehend, I am going to succeed. I will not fail. I cannot fail.'

A door opens and closes behind him somewhere as he continues to stare at the camera, a whirlwind of thoughts and emotions causing havoc inside his mind. A pretty lady comes into the shot just beside his right shoulder, perfectly straightened black hair cascading down her cheeks, outfitted demurely in an off the shoulder black dress ending just above the knees. A questioning look contorting her otherwise cute features, a cherub nose and small but full lips.

'Tempus?' her high-pitched soft voice calls. The man in the video, Tempus, turns around, startled.

'Gemma? What are you doing here?'

'What do you mean? You promised, Temp.'

Tempus swivels around to the screen and reads the date on the videolog. *Thirtieth of January*, he reads. His face falls and his dark skin lightens as it drains of most of its blood. His eyes dart from side to side as he splutters a made up excuse.

'Oh...G...Gem, I uh, I thought that you were not going to be well enough. Didn't you say something in the morning like that...you were feeling...' He stops as Gemma's face changes, and not for the better.

'Tempus. I said no such thing and you know that I didn't. I told you that however sick I'm feeling today, you are taking me out for a nice romantic birthday dinner. The one day in the year that I might be able to get an ounce of attention from you. You haven't had to do anything, just be ready. I've booked our special place already and all you had to do was care for once. You'd better not spoil this for me.'

'No, sure I won't. I promise. I haven't, I mean. Give me two shakes and I will meet you in the car.'

'Five minutes, Tempus,' Gemma says sternly as

she stalks off out of shot in a cloud of displeasure.

Tempus sheepishly looks at the camera, shakes his head and sighs at himself.

'Idiot.'

Videolog 1 - 17th February 2017

The screen flickers on and finds Tempus adjusting the camera lens to make sure that he is centrally set in the shot while sat at the desk. Bright-eyed, clean shaven and sporting a trendy side-parted hairstyle, he is dressed in an immaculate white lab coat, a well-pressed light blue shirt and matching tie visible where the lab coat is undone in front. He is smiling and looks excited. Ocean coloured blue eyes glowing with purpose.

'Right. Good,' he begins, giddily like a school boy with his first girlfriend, overdoing the hand movements and facial expressions. 'Hello, my name is Professor Tempus Sorsman, theoretical physicist. Here in my laboratory on the grounds of Queens University, London, England, Europe, Planet Earth. Sorry, sorry, let me try to be a little more professional as this occasion should demand.' He takes a deep lungful of breath and mumbles a few unintelligible words to himself to steady his nerves. 'I have recently and very generously been given funding to continue my work in the realm of...*time*. More precisely, in the prediction of time, and its real world application. I am here to embark on a historic voyage with my engineering and computer science team who…I think you can make out behind me. Come and say hello team.'

Tempus wheels himself to the right edge of the shot and allows his team to come forward into the shot. A petite oriental woman and a short young bearded man wave at the camera, their own enthusiasm shining from behind their large safety spectacles.

'This is Doctor Edward Transwill, our engineer who will endeavour to realise our theories and Professor Xun Wan, an exceptional computer scientist and IT expert who will be in charge of programming all of our systems to carry out the required processes.' As quickly as they wave to the camera, the pair are back to work on their equipment, not wanting to waste a second more than is needed on the frivolity that is recording media. Tempus returns to the shot.

'This project that we are working on has the potential of discovery in a similar vein of importance to the human race as Newton's discovery of gravity, Einstein's theory of relativity, even the first steps on the Moon by Armstrong and his other team members. We have been given this opportunity to work on a theory of mine that I have been developing for the past four years based on the prediction of events to occur in the future. Now while this may appear at first like science fiction, it has definite roots in scientific fact.'

Tempus stops to take a sip of steaming hot coffee from his brand new mug.

'Hmmm, lovely. Thanks Gemma,' he says, raising the gifted mug to the camera. 'So, let's take for example the age-old analogy of the person catching a ball. Simple enough. When a person is told to catch a tennis ball, or any kind of ball, that is thrown at them at a reasonable speed from five metres away, that person will not simply stand there until the ball reaches them and then attempt to pluck the ball out of the air. No.

'That person will look at the ball, judge the speed at which it is travelling, check the height at which it is thrown and the direction, maybe if there is a looping curve and then calculate roughly. The individual will factor in as many of these as possible before the ball reaches them. They will then adjust their own body position and place their hands in a place where they think that the ball's flight will take it, thus being able to be best positioned to catch it.

'So if we think about what has happened, based on rough data, the person has *predicted* where the ball will be in the future, so they are able to catch it. Granted, the future that we mention is about a second away, or however far away the ball is travelling from but the premise is sound. Based on analysing *real* data we can predict an event to take place before it has occurred with a degree of certainty.'

Tempus spins around excitedly on his swivel chair. When he is back facing the camera he bangs both palms on the table to stop himself.

'Now,' he continues as his hands strike down on the desk, 'if we return to the individual catching the ball, let's call this person, Bob, for arguments sake. If Bob, having caught the ball once, were to do the same thing again, he would presumably learn about the behaviour of the flight of the ball and would be able to position himself earlier, thus increasing the amount of time into the future he is able to predict. That's number one. Number two pushes this scenario further. If Bob were to repeat this process a number of times, he would be able to attempt a more complex procedure. He would be able to increase the five metre position to twenty metres away. A considerable increase. And if Bob is able to catch the ball successfully from this distance, he may begin to observe other factors affecting the catch. Maybe wind factor plays a role. Or he may have to shuffle his feet or even sprint a short distance to position himself. Whatever else he has to factor in, can be learnt so that his prediction of the future is over a longer time frame and involves a more complex set of internal calculations.'

Still looking at the camera, Tempus smirks

cheekily, as if he knows something that no one else does. He takes a pencil and draws something on a plain pad, making quick and fast strokes which betray his eagerness to display.

'What if we then subject poor old Bob...to this?' Tempus rips the A4 piece of paper from the pad and holds it up horizontally to the camera. It shows a crudely drawn stick man at the bottom centre with five small circles around him in a curve, each circle has a line joining up to the stick figure. 'We throw five balls at Bob, all at the same time, and all at the same speed. He can never learn to catch all five at the same time. But what he can learn after multiple repetitions of this disastrous experiment, or however many times it takes for Bob to learn depending on his IQ level...is that sometimes...you have to...move out of the way.'

He scrunches up the piece of paper and launches it back over his head where it hits Edward on the nose. Tempus doesn't turn around but to the left of him Edward is standing there shaking his head in annoyance before carrying on with his checks.

'Sometimes...Bob doesn't learn.'

Tempus winks at the camera and spins once more on his chair. 'So...what this means is that with the correct level of data available to us, algorithms complex enough and a computer system more powerful than anything the world has ever seen...we can predict the future before it has happened and on a scale that is...,' Tempus glances above the camera and an expression of realisation cloaks his face, '...but before we get into the real world application, I have a date with my wife to celebrate our fifth wedding anniversary, the wooden anniversary I recall, and I would be insane to keep her waiting. We shall continue this introduction tomorrow.'

Videolog 949 - 17th February 2019

Tempus is hunched over at his desk, his hand clasped around a bottle of red wine. No glass in sight. He raises the bottle to the camera in salute.

'To my dear darling wife...happy anniversary,' he slurs as he takes a long swig of wine, a few droplets falling down his shirt staining the already soiled material, 'and all I got was this lousy text message.'

He holds up his phone screen to the camera showing a message:

Happy anniversary...I'm staying at mum's for a few days, feeling unwell. I'll call you in the morning.

'I guess it's my fault,' he says, letting his phone drop carelessly onto the desk. 'I should be there for you. Caring for you. Looking after you. I'm sorry, Gem. I promise that I will make it up to you as soon as I solve this damned problem. That's all it is, a problem. You know that I'm a great one for solving problems. This is what I do. I know that the more I focus on it, the easier it will be to solve. And once I do, I will be everything that you want me to be, that *I* want to be. And one day, I will be able to explain everything to you.'

Tempus tries to take another gulp of wine but finds there is nothing left in the bottle. Disgusted, he flings the bottle away where it thuds against something hollow then shatters, the sound of breaking glass making him flinch. With a limp wave of his hand, he dismisses the mess that he has caused.

'I'm doing this for you, Gem. It's all for you. I want you to know that. I'll show everything to you one day, all of these stupid recordings, all of my work…and we'll have an amazing future together…you and me…I promise.'

Videolog 2 - 18th February 2017

'Right, now where did we leave off last night?…Oh that's it, the imaginary Bob and his ball catching exploits,' Tempus chirps happily. 'So, the position that we find ourselves in is one of amazing possibility…being able…to predict the future. There are obvious issues with this. Does knowing the future then change it? Are we able to change the future once we know it? If this is a prediction, does that leave room for error? How much error? If a lot of error, does it then simply become an educated guess? You have the normal morality and ethics based objections to carrying out this kind of work as well. The data requirements of this experiment being vast, are we tapping into areas that we shouldn't be? And then we have the real world applications for a project of this kind. Will it be misused by governments or even worse, corporations, even the military? So we have a lot of considerations here. All of which are very valid and will be addressed as and when the information becomes available.'

Tempus stops to adjust the camera and his seated position so that he is moved to one side of the picture and the lab background can be seen more clearly. Xun and Edward are both busy at work, looking extremely dedicated to their respective tasks at hand.

'To discuss one of those issues - the real world applications, I have to show these guys behind me. The team. They have been handpicked, not only because they are leaders in their respective fields, but also because of their characters. These are nice people. They want to do good, as do I. And though that may seem like an irrelevant note to make in the world of science, when we are dealing with a project like this, it makes all of the difference further down the road when important decisions are to be made.'

He swivels the camera back into its position so

that he fills up the screen once again.

'If we have success in any way shape or form, there will be demand for our technology.' A solemn expression takes hold of his features. 'We will only allow the use of our knowledge to go towards the betterment of our society, our environment, forwards progress and the betterment of the collective known as the human race. Profit, power and manipulation will be avoided at all costs.'

Videolog 978 - 26th May 2019

'Is this thing even on?'

'Of course it's on, can't you see the bright flashing red light?'

'Oh yeah.'

'Moron.'

'Smart arse. We're not all computer experts.'

'Computer expert? It's a flashing light. A five year old could work that out.'

'So it's on then?'

'Yes! Oh my God!'

'Good'

'Well?'

'Well what?'

'Get on with it then. Hurry, before he comes.'

'Didn't you see him drinking last night? It's going to be a while before he's even conscious again.'

'Whatever. Just get on with it.'

'Okay, okay.'

Edward clears his throat...for a long time. Just as he is finally about to speak, he holds up his hand to the camera and attempts to clear it once again. He receives a solid smack on the back from Xun for his troubles. His eyes water slightly. But he does not show his pain. He nods tightly at his colleague and turns back to the camera.

'Good morning, Professor Sorsman. I am not entirely sure who else this video of the official project transcript will be viewed by once the project eventually completes. Whether it be the university council, review boards, future generations and members of the public, a combination of them all, or even none at all. Whoever views this, please be aware that I, Doctor Edward Transwill and my project partner here, Professor Xun Wan are recording this with very heavy and sorry hearts. We do wish to let it be noted however, that we have positive personal relations with Professor Sorsman, regard him highly and have been in awe for the past two years working with him and his brilliance. It has truly been a pleasure and an honour.'

'That said,' Xun interjects taking over from Edward, a stern brow creasing her skin, 'we have recently come to discover that much progress that we *should* have made in this extraordinary project has been hampered, sabotaged and ultimately lost.

We are not pointing any fingers of accusations at anyone, but what we were promised pertaining to the moral and ethical use of the discovery has been purposely sidelined. Not blatantly, and very difficult to see at first, however after two years of work, we have gently but definitely been manipulated along the way.'

Xun opens her mouth to say more but nothing comes out. Edward notices the stall and minute tremor of emotion on her last words and picks up the slack.

'Yes. Manipulation,' he says. 'It is a strong word with very negative connotations. Nevertheless, there is no more adequate way to describe it. For the past five months at least, we have been lied to about the success of our work and made to repeat confirmations needlessly and solely for the prosperity of an individual. As we said, we are not here to point fingers or to see anyone punished. We are also not looking for any kind of compensation. We simply want the record to reflect the truth as to why we left the project. If any lies are told furthermore, please note that we have indisputable proof which can be distributed and publicised if necessary, although we would prefer not to.'

Xun has composes herself enough to rejoin the video.

'I think that is all that needs to be said. Myself and Edward are moving on to join other projects and hope that the integrity of this project is restored for its own sake. We also wish everyone here our best wishes and luck for the future. But please understand that any attempt to contact us regarding this matter will only be done under recorded circumstances and in the presence of our legal representatives. So…we'd rather not.' Xun looks over at Edward. 'Is there anything that you want to add?'

'No, I think that's everything.' Edward looks seriously at the camera one last time. 'But, I do want to say something directly to you, Professor. We have been very reasonable with you upon discovering what we have. You know exactly what we are talking about. I am sure that you won't want this to come out so you will leave us alone. But for your own sake, stop this madness. Remember why you are doing this. Do the right thing.'

Videolog 639 - 24th August 2018

The light is dim in the lab. A single low light bulb providing the illumination. Possibly a lamp or a low-light in a corner. The digital clock high up on the back wall is displaying 23:45, the time showing there as well as on the face of Tempus. He looks skittish. Pupils darting from side to side. Fingers tapping quickly on the desk in some repeated rhythm. The fidgeting is obviously an outlet for the mass of thinking going on in his mind. He is tussling with something. An issue.

'Look man,' he says much too quickly. The caffeine jitters being released into his voice, 'I'm happy okay. I'm over the flipping moon. It works. The damn thing works. We have done it. On a small scale granted but yes, we have done it. We have predicted the future with a success rate of over ninety eight percent on the ink blot test. Location decision was over ninety five percent and weight repetitions came in at over ninety six percent. The thing works.' Tempus suddenly appreciates how fast he is talking and takes a deep slow breath to calm down.

'I am aware that we need results to hit the ninety ninth percentile before we can move on to the next stage but that is purely a matter of time. Not a great deal of time, either. I'm guessing months, if not weeks.'

He jumps out of his chair and begins pacing back and forth, perspective making his form smaller then larger, smaller than larger. His hands are locked behind his back as he walks making him bend over a few degrees. A typical scientist form. The thoughtful form.

'I know that we've had to scale down the scope of the project recently.' Tempus is back at the desk, a line of thought organised enough to articulate. 'To come in line with what we've learnt about this prediction process and just how complicated it can be. We can only involve a single person in the primary prediction phase because of how much data is needed. But the rest of the theory is sound; the individual's data collection from DNA mapping, physical assessment, psychometric testing, medical records, full online browsing data, shopping and pastime activity, all of it. The cross referencing with environmental factors regarding the individual - political, religious and educational choices, peers, fashion, their romantic escapades. Basically pulling every piece of information available about that person from under the Sun and compiling the data in a usable program to predict what their future may hold in a certain circumstance. Sure, we have to use one of the most powerful and expensive computer on the planet for severely limited periods of time and we can only ask the most basic questions at the moment. But yes. We can do this.'

Tempus leans over the desk, plants his palms down flat. His eyes focus at the camera unblinking.

'But the information that I have just discovered troubles me. It troubles me greatly. I have made a promise to my team for God's sake. How am I meant to keep that promise now?' The desk shudders as he drops heavily into his seat, his worry zapping the energy from his body. 'The funding for this project isn't from the university alone. The majority is from AAB Systems. The weapons manufacturer. What level of morals and ethics will they have once the results are concluded and finalised? All they will do is try to weaponise it and sell it. For profit.'

Videolog 640 - 25th August 2018

'A wise man once said that you must help yourself before you help others.' The bags under Tempus' eyes are worse than yesterday. Sleep must have evaded him once again. Although his mood appears to be more positive. He seems calm.

'I think what he meant was that, to give to someone else less fortunate, you must have something to give in the first place. Whether it be a thing of physical or emotional construct. It has to exist. And right now, nothing that can be of use to humanity exists, except as an idea. And when that idea turns into something of use, it will be placed into the hands of evil. I cannot allow that to happen. I feel terrible about what I am going to do, but I want the record to reflect the position that I am in. An untenable position unless I take an action that I would normally never take.'

Tempus pauses, readying himself to take a plunge.

'With a heavy heart I say this...I will delay the progress of the project in a manner that is unknown to my team. Fudging results, ordering retests, changing reliable settings for unreliable ones. I will upload my personal data for use with the system and use it for one purpose only. Money. That very thing that I vowed not to do. I can't believe that I am even saying this. Nevertheless, I will use this machine to indicate future visions of events that I will be a part of and amass an amount of money that will free this project from the grips of a war-mongering corporation. Use that money to help society, feed the poor, educate those who can't afford to, support those who find only obstacles in life. Do all of the things that I wanted this project to end up doing.' Tempus blows a puff of air out of his nose in amusement at the irony of this new situation.

'I have to tread the path of evil to overcome an evil. I must be careful not to fall in too deep.'

Videolog 1248 - 13th August 2021

Tempus switches on the recording. He looks lost. A hollow shell of the man he used to be. A rough uneven patchy beard has sprouted, black has turned to grey, flecks of grey becoming white and lifeless. His once plump flesh has shrivelled, wrinkled skin sagging and robbed of its tautness. Shoulders hunched over in a way that they are long used to, lacking in the energy to be held up strongly and firmly.

'Day five hundred and...and...something. I

forget where I have reached to sometimes.' Tempus' voice is that of an old man who has spent a life regularly employing the services of whiskey and tobacco. The vocal wavelengths struggle to pass through the air, barely registering as a whisper.

'Yesterday's test results have come through. Another fail…as usual. Altering the diet to vegan-based has had no effect on avoiding the initial prediction. It remains…as it always has. I cannot find the cause behind this effect. I am unsure now whether it can be affected by my actions now or if my actions are contributing towards it. It seems inevitable. Whatever is done or not done in the present, the event will always occur. Like the exploding of the Sun at some point in the future. Unavoidable.'

A knock at the door shakes Tempus out of his train of thought.

'Come in,' he says, although he doesn't turn around to see Gemma, his wife, who has come into the room.

'Temp?' she says softly, as light as the breeze. He lets out a heavy sigh, leaden and weighed down with tiredness but doesn't turn around.

'Gem. Can't this wait until I get home?'

Gemma stays quiet, considering her response. It seems that they have been over this issue many times before and she is weary of retreading old ground. She looks exhausted. Empty of the will to move her body with anything resembling force. She appears frail and gaunt from what can be seen of her in the distorted background.

'I'm leaving Temp.'

'Off to your mother's again?'

'I'm leaving *you*, Temp.'

At last Tempus turns to face his wife for the first time since she has entered the lab.

'What?'

'I can't carry on like this, Temp. Playing second fiddle to your work. Living off of the scraps of your time that are so devoid of emotion that you may as well not be there. The few seconds when I feel you climb into bed at two in the morning. Or watching the wave you give me as you leave again early in the morning. But as much as I can learn to live without you, I won't let our baby feel your absence as I have.'

'But...' Gemma holds up a hand to stop Tempus from replying. She has more to say. She tries to stifle a cough which comes out anyway.

'Please, Temp. I have made up my mind. I am going to be at my mother's from now on and I am taking our baby with me. You can come and see her whenever you want. It is up to you to find the time and the will. If you can prise yourself away from this...place.'

Tempus stands up and attempts to approach his wife. To his surprise Gemma takes a small step back and shakes her head.

'Please Gemma. Don't do this. You don't understand.'

'Understand what, Temp? Tell me please.'

'I can see that my behaviour seems…obsessed…out of proportion. That I'm cold towards you. But nothing could be further from the truth, Gem. Everything that I am doing, all of this…is for you, for us and our sweet baby, Pretio.' Gemma shakes her head disbelieving.

'I've heard this many times before, but you never tell me how. How is this for me? How is this for our child?'

Tempus stays silent. He looks down at the floor.

'I can't tell you right now, Gemma. I just need some more time.'

'Time? You have had plenty of that. And you've wasted it. Your time has run out. If you don't tell me something that I haven't heard for the past two years, I am going.'

They say that silence is golden.

This silence is the exact opposite. Devoid of warmth. Black.

As Tempus remains quiet, Gemma keeps hold of what little dignity she has remaining and slowly walks out of the room. Her body stiff with the pain of emotion, her insides collapsing.

Tempus doesn't move for the next few minutes. He is lost in his own mind, an avalanche of scenarios that he must navigate in order to make sense of the world that is crumbling down around him. When he returns back in front of the camera, he looks conflicted.

'This is…crazy.' His eyes dart from side to side, chaos raining throughout his thoughts. 'I can't possibly tell her why I am working so hard here. She would be destroyed. But does she deserve what I'm putting her through right now? I can't…won't…'

Wracked by indecision, Tempus loses any shred of determination that he had in him. The back of his chair shudders as he lets his body fall backwards. And there he remains, not daring to move. He lets time pass by. Every second that ticks on the clock bringing him ever closer to that which he has tried to avoid.

Videolog 729 - 25th December 2018

A curled ribbon of colourful wonderment unravels at speed and strikes the camera dead in the centre, exploding with a blast of irritating noise. As quickly as it unravelled, it retreats back to its curled up state with its teat nestled between the grinning lips of Tempus. He has his Christmas party hat on at an angle that some may call *street*, although knowing Tempus, it is simply because he is inebriated beyond measure. His party whistle dangles limply from the side of his mouth, looking as though it wishes to commit suicide by leaping.

Tempus takes a long dazed second to scoot his chair closer to the camera.

'Merry Christmas project!' he yells at the camera, tooting again on his poor abused whistle.

'Now you are probably wondering what the afterlife I'm doing here on Christmas day when there isn't another soul to be seen. Well, let me tell you, future *me*...,' he says conspiratorially with an unnecessary close up of his pudgy face. He ducks away to rummage around in his draw, 'I have come to collect Gemma's Christmas present after giving her a fake one this morning containing a pair of socks.'

Tempus bursts into uncontrollable laughter and rocks back on his chair which decides to abandon him by spinning away to the far corner of the room and sending him crashing to the floor. Though he is not in screen shot, his manic laughter screeches out from beneath the table for far too long, briefly stopping as he attempts to literally climb back up. The table doesn't appear to appreciate his efforts as it shakes dangerously, stopping once he is up and back safely in a nearby substitute chair.

'Check this out. Look at the real Christmas present I have bought for my gorgeous wife.' Out comes a fancy maroon box from underneath the table which he plonks in the middle of the desk. The embossed gold script on the top gives up the brand.

Cartier.

Tempus flips open the lid and spins the open box around to face the camera. Inside are a set of brand new sparkling diamond encrusted his and hers platinum watches, both nestled on white silk cushioning. A small card says, 'with love, Temp'.

'Huh? How is that looking? Gem is going to be bamboozled and blown away with my wiliness! And to think, I told her I was going out to look for some sherry. Ha! As if I'd ever run out of sherry. And at Christmas no less. The lord himself wouldn't forgive me for that mortal sin.'

Tempus manages to place the box in the gift bag without damaging it or himself. He looks rather proud of himself. Like a preening cat.

'You are probably trying to remember where I got the money for this, aren't you future me? Well, I'll let you in on a little secret...which you probably know already, don't you? Ha!' Tempus sways in the air as he takes the time to enjoy amusing himself.

'So anyway, our little enterprise is making a nice pot of cash...obviously for good causes but that doesn't mean to say we can't enjoy the fruits of our labour a smidgen, does it? Of course not. The way I see it...we'll see it...or is it *you'll* see it? All of the above! Ha!' He leans in to the camera once again, lowers his voice. 'You see...there would be nothing without me. No money, no project, no predictions. I am the reason for this whole shebang that you see before you. This new sect of science that I am the leader of will revolutionise the globe. I will give the power back to the little man and take it away from those with too much. Nothing can derail me. Nothing can hold me back now. Nothing has the power to ruin my life...except death that is...'

Tempus has his arms raised over his head in self praise, but he freezes. A look of contemplation taking over from the exaggerated lust for domination he was previously displaying.

'Death?'

He adopts the thinking man's pose he often takes.

'Why hasn't this question come to me before? It's very obvious. The only thing that can bust up this party is an unexpected departure from this fold, taking with it all of my plans...I wonder...'

Tempus propels himself backwards on the chair until he reaches the computer controls for his prediction system, the alcohol in his system instantly evaporating. Tentatively, as though he is at the controls of a nuclear weapons device, he begins to tap some commands into the computer. Slowly at first, very slowly. Each keystroke is given his total presence so as to avoid any mistakes. But as the excitement builds inside him, he moves faster and faster until his fingertips are just a blur, tapping away at incredible speed. His head bobbing to an undetectable rhythm in his mind.

The huge contraption behind him turns on and for around twenty minutes, it shudders and hisses as it completes the tasks given to it by Tempus. Soon he is finished. He downloads the data onto a thick portable hard-drive and takes it with him to the main multi-computer station at the other end of the university, almost running out of the room and forgetting to shut down the camera feed.

Tempus is gone for a long time but eventually he does return. However he does not look like the same excited man who almost sprinted out of the lab.

Gently placing the hard-drive down onto the desk, he sits timidly, the blood drained from his face so that he looks sick. Actually, he doesn't look sick.

He looks scared. The way a man looks when he knows that he is heading for doom yet can't avert it in any way.

'I die...,' he whispers. '...I die...soon...too soon...'

His face crumples up with emotional agony at this new revelation. His shoulders heave as he breaks down into loud sobs. In an instant he has been thrown down a deep hole from his position at the top of the world.

'No...this can't be...I can't be dead...,' he says finally, wiping the wet from his cheeks and gaining some semblance back, '...this isn't what is going to happen. I will change this...this...future, where I have committed...*suicide*. This cannot be right. I mean, why would *I* of all people commit suicide? This just doesn't make any sense at all. There is so much yet to do, in my research, with the world...with my wife...' Tempus looks at the gift for his wife.

'My wife...Gemma...No, I can't leave her alone in this world. That is the last thing that I want to do. We love each other in the purest form there is. We have a future family to create, to build and grow, to instil our passion in them so that they may also one day make a positive difference in this world. No. I will find a way to defeat this future. Even if it takes my last breath, I will not commit suicide and leave all of this behind. Gemma will not attend my funeral. No...No!'

Tempus throws a piece of paper onto the desk, crumpled yet viewable. It is a print out from the universities main computer, a generic picture showing a black funeral casket with Tempus abstractly hanging by his neck next to it, his face identifiable from an old passport picture the system has used from old input data. Around the edges are more generic figures of men and women, with their faces replaced by real pictures found on the web of who they really are. Ironically, Gemma has a smiling face for hers from an old holiday picture.

Underneath the casket is a date: 08-2023.

Videolog 1294 - 22nd August 2023

The video comes to life. Yet the setting is different than before.

Gone is the lab with all of the equipment in the background, the sterile white environment in which modern magic was occurring.

Instead, in its place is a small dark dusty room with no windows and bare red brick walls which have long begun to crumble. A workbench lines the full length of the wall with a low shelf below it packed with unidentifiable junk and cardboard boxes. A sole light bulb hangs from a kinked wire in the centre of the room, its light fizzing away every once in a while.

Tempus walks into view from around the back of the camera. Gone is the lab coat, replaced with a simple grey sweatshirt and blue jeans. Though he is visibly older with a mesh of wrinkles at the edges of his eyes and mouth, he is clean shaven and fresh. Sleep no longer appears to be a stranger. He has adopted a serene accepting aura which emanates about him, making him seem almost other-worldly.

He sits on an old wooden stool in the middle of the room, on top of the hard concrete floor. The foot high seat squeaks as it takes his weight.

'Good day,' Tempus says, tiny beginnings of a smile developing at the edge of his mouth, 'it has been a long time since my last video. For that I apologise.' Though the stool is backless, Tempus does not slouch. He has found an inner strength with which to hold himself up. He draws in a deep breath.

'Fate. Destiny. Are certain events preordained to happen? Probably. Is everything that we do pre-written? No, I don't think so. But are aspects of our lives more likely to unfold in a predictable way because of our journey leading up to that moment? Absolutely. Does it really matter? No. As long as you live your life in the best way that you can, your final moments on this earth play a minuscule role in the definition of your life. What matters is how you got there. The journey.' His voice is different than before, like that of a man who knows something important.

'A lot has happened over the past few months since the university lost the funding for the project. I acquired a little more time in my life. Time to reconnect with my family. Time to analyse where I have gone wrong. Time to create a path to make amends which will never truly be enough. Since the moment that I learnt about my looming death, I lost all perspective and became selfish. Greedy. I was looking at the knowledge from only one point of view. My own. What would happen to *my* work? What would happen to *my* wife? What would happen to *my* dreams? I have wasted the last years of my life trying to change a future that hadn't occurred at the expense of a present that was yearning for my attention. I wouldn't give it.

My wife left me. Took my child with her. I lost my job because I wasn't progressing in the research that I was meant to be. My reputation is in tatters after the revelations that my former colleagues had let slip about me. But the time that I have gained since all of this has happened has been invaluable.' A little mist builds in his eyes.

'I have finally discovered the fatal disease that my wife, Gemma has been hiding from me all of these years. The reason that she needed me and my time to help care for her. But I wasn't there. Her mother had to replace me as support for her and our child. My own child! She never asked anything of me. Not even divorce or finances. She needed *me* and I wasn't there. And now she is on a waiting list for a lung transplant that will save her life if it ever comes. And it will come. I will make sure of that.' Tempus stands on his feet.

'Because that lung will come from me.'

He stands on the stool and pulls down a rope from the ceiling. A noose at the end is looped around his neck.

'Gemma, I am sorry for trying to live my life without you instead of by your side. By thinking that by having money and being the smartest man in the room would make you happy. I should have been what I promised you that I would be. Your partner in life.'

Tempus pulls the noose tight around his neck.

'An ambulance is on the way. They will find me

dead but with instructions to donate whichever of my organs is needed to you. My recent will that is with my lawyer will make sure that you and Pretio are well taken care of. Please understand why I have done this. All of my video recordings will be yours if you ever want answers. In life I wasn't able to provide what you needed. Maybe in death, I will be more successful. I love you.'

Tempus kicks the stool from beneath his feet.

Twenty minutes later a paramedic crew find him hanging in the room. They carefully descend his body to the floor. They find the laptop recording and shut it in disgust.

Videolog 937 - 28th January 2019

'Hey Professor, we're going to call it a day.'

'Yep. We'll try and figure this issue out tomorrow.'

Tempus is adjusting the level of the webcam as Edward and Xun are in the background collecting their coats and making their way to the door.

'Still no joy with finding out the issue with the predictor?' he replies without turning around.

'No,' Edward says, 'I can't understand it. We were getting really solid results a while back and now...well...it has reduced to the level of chance and we can't repeat those early results.'

'I'm sure we'll figure it out soon,' Xun says.

'Sure. No problem. Have a good evening guys.

See you in the morning.'

Tempus shiftily looks behind him once they have left to make sure that they have gone. Once he is satisfied, he sits at the computer and begins typing rapidly. He doesn't even notice Gemma has entered the lab.

'Temp?' she says quietly.

'Oh! Gem. You scared me. Come in. Take a seat.' Tempus turns back to his computer as Gemma sits at the desk. 'So how are you doing? Did you go to the doctors today?'

'Yes. I went in to see them.'

'Hmmm...,' Tempus replies, still concentrating on the computer.

'They gave me the results of the tests they took last week.'

Gemma waits. She doesn't continue talking. She sits and watches her husband engrossed into his work. With an unblinking glazed look as he stares at the screen, simultaneously typing furiously.

'How is your work going, Temp?' Gemma asks, changing the topic.

'Hmmm...well, I have a problem that I can't solve...and I refuse to stop until I have,' Tempus replies absently.

Gemma spends the next few seconds trying to recover from an uncontrollable coughing fit while Tempus carries on with his work.

'Okay. Well, I'll see you at home. Dinner's at eight.'

Gemma begins to leave the lab, tenderly holding her chest with one hand.

'Don't wait for me, Gem. I might be late. Much later than that. You eat without me if I'm not there.'

Without responding, Gemma makes it to the door.

Suddenly, Tempus straightens up in his chair and stops what he is doing. He turns to his wife.

'Oh Gem. What did the doctor say?'

'We'll talk about it later, Temp,' Gemma says without breaking her stride, 'there is plenty of time for that.'

THE HOLIDAY

Machine gun fire rings out all around. A crack guerrilla team descends on the camp deep in the jungle, destroying any hostile with the full force that live rounds will allow.

The captain of the team begins to clear the inside.

He takes cover behind a pole.

Enemy soldiers ahead.

He breaks, unleashing the lethal power of deadly ammunition, his bare forearms pumped while gripping the weapon as it fires and shudders.

Out of his periphery, a movement.

A threat.

Despite being six foot two inches of pure rippling muscle, he pirouettes like a ballerina, simultaneously pulling out a nasty looking army knife from a hidden clasp and launches it into and through his enemy's chest, pinning him to the wall.

Without skipping a beat, he says those now immortal words.

'Stick around.'

Arnold Schwarzenegger's face fills the screen. He grins as he is saying his line. A grin to indicate that he is obviously very pleased with himself to have come up with such a witticism especially under seriously life threatening circumstances.

Heavy fire, grenades, explosions, all of that.

Yet he can still come up with a line that the rest of humanity would only think to say a week after the event while in bed and trying to sleep but not able to because of the constant nightmares and bed-wetting about the mission in the jungle. That's only if we actually made it out of there in the first place without severe psychological problems and a loss of a limb or two.

That's why I love Arnold.

I have always loved this guy.

Arnie. The Austrian Oak. The Terminator. The Governator.

What an inspiration!

The man who has undertaken one of the greatest rags to riches stories in recent history. While providing humanity with some of the most awesome catchphrases ever heard, especially since they all need the Arnie Austrian twang to go with them. 'Billy! What are you doing? Get to the chopper!' anyone? We have been imitating this mountain of a man ever since the 1980's, finding joy and humour in getting as close to his original accent as possible, often taking the inflection much further than it needs to go. Never has Arnold shown offence at the imitation, always seeing it as a positive instead of ridicule.

I first saw the movie *Predator* when I was seven. The unique heady mix of sci-fi, action, mystery and a little comedy. Back when it was on VHS tape, I could rent the over-eighteens video from the local newsagents slash video rental slash arcade shop by telling the owner that my dad had sent me to pick it up.

It was a revelation for me. This shy awkward chubby kid from East London seeing on screen the ultimate hero. A man's man. A tall, strong powerhouse with classic chiselled looks, a great sense of humour and who never took himself too seriously. A man who turned the obvious handicap of a heavy foreign accent into his greatest selling point. Five time Mr Universe turned Hollywood legend, shattering box office records all over the place and doing it while coolly smoking a fat Cuban with one hand, dropping people upside-down off mountain sides with the other.

What a guy!

I watched an interview with him once. He spoke of the reason of his success. The factor that opened up his path to stardom, he said, was his ability to set a goal, a vision, and to do everything in his power to reach that point. Everything that he did was done with positivity and expectation, a belief that he was getting closer and closer with each rep and each squat. He knew that the secret lay in his dedication to keep in peak physical shape to attain his goals.

I was a fan. Instantly and completely.

I wanted to be like Arnold.

I grunt as I take a load onto my shoulders. Squat down and push back up with close to two hundred kilos loaded onto the thick iron barbell. Every rep is a challenge but the last of the ten really pushes me to the limits. Every piece of me wants to rest but mentally I kick their lazy asses and ignore the fiery burn that is incinerating my pulsing muscles. Digging deep down, I find a final hidden molecule of energy and use it to push. With a roar I straighten my knees and manage to lift the bar back onto its rack.

Now my body can rest.

Or collapse.

Either is good.

I crash down onto a nearby bench and lean over. My chest is heaving, my heart is pounding. I suck in as much air as I can while sweat trickles off the end of my nose. Though I am shattered, it feels good. Great, in fact. Knowing that the last couple of reps have ripped the fibres of my muscles to shreds is knowledge enough that they will rebuild stronger and bigger.

As long as I feed them the right way. And fast.

Once I'm feeling up to it, I make my way out of

the gym after an hour of abusing my body. I pass a couple of athletic lithe girls on the treadmills. I smile at them as I go past. They both respond the same, though a bit more enthusiastically than is necessary.

I often get this response.

From both males and females.

The over enthusiastic part, that is.

The ladies usually begin unconscious preening, head tilting and teeth-displaying eye-reaching smiles, a gentle arm touch if they're in range. The men? They do things differently. They prefer puffing out their chests, strengthening their handshakes and reducing verbal syllable usage, i.e. 'sup? (what is happening?), bare (a lot of), fam (family and/or friends), seen (I understand what you are saying to me) or link (to meet up at a later date).

I think that it has something to do with my having transformed from an ugly duckling into an entity reminiscent of a human form of a Greek God somewhere over the last decade. Almost daily sessions at the gym and a strict diet have seen me appear as though I have been chiselled out of a dense material, more granite than the pdf of yesteryear. Or so I've been told.

I make my way to my usual eatery after my solid session. My local cafe, aptly named *The Local*, is a normal cafe which serves the traditional full

English breakfasts and other heart disease inducing accompaniments such as the greasy bacon sandwich or the double cheese, double bacon, triple burger heart-bypass special that many patrons call 'the usual'.

I rest my cheeks on a stool at the front counter with a cracked red leather cover and sponge sprouting out of the sides. The place smells of coffee and fat, and has a steamy hue hovering in the air from the open kitchen manned by Demetriou, my old school-time friend and the cafe owner and pretend-chef. Though he came to this country from Greece almost twenty years ago, he still retains his accent. I think on purpose sometimes. And I say 'pretend-chef' because outside of frying the components for a fry up breakfast or a variety of toasted sandwiches, there isn't much that he can cook. A roast leg of lamb would defeat him as if he were George Foreman being mentally and physically maltreated by Mohammad Ali. He would assume it would be roasting beautifully. But at the last second, as his carving knife would slice into the glorious piece of meat through the crisp skin and tender meat, a squirt of blood would fly through the air from its origin of the raw underbelly.

Defeated. At the last second.

'Hey Valens, looking good as usual, bro.' Demetriou is busy at the hot stove but always finds time to smile, his perma-stubble never not groomed.

'Got to represent, D, you know me.'

'The *Usual*?'

'Hit me, dude.'

'You got it.'

My usual is different from the *usuals* of other customers. I don't indulge in anything that is bad for my body. No bacon, cheeseburgers, buttery bread, sugary tea or coffee. No processed meats, fizzy drinks, sweets or chocolates. Basically anything that tastes really great has to be closely analysed before eating.

Demetriou lays down a bowl of freshly cut fruit with a nut and seed mix in front of me to go with a plate of steamed vegetable and grilled soya steak, lightly seasoned. Next to it goes a green leaf and berry smoothie, for a generous hit of anti-oxidants and nutrients. As I steadily munch my way through my brunch, chewing each mouthful repeatedly, Demetriou flickers his eyes onto me every now and again while cooking the steady stream of orders coming at him. His cafe is very popular.

'Vee, don't you get sick of eating that stuff, man?' I pop a piece of broccoli into my mouth and chew, liquefying it quickly.

'You do realise that you just made all of this stuff for me?'

'Yeah, yeah, I know.' Demetriou artistically flings a piece of sliced tomato onto the hotplate. It misses the target and drops down the side onto the floor. 'Damn slippery tomato,' he mumbles as he places a replacement slice more carefully, 'I can make a soggy paper towel taste good, that's not my point.'

'What *is* your point, D?'

'My point is that I only have this stuff on the menu because you wanted it when you made your 'change' all those years ago. Yet no one else touches it.' Demetriou raises his hands to physically demonstrate the air quotation marks around the word *change*. He does it while still holding the steel spatula he is cooking with and semi-cooked sliced mushrooms fly around the cafe like defective boomerangs. The cafe patrons don't bat an eyelid. They are used to these dangers. 'Your ingredients even have their own fridge, man.' He points to a small fridge behind him with a glass front. The top shelf is lined with fruit, vegetables in the middle and other exotic looking healthy treats in the bottom.

'Dude!' I put my utensils down. He goes through this charade every time he has to order more stock just for me. He tries to convert me back to eating the same grub as everyone else, all of that artery thickening, heart attack inducing fat laden food, tasty as it may be.

'Sorry sorry. I let you eat, huh?'

'Thank you!' I'm about to plunge into my juicy soya steak, essential in providing plenty of protein for muscle rebuilding.

'But you never miss the salty goodness of a slice of smoked bacon, huh?' He smiles in his cheeky way as I drop my cutlery to the counter. Sometimes it's best to indulge him otherwise he keeps on prodding away.

'Alright. Yes. I do miss the taste of all of it. The junk, the ice cream, burgers, greasy chips, sausage in batters, all that stuff. But do you know what I don't miss?'

'What's that?'

'I don't miss my big wobbly belly.' Demetriou rolls his eyes. 'I don't miss getting out of breath running for a bus or pulling a muscle trying to pick up a used sock up off the floor. And you know what else I don't miss?'

'No, please enlighten me dear sir.'

'I don't miss having multiple chins...although I can see that you're a big fan of that particular bodily growth.' The silence I receive is all the permission that I need to carry on eating. Demetriou is self-conscious about the roll of fat around his thick neck. It looks like he is wearing a scarf sometimes, especially when he doesn't shave and clean up underneath his chin. It's a blow a little south of the belt, but damn, I'm hungry. And a hungry man is a dangerous man.

Out of the corner of my eye, I can see Demetriou trying to raise his head while cooking so as to lessen the bulbousness of the chin fat. It doesn't really help.

But I feel bad.

Once I finish my food and move onto the smoothie, I lean back on the stool against the tiny lower back rest. It is small but does the supporting job.

'Hey man. Your food is tasty though.'

'Ya ya, whatever. Don't look at it too hard, it might give you a pulmonary embolism.' My eyebrows shoot up like a pair of jumping caterpillars in surprise.

'That's a pretty complex medical condition you just threw at me,' I say.

'What you think? You're the only one who reads around here?…Anyway, there was an article about it in FHM magazine.'

'I thought you just looked at the pictures.'

'Ah…when you seen one body, they all kinda look alike after a while, you know? But I have a point to make. I tried to diet a couple of times. But I couldn't deal with the taste of healthy food. Once in a while is fine…but every day? Day in, day out? Life's too short, man.'

'Life is even shorter if you don't eat healthy. But I hear what you're saying. You can't realistically compare the taste. But there is no way I'm going back to the chubby version of me. I had boobies, remember?'

'I remember…' Demetriou laughs…a little too much for my liking. 'Swim class was the best! You didn't even need the floaters!' He bends over double, cackling away. He doesn't even realise that his chef's hat is being lightly toasted where it's hitting the hotplate. 'Ah…good times man.' He straightens up. The top of his hat has blackened. It suits him.

'Yeah, very funny. Hilarious,' I deadpan.

'Why don't you just take a break every now and again? Everyone needs some downtime, otherwise they just burnout.'

'No. I mean, I would love to. But I remember how difficult it was to give up all of that food in the first place. I don't think that I could do it again. And I like the way that I look and feel now. It would be like I'm punishing my body just so my brain can indulge in a few happy hormones.'

'You and your over-thinking, man.' He puts together a quarter pounder burger with cheese, the bun lightly fried till beginning to turn crispy. 'Just look at this. This is a thing of beauty.' He holds the burger up on his palm displaying it in front of me. 'As you bite down, the crispy bun gives you texture. The melted cheese oozes into your mouth. The thick beef burger, so succulent with juice and flavour. Cool relish contrasting the earthy flavours with a pickling sensation. Your serving of veg for the day with perfectly seasoned mushroom and tomato…hmmm…' Saliva is building up in his mouth. I can tell by his repeated gulps. He lingers closely to the edge of the burger, taking in its aroma in his nostrils.

He takes a big bite.

'Demetriou?!? Mate! Is that my burger you're eating?' an angry voice rings out.

A guy dressed in workman's fluorescent vest on a stool a few down from me is looking at the chef in anguish as Demetriou quickly chews and swallows.

'Sorry...sorry my friend. I make you another, okay. Very fast.'

'Dude...not again!'

I slowly sip on my smoothie.

The walk home is lovely. I take the scenic route via the high street, finishing off the last of my smoothie; spinach, kale, blueberries, raspberries, oats, almond milk and ice - a dream sensation, also super healthy. Even though the shards of ice have more or less completely melted, it is still a pretty thick consistency. I find myself having to grind down some of the larger chunks before swallowing.

I don't usually take this path home. My flat is just a few minutes away if I cut down an alleyway next to the cafe. But today has turned out to be one of those unexpectedly warm days, the first of the year in fact to break twelve degrees. The onset of spring has announced itself.

It makes a change to the huddled rushing around that everyone does in winter. Head down, hands stuffed in pockets and a step that is quicker than normal. I can see people more relaxed, less tension in their facial muscles. Though the build-up of traffic is the same, human and mechanical, people don't mind slowing up a little and waiting a few extra seconds.

I finish the last of my drink and dispose of the empty cup in a bin, must keep Britain tidy and respect the street sweeper. A mother and her child dawdle past me. The cute little girl has her mother's arm across her tiny shoulders, guiding her down the road because the little person has no interest whatsoever in where she is going. All of her concentration is going into eating her McDonalds McFlurry. It looks like the Crunchie flavour. Her face is frozen in an expression of angry focus as she battles to scoop a piece of the delicious chocolate along with some ice cream. No easy feat at an age where tying your shoelaces is like defusing a bomb with ten seconds left to blow.

The pair disappear past me and thoughts from my own childhood come flooding back to me. That little kid used to be me. When my uncle used to visit and take me out on adventures, when the time came to eat, all I wanted was a burger, sweets or ice cream. Usually a combination of them all or a replacement here or there; fish fingers was good too, or candy floss and a strawberry milkshake. I quickly learnt that my uncle was soft and could easily be turned to my dark side by a minute or two of stroppiness and pouty face. My mum on the other hand would deal with my demands in a more dictatorial manner. Less of the democratic every-vote-is-equal way; more of the do-as-I-say-or-suffer method. So my sulking was a considered approach which I only used on certain individuals.

Nevertheless, like almost every other kid, junk food was held in high esteem. I didn't care what went into it, all I knew was that it tasted great and I wanted it whenever I could get it.

I didn't concern myself with high sugar content, rotting teeth or my growing waistline.

I miss those days.

It does get difficult to stay clean and healthy sometimes. Especially on the odd occasion where I've had less than my usual eight hours of sleep and my energy and will power are lower than normal. I was addicted to junk food as a kid and those memories of gorging on snacks while watching Blue Peter are actually happy ones. But I know that if I go back and break my healthy way of eating, I could undo years of good work.

On my left a couple of school kids run past me, their rucksacks jumping around on their backs. I wonder what they are running for. My curiosity doesn't have to wait long for an answer as a bus flies past me and stops at the bus stop about fifty metres ahead. It looks like the bus driver has seen them as he waits patiently until they reach the front doors and stumble on board.

It is nice of him to wait.

I've seen many a bus driver wait until a running passenger is just at the doors and then close them and drive away. I guess they need some laughs too in their line of work. That seems like one of the easier ways to get them.

As I get closer to the bus shelter, there is a rolling advert on the board facing me. It looks like a new one. Instead of there being a different advert on each section, each time it changes, the next part showing is a continuation of the same advert.

They've gone for simplicity (usually a good idea, with the steadily declining average IQ of the nation). A bright white background with luminous green text, glowing with a three dimensional effect.

Does the grass always look greener on the other side?
(scrolls down)
Do you want to experience their greenness yourself?
And have a well earned holiday at the same time?
(scrolls down)
Now you can...at Soul BnB
Refresh your mind, body and soul...any way you desire

The advert scrolls down a final time, showing contact details along with their logo before repeating itself from the beginning. The logo has the company name, Soul BnB, in vibrant green, a curved baby blue arrow underneath it pointing from left to right. At the tip of the arrow, three enlarging bubbles rise, the final one turning into a bright yellow Sun.

I stop in front of it and read the advert all the way through, twice.

It grabs my attention.

I saw the same advert in the paper the other day. A revolutionary way to take a break. Great reviews too from what I saw on Trust Pilot and Trip Adviser. Especially from fitness and health freaks such as myself. Completely controlled and in compliance with the Department of Justice for the legal aspects. I remember a guy at the gym talking about it a few months ago. He said it was the perfect way to take a break, with a price bracket available for most people, depending on what you want.

The address isn't far from where I am.

I'm not working today.

I think I'll check it out.

As I walk through the automatic sliding doors of the Soul BnB practice, I am enveloped in a warm glow of bright light. Not that sterile white light of a dentist's surgery but more of the natural brightness from a hot summer's day. However, the store look is a bit odd. Matt white, square tiling covers the floor and walls up till about shoulder height. A soft shade of pastel green continuing from there and a very faint blue on the ceiling. But that isn't what is odd.

What's odd is, that's all there is!

A smartly decorated room, about ten metres square with nothing inside except a small young lady standing in the centre. She looks at me and smiles genuinely. Her shoulder length hair is tied back into a ponytail and she is dressed in a tidy smock of yellow, green and blue shapes, randomly arranged in abstract shapes.

'Good morning, sir. I am Sasha. How are you today?' Her voice is light and friendly, the smile never leaving her features.

'I'm good, very well. Thank you. How are you doing?'

'I am great. Thank you for asking. How may I help you today, sir?'

'I just wanted to enquire really. Have you guys just moved in here?' I gesture around the room at the...well...the nothing.

'No sir, although we have just opened up this morning,' she replies, not catching my drift.

'Okay…well, I wanted to speak to you guys about your holidays. I have heard of you before but haven't really looked into how exactly it all works. Could you fill me in?'

'Sure. Not a problem. There is quite a bit of information and various choices to make. We can show you our introduction video first and then if you're interested or have questions, we can help you from there. How does that sound?'

'Yeah, that sounds good.'

'Great. If you'd like to come this way.' I follow her to the far corner of the empty room where she presses her thumb to the edge of one of the wall tiles. The tile illuminates and transforms into a touch screen LED. She very quickly rifles through some screens and options and turns back to me. My eyebrows are raised.

'Please could you step back for a moment?' I shuffle backwards not understanding the reason for her request. Until that is, one of the floor tiles, about two feet away from the wall begins to slide upward until it reaches chair height. Sasha pulls off the top section of the cuboid, removes a pair of wireless headphones and replaces it upside down to reveal a padded side. It reattaches by what appears to be a magnetic force. My eyebrows have leapt off of the top of my head and are somewhere on the ceiling.

'Take a seat, please.'

I do as I am told and put on the headphones as instructed. Sasha plays a video on the tile screen, and the rich sound blares out through the headphones. The quality of both picture and sound are amazing, I feel totally immersed in the video within a few blinks of an eye.

After a company logo introduction, a middle-aged man dressed in a lab coat appears on the right of the screen. I recognise him. Dr. Sebastian Graves. The founder of Soul BnB and inventor of its technology. I remember reading about him in the Metro. I'm sure he passed away a while back.

'Dear friend, thank you for taking the time to watch this introduction to Soul BnB and the wonderful new technology that we have created.'

His voice is gravelly and rough, but in a grandfatherly type of way which puts me at ease immediately. I'd expect him to slip me a Werther's if we ever met, despite me being an adult. He continues.

'I have spent my life in the pursuit of greater knowledge. Primarily in the field of the human brain and understanding it as best as I can. Now I won't bore you with the details of my history and the founding of the company. I'm sure someone there can give you a pamphlet for that or you can read about it on Wikipedia. But I can tell you that my aim was always to improve the human condition. To make life that much more cheerful.'

As the figure of Dr. Graves speaks, a colourful animation begins to play to Valens' left, illustrating the things that he is speaking about. A female cartoon character who looks exhausted at work, suddenly is whisked away to a sunny sandy beach where her frown becomes a smile as she lounges on a deckchair, sunglasses on and exotic cocktail in hand. A light merry ditty plays in the background.

'We all know that taking a holiday is probably the number one way in which we like to relax and unwind. To travel somewhere far and beautiful, meet different people, enjoy postcard scenery, eat delicious new foods and so forth. But what about the problems with going away somewhere?'

The animation morphs into an endless run of obstacles endured by our holidaying toon. She struggles to lug around a heavy suitcase, then her taxi to the airport gets stuck in traffic with the departure time ticking closer and closer, worried sweat drips down her face like Niagara Falls. She does manage to get on her flight on time but gets stuck between two larger passengers who squeeze her off both arm-rests. She has a bout of travel sickness brought on by a turbulent flight, then goes through multiple sections of waiting and standing in queues as she makes her way out of the airport. But before she can leave, she finds herself in the lost luggage department as it transpires that her suitcase is on its way to the opposite side of the world. Our traveller is not a happy bunny. The cartoon makes me chuckle, knowing first hand of some of the situations displayed.

'And apart from those possible travel issues,' Dr. Graves continues, 'what is the one thing that is the same every holiday?'

A big blue question mark. Our heroine

checking her watch, tapping her foot and staring at me with a simple quizzical expression.

'*You*! That's who. You are the same person every single holiday. Doesn't that get a little tiresome after your fifth trip to Majorca? Well, using our advanced technology, that does not have to be the case anymore. Here at Soul BnB, you can transfer your consciousness into any one of our Soul renters and you can live in their home, in their country and most importantly...in their body!'

Our figurine steps into a Soul BnB outlet, lies down on a couch as a fancy helmet is placed on her head. She then drops off to sleep as a ghostly version of her is sucked down into the attached wires and seen journeying to the other side of the globe to Australia. Here we see an Australian Soul BnB outlet where an unconscious woman has a helmet on her head, wires attached to it. Our ghostly toon continues her journey through these wires and gets sucked into the Australian toons mind through the helmet. She wakes. A big smile on her face.

'No travelling. No wasted time. No jet lag. A truly new experience for you to enjoy. And what happens to your own body, I hear you ask? It goes into a refreshing hibernation...or rent it out yourself for a fee that goes into your pocket...minus our small costs, of course. The choice is yours.'

The animated consciousness of the

holidaymaker undergoes a series of transformations from body to body and from place to place; scenic mountains to a glittering mansion, youthful body to old, tropical weather to snow, Japanese body to African, and on and on. Finally morphing back into the company logo.

Dr Graves enlarges, his head and torso take up the majority of the screen.

'Do you have any questions?'

Huh? Is he speaking to me?

'Oh, hi...um. Yes I do. Do I just...ask you?'

I'm confused now. Is he really there? He can't be. It must be like Siri, an artificial intelligence program.

'Yes, please do.'

'Okay...well...so let me get this straight. I can send my consciousness on holiday into the body of someone else?'

'Yes, that is correct. We would send your consciousness into the body of one of our participating members, while their own would either go into a dream-like virtual environment or on to a holiday of their own. You would wake up in their body at one of our nearby facilities, orientated and then dropped at their home to begin your break.'

'Whose body would I go in? And where?'

'We have a database of members of almost thirty thousand which is constantly growing. These members are located across the globe, although mainly concentrated in the busiest cities of those countries. Our members are from all walks of life and the majority of social classes, ethnicities, sector occupations and religious backgrounds are available. The members also charge their own fee. A member from a New York penthouse, for example, would charge more than someone in Bolton, England.'

'And genders?'

'You can choose which gender you would like to holiday in. Some of our members are not concerned with the gender of the tourist, others are. If the option of opposite sex transfer is made available to you, it will be on offer, although it is rare. We do however, have a strict over twenty one years of age policy. No children are allowed to be involved in the transfer at any stage.'

'Okay...I was just asking, you know. I'm not like a pervert or anything.' I'm not, I think.

'That's absolutely fine, this is the place where you ask your questions.'

'Sure, okay. So how long is the holiday for?'

'It is similar to a normal holiday. The longer you travel for, the more it costs as you book at a daily rate. But the minimum duration is two days, the maximum is one month at present. Longer durations may be available in the future.'

'One month! Do people actually do this for that long?'

'You would be surprised. This is for some

tourists an escape, like any other holiday. Some like to escape for longer than others.' Dr Graves smiles. This artificial intelligence program is great, it's like speaking to an actual person.

'And the cost?'

'Prices begin from £500 per day. The top rate at present is £25000 per day for a member of a European royal family. I am not at liberty to say any more just yet. A non-disclosure agreement would have to be signed and your credit checked before more details would be given.'

'Oh, that is fine. There is no way in hell that I could afford that. Damn. I had no idea you guys were so widespread.'

'Yes, indeed.'

'But what happens if something goes wrong?'

'Wrong? In what sense?'

'Well, in every sense, I suppose. I mean, what if the transfer goes wrong? Or I have a heart attack in the new body? Or I decide to steal a car and go joy-riding?'

'With every transfer, you are entering into a legally binding contract. No transfer will be done until you sign our terms and conditions and pass our background checks. Full life, home and contents insurance must also be taken out to cover any mishaps or accidents, both during the transfers to and fro, and also while you are in occupation of the host body. All accidents must be reported to head office immediately. If you decide to commit any sort of crime or misdemeanour while in the host body, *you* personally will be criminally liable. We will end your holiday immediately and you will be handed over the police in your actual body. All transfers are logged with the Home Office so your comings and goings are fully documented. With regards to the actual transfer procedure, we have never to date had a single problem since our launch. It is very safe with a perfect record.'

'Okay, good stuff. Sounds like you've got all of your bases covered.'

'Yes, the system has worked very well. All of our tourists leave feedback on their hosts and their experience. You can find this on our website. I am sure you will find it all very encouraging.'

'I'm sure I will. I guess that's all the questions I have for now. Thank you.'

'You are very welcome. Please feel free to contact us with any other queries that may arise. Thank you and have a great day.'

The interaction ends and the screen returns to its state as an unassuming wall tile. Sasha comes over once she sees that I'm finished and descends my seat back into the ground, the cushioned lid flipped and my headphones back in its nesting place.

'So Mr...?'

'Novo. Mr Valens Novo.'

'Mr Novo. So what did you think of our

presentation?' Sasha smiles at me expectantly. I reckon that she can see the wonderment dancing behind my eyes. I'll play it cool for now.

'Hmmm...interesting. Is it for real? You can do that without turning the person into a vegetable?'

'Oh, absolutely,' she chuckles, 'the process is very successful. There have been multiple studies conducted by independent labs confirming our own results which you can peruse.'

'I have to admit. Your service is intriguing. Actually more than intriguing. It's bloody amazing. It's like Total Recall, you know that movie with Arnie. But for real. Except that you can't go to Mars. At least I think that you can't go to Mars. I didn't ask the doctor there. And that interaction interface is flipping off the chain! You know the bit, where you ask any questions. It was like I was really speaking with him. He replies just like a normal person. Well, a normal genius, that is. You guys are out of this world. I had heard good things about you but I never realised that you were at this level of awesomeness. Incredible! Absolutely incredible!'

Way to playing it cool, man.

'Thank you sir. That is very kind of you to say.'

'No, it's not being kind! It's the truth. I mean, this is the future. We are in the future right now, here in this place is what Philip K. Dick and Spielberg were talking about with Blade Runner and Minority Report. All that stuff!'

Sasha doesn't reply. She just smiles, but her mouth is beginning to strain and falter a little at the edges. I need to go back to playing it cool for real. And fast. I'm coming across like a bit of a nut job.

'Anyway...Sasha. How would we go on from here...*if* I was interested, that is?' I fold my arms in front of me. It usually indicates a defensive body position, but I'm simply trying to get back under some sort of control. My heart is beating faster than it should be. Folding my arms also shows off my bare biceps in the t-shirt I'm wearing, always a good look.

'Quite straightforward really. You would go through the holiday options with our adviser, decide on the specifics of your trip. Then if you're happy to proceed, we'll book you in for the transfer here in our clinic. As long as the paperwork has passed the checks, you're good to go. That bit's usually just a formality though. I wouldn't worry about it.'

I'm feeling tempted to dive right in and go and see the adviser. Maybe I should go and think about it before I do something I regret. I don't even know when I could book the time off work. Or if I'll be able to. Time off at work is first come, first served.

'Look, let me go and think about things. I'll do some research, check out your website, see where I am and then get back to you. That okay?'

'Sure, of course. It was lovely to meet you today.'

'And you.'

The next morning, I find myself pounding the streets. A five mile jog which sees me aim to be home before six am as I do on a daily basis regardless of the events of the previous evening. This early in the morning is a strange time. Depending on the time of year, it can be pitch black outdoors or as bright as day. The most thought provoking runs occurring when the sun rises whilst I am out there, lost in my own world of swirling scenarios, life altering ideas and mundane checklists to complete during the day, among many other deviations. Being out on the paving as the black of night slowly, but noticeably, becomes the white of morning, often passes me by without a sparing sliver of attention. But on those occasions when I do notice, it jars me to realise that the entire planet Earth is spinning in space at a thousand miles per hour. And where I am entering a period of sunlight, others are right at that very moment, being plunged into its absence, evolution informing them that it is time to sleep. To recover and recuperate from the day's events.

Who are these people that live in constant contradiction to us? Asleep as we wake. Warm while we are cold. Always far away from us, existing in cultures and traditions unknown.

How are we ever to know them, truly? I could visit their countries, over and over. Live side by side. Work with them, celebrate life alongside family and loved ones. But once the day is done and the door closes, the facades drop, intentional or otherwise. How much can I really understand about another?

And isn't it understanding others that brings us all closer together? One step more toward the goal of peace; live and let live. Celebrate our differences instead of using them as ammunition for prejudice and fear.

To live as another, that would be the path to ultimate empathy. To walk that mile in another person's shoes, to experience life as that other even if just for a fleeting moment. That would be worth more than studying an avalanche of lectures and interviews.

As I reach home, I find myself more out of breath than I usually am. Checking the time I am surprised to find that I have been running a lot faster than I should be. The morning jog is just a warm up for the day, not something to exhaust me. With the weary load slowing me down, I carry out the rest of my morning routine. Warm down stretching, lemon and honey mixture fluids, granola cereal with nut milk, plain rye toast ending with a selection of freshly cut fruit and some seeds. The revelations I have reached seem to have spurred me on subconsciously.

I soon conclude the reason why.

I am excited.

Three days pass as I finalise details of my holiday and book the necessary time off work. My boss wasn't too happy with the short notice that I gave him, but as I only decided on a three night trip, I wrangled the holiday through somehow. I'll probably be facing a desk load of work left for me on my return, sadism being a hobby of my boss, but I think that it is totally worth it.

As Sasha had told me before, passing the physical and mental evaluations was pretty straightforward, as was completing the criminal and credit checks, and taking out the required insurance. I had a few additional questions which she cleared up for me and after seeing the scores of positive reviews from previous tourists, I was more or less made up.

'Mr Novo. Great to see you this morning. Are you ready for your holiday?' Sasha is chirpy as always.

'Yes thanks, Sasha, I think. I'm nervous to be honest,' I reply, the unknown taking away strength from my body. I feel light headed.

'Oh, you'll have a great time over there, I'm sure. Come with me and I'll take you straight into the clinic. You're right on time.'

We head to the back of the room where Sasha presses her thumb to one of the wall tiles, revealing a hidden door that swings open with a low pitched swoosh. Sasha gestures for me to pass through with a wave of the hand and a gentle bow of the head. Ever the polite professional.

I am greeted by a typical lab-coat clad scientist, wearing generic clothing underneath and sporting a scruffy hair style on top. He is concentrating on a file he is reading as I come in, making notes on the page with a blunt pencil.

'Hello there. You must be Mr Novo.' He stops and greets me with an outstretched hand. His handshake is surprisingly yet reassuringly solid. 'I am Dr. Young. Please, come in and take a seat here for me.'

The room I enter into is not what I had expected. After experiencing the marvel of the front of house, I thought that the actual portal into another entity would continue that theme; push the boundaries of what I knew to be possible.

What assaults my eyes is a chair and a computer. A few wires running from it and connecting to a shiny helmet on a stand that a child could replicate with a coat hanger and some tin foil. Probably even improve on. The room isn't much better. A cheap light brown lino with cream paint on the walls. A tiny sink fitted into the corner and a workbench that runs around two of the walls.

Dr Young must have seen the dumbstruck

gormless expression on my face. 'Don't worry Mr Novo. All of the clever stuff is hidden away on the inside.' He leads me to the seat.

'Are you sure? I mean, it just all looks a little...basic.'

'Oh, you're in good hands, I can promise you that. I admit the decoration needs some updating, but bear in mind that this was the original clinic for Soul BnB. The new guys get most of the newer toys and sets, although we take care of the majority of the...prestigious...clientele here. And don't let looks deceive you, there is more going on here than you think.'

'Hmmm...'

I'm not very convinced. Nevertheless, this isn't the time to falter and bail.

The good doctor is oblivious to my unease and continues with the preparations, always returning to his file and making notes after each step of progress. He is deep in concentration as I sit on a chair not dissimilar to a dentist's chair, or a barber's chair, same thing really. After fifteen or so minutes of what appears to be a box ticking exercise, he gives me some attention.

'Right Mr Novo. Everything is perfectly set up. Your vitals and essential levels are in great areas, probably as you do look after yourself pretty well.' He lightly slaps me on the shoulder, my protruding deltoids solid even as I rest. 'Your host body is ready and waiting for you in sunny,

California. I have to say, location-wise, a great choice.'

'Thanks. And host-wise?'

'A fairly run-of-the-mill body. But I get it. It must be tough to maintain a physique such as yours. Being so disciplined on a daily basis. You must look forward to a break.'

'Yeah. Something like that. But how are you checking my bodily details? I'm just sitting here. You haven't stuck or prodded me with anything.'

'Ah. That's the deceptive part I was telling you about. This room has been monitoring you remotely since the moment you entered. Brain waves, blood pressure, heart rate.' My mouth opens in shock.

'You can really do that?'

'Oh, so sending your consciousness into the body of a man thousands of miles away for a holiday is fine, but *this* you have an issue with?'

I am in the realm of the impossible. I'm going to take it all in my stride from now on.

'I suppose you're right.'

'Good. Are ready for transfer?'

'Yes.'

Dr Young places the cranial contraption onto my head. Despite looking messy in its build, it is cushioned on the inside and comfortable. It weighs a fair amount too, indicating that it has a lot going on within its surface.

The doctor confirms with me the details of the

transfer, duration and host. Takes me through a few last minute pieces of information, much of which I already know but it is helpful to reiterate them.

It feels very strange. I am going on holiday without taking a single item with me. Normally I have a long checklist of clothes, documents, creams and toiletries, electronics and chargers, money and bank cards as well as a full itinerary of travel specifics. But here I have nothing. Simply me.

'Okay, Mr Novo. We are ready to transfer. As soon as we activate our module here, you will become unconscious. It may be possible that you go into a dream state and experience very vivid scenarios. That is perfectly normal and will only last for a few minutes in reality. The next thing that you will notice is waking up in your host body at our California clinic in Santa Monica. The team there will look after you from there. Your body here will be kept in our hibernation unit at these premises and you will receive it back in exactly the same condition as it is in today. No loss of muscles mass so don't worry. Any questions?'

I stare at the doctor and try to think of something to say. More to delay the activation than anything else. I'm about to pee my pants. I shake my head.

'Good. Now just relax. We are transferring in five...four...three...two...one...'

I don't hear what Dr. Young said after one. It was probably *blast off* or something similar that he finds humorous. Me? I feel as if I'm in surgery and they have just turned up the anaesthetic. Darkness clouds my mind and I'm falling…fast…asleep…

I open my eyes easily. But everything is blurry and out of focus.

I try and sit up but I feel really weak and heavy, lethargic.

'Mr Novo. Please don't move. My name is Dr. Ramchand. We just need to go through a few checks and we can have you on your way. You will feel disorientated for a period, but that will pass. Oh, and welcome to California, USA.'

I look around to see the origin of the lilting accented voice. Dr. Ramchand is the polar opposite of Dr. Young who sent me on my way. Big brown eyes stare at mine, I'm relieved that there isn't any concern showing in hers.

'Hello there.' The words croak out of my throat, raspy and breathless. *I* said them but they don't sound like me. My English accent is still kind of there but also not, and my pitch and tone is lower. A lot lower. This must be the voice of my host. I hope the rest gets better.

'Don't speak for now Mr Novo. You can go ahead and close your eyes. You'll feel better. Once I'm happy, I'll get you on your feet.'

I do as she says and almost go back into a

slumber. I hear a lot of shuffling around and noises. Electronic noises, beeps and hums, tones which come from button pressing. It sounds a lot more active than the clinic I just came from.

As I am waiting, I try to ground myself. It's a technique that I learnt from my father about dealing with peculiar or stressful situations. This certainly comes under the category of peculiar. I take a deep breath, feel the air rushing into my lungs. Flex my limbs, feet and hands to feel my boundaries. I smell the air and recognise that nothing dangerous is around me. I delve into my psyche and remember who I am and what strength I have within me, that I am able to do whatever I will.

It works. Soon I am relaxed and ready. But something still feels out of place. I know things that I never knew before. Names, places, people. I was told that this would happen and is actually part of the trip. But it feels like I am looking out of someone else's eyes.

I guess I am.

'Alright. Mr Novo. All checks are complete and successful. You are officially on holiday!'

After a short uneventful car journey passing through a residential area, a member of the Soul BnB team walks me into my holiday home for the next three days, located just off Ocean Avenue. He shows me around the smart one-bed flat in a nice residential complex, gives me the keys and contacts for any questions, although the host has left me a required set of instructions for all of the essentials. I don't pay too much attention. I'm in a daze. I feel as though I'm living in a virtual reality. I wait till he goes and leaves me in peace.

The quiet is jarring. It makes me question what I have done. But I now have time alone to investigate this new body. Or this thirty-five year old body. Just *new* to me.

I walk around the flat, taking in the new environment. The front door opens into a passage. To the right is the front room, open plan with the kitchen to one side. Large windows ideally facing east letting in maximum light and heat for the day. The kitchen attracts the eye with its black, white and chrome colour combination, fitted appliances and cupboards for a sleek look, though the majority of them look barely used. The living room has a sixty inch led television hanging on the far wall, a complicated remote control on the glass table in front of it.

If this were any other normal rental, I would need some experimentation before understanding the buttons on all of these contraptions. But here I know exactly what does what. It is one of the most important positives of the Soul BnB trips. As Sasha explained to me, markers are left for me in this brain with the basic information that I would need to live in this body; allergies, diet, emergency contacts, the local layout, everything that I would need to function in a strange area with the minimum of fuss.

Also on the table is my credit card. A special one made up just for this trip which I use as this host but is pre-topped up beforehand with my own spending money. Any amount that I go over my pre-paid value gets charged at interest to my debit account. For convenience, I have a hundred dollars in cash on my person from the clinic. All of that, along with the hefty rental for this three night trip has put a large dent in my wallet.

Hopefully it's worth it.

The bedroom is at the other end of the passage. Reasonable size, a comfy looking king-size in the middle of the room. On the left door of the wardrobe is a full length mirror. Time to examine this host properly, see what I'm working with here. I strip down to my underwear.

This is freaky.

I am gazing at my reflection in the mirror, but the face looking back at me is not me. A man by the name of Juan Marcos looks back at me. Short haired with a receding hairline and protruding belly. The same height as my own body but slightly hunched and a lot curvier. The curves are very soft.

I wave my hand.

The man in the reflection waves back.

I drop into a squat position.

So does the man.

I push back up to my standing position.

So does he. That movement is harder than I can ever remember it being.

This guy doesn't look after his body.

I smile.

In the living room is a phone. One of those trendy upright circular phones. The top half of the circle is the handset which comes away in my hand as I pull it free. I'm not wasting any time. I speed dial number 3 and listen. When the person picks up on the other end, I begin talking.

After a couple of minutes, I put the phone down.

And I wait.

This should be good.

To while away the time, I take a trip round the flat, looking to get a feel of the host's life. Pictures, books, movies, newspapers. Anything to get an inkling of who this person is that I have suddenly become so intimate with. In the passage, a wooden framed photograph hangs on the wall. In it are two men on a boat during a sunny cloudless day. One of the men is Juan, smiling and displaying both rows of teeth. He has an arm around the shoulders of an older man wearing a blue baseball cap, skin tanned and leathery from regular hours outdoors. The similarity between the two men is striking, their features though decades apart in age, are cut from the same cloth. He must be his father or at least a blood related uncle.

It makes me wonder.

If that is Juan's father, what must he be making of his son signing up with Soul BnB? The son whom he raised from a tiny baby into an independent man is renting out not only his body, but his life and essence as well. *Does he even know?* What if I happen to come across him out of the blue? Surely these instances must be common place with this type of endeavour and the people involved have been notified already.

Or have they?

As I stand there, pondering, the front doorbell chimes, knocking some reality and presence back into me. I completely forget that I am in my underwear and scurry around looking for some clothes to put on.

'Hold on! I'll be right there.'

This body is not as deft and agile as mine is and I keep bumping my shoulder into door frames and wall edges, but I manage to fit into my trousers once again.

I make it to the front door, out of breath from that thirty second dash. Not what I'm used to at all.

'Hey, wus up man?' The personal salutation knocks me off balance.

'Oh...uh...hey man.' The guy squints at me

suspiciously.

'You okay? You don't look so good.'

'Yeah...uh...just been exercising. I'm pretty out of shape.'

'Okay…You sound different too.' I'm at a loss. I can't just go and tell this guy that I'm on vacation in the body of his friend. Some of Sasha's advice comes back to me and I search my memory banks for some guidance on who this fellow is.

It works.

'Uh…Caesar, right? I mean, my man! Ha-ha, I'm just kidding with you, been watching some of that Downton Abbey, that English stuff is dope, yo!' I put on my best New Jack City accent. Wrong city, I realise.

'For real! The ladies love that accent, man!' It seems as though I have passed it off. 'Here's your order, man. All paid for. Enjoy.'

'Thanks. I'll see you.' I take the large brown paper bag from him, slide him a ten dollar tip and close the door. I can hear Caesar walking away laughing to himself, '...English accent, I gotta try that shit, man...'

Hurriedly, I move like a rhinoceros trying to tip toe into the front room, banging and scraping against the walls. I have been fervently awaiting this moment from the instance that I decided to go on this trip. The time has come.

I pull the small glass coffee table towards the two-seat sofa which I crash down onto, placing the bag on top. I turn on the flat screen, the comedy channel comes on, my favourite. This cannot get any better.

I tear open the bag and distribute the contents all over the table. They barely fit on. I have to double stack a few items. But I don't care. The time has come. My time has come. My mouth salivates, drools copiously as I gape and survey all that lay before me.

My bounty.

My treasure.

Junk food!

And lots of it!

Dr. Young is smiling at me back in my local Soul BnB clinic.

Am I back already? Wow, that holiday went fast. Well, you know what they say, time flies when you're having fun. So much so in fact that I don't even remember the homebound journey. Maybe, it will come back to me once I pull out of this daze that I'm in.

Even so, despite the success of the trip, it's good to see Dr. Young's face again. Someone from my home town. Kind of lets me know that I'm back and all is well. I have to say though, the good doctor's smile is feeling curious. I don't remember him to be a chirpy smiler. He was quite a dour fellow on the outbound section of the trip.

Actually, the more that I look at him, the less of

a smile his expression looks like.

It looks more like he is baring his teeth at me like he wants to eat me.

Out of anger.

Or is it more than that? Rage.

My vision is a little blurry. I blink rapidly three or four times.

Ah...that feels better.

My vision has sharpened up a tad.

Oh. There is someone behind Dr. Young.

Is it Sasha? She certainly is female.

The uniform is all wrong though.

That is a police officer's uniform.

Actually, now that I'm looking around, there is a whole team of officers surrounding me as I sit here on this chair. Other stern faced official types too.

I can't move my arms.

I'm strapped in.

What the hell is going on?

'Mr Novo, I am arresting you on behalf of the government of the United States of America for the murder of Mr Juan Carlos. Anything that you do say may be...'

I don't hear the rest of it. My mind is spinning. I black out.

When I come around, Dr Young notices. Instantly he is upon me. He leans down to my ear and whispers harshly.

'You stupid bastard, how could you? You've put this whole company at risk!'

An officer grabs him by the arm and holds him back, not liking the level of aggression he is showing me. But even from a distance, I can feel the hatred being levelled at me.

'Wh...what's going on, doctor? Murder? I haven't murdered anyone.'

Dr Young shakes free of the officer, tells him that he has calmed down. He turns back to me, an angry bull puffing out of his nostrils.

'Valens, while you were in the body of Juan Carlos, you gorged yourself on so much junk and crap, that you ate the body to death. You pig...no, no...actually you're not a pig. That is an insult to pigs. You, my friend, *you* are something else.' He comes closer. The officer positions himself between the two of us, but lets him continue speaking. 'You...Mr Novo...you are a disease, a parasite, a virus. A blood sucking vampire, greedy, weak and a fake. You...'

'Okay doctor. That's enough,' one of the stern faced officials interjects, cutting off the doctor before the throttle is revved any further, 'I'll take over from here, James. Go and get some air.'

Dr. Young lavishes me with a final lingering stare filled with an unadulterated passion to kill and storms out, muttering to himself.

'I apologise for the doctor's conduct,' the man says, his bald head glistening, round rimmed glasses perched on the tip of his nose, 'but your actions have put him in a stressful position...being the one responsible for your transfer.'

'No, I understand. I didn't mean to...I wasn't trying to kill anyone...it's just the hunger that I had...after all these years...'

'Mr Novo. Please. You have just undergone an emergency transfer so you will be disorientated, a little hazy on the details. I am Dr. Jones, executive officer of Soul BnB. This is a very serious situation so let me fill you in on the precarious position that we find ourselves in right now.'

'Sure...sorry, sorry. Go ahead, please.' My heart is beating fast.

'Now, Mr Novo. While you were in the body of Mr Juan Carlos in America on a holiday transfer, the body passed away. Fortunately, the body was found just in time for us to be able to retrieve your consciousness and return you to your original body, as you are now. However, Mr Carlos had in-house surveillance equipment from which we were able to access footage of the events leading up to the death.' I open my mouth to defend myself, but get cut off. 'Before you say anything else, watch the video with me and then we can talk, okay?' I nod nervously.

Sasha enters the room with a tablet and hands it to Dr. Jones. She makes no eye contact with me whatsoever. I can't blame her.

A clip plays on the tablet showing the angle

from the front window corner and taking in the entire living room and kitchen. It shows me as Mr Carlos sitting down with a large paper bag, emptying it of its contents. Before long the coffee table is full of chips, burgers, a kebab, pizza, fizzy drink and ice cream; me attacking it all like a ravenous dog.

'These are your actions, yes?' I nod once again. 'Good. Thank you for being honest. Now look at the time mark on the video. One pm. Now if I scroll to four hours later.'

Dr. Jones shows footage of me entering the room with another large bag, this time unloading a mound of desserts onto the table, chocolate cake, more ice cream, pastries, tiramisu, and more. Not even an hour later, it has been demolished.

Dr. Jones scrubs through the clip and shows time after time after time of me ordering excessive junk food and eating again and again, taking small breaks in between. Watching it is disgusting me. I can't believe I did that.

'Now if we go to the next evening after your arrival.'

The clip shows me again as Mr Carlos, sat with huge hot dogs, steak sandwiches and a large pizza. My rate of eating has slowed but I continue consistently nevertheless. The definition of the clip is good, I can see that I am sweating profusely while I eat and showing signs of struggling to breathe.

'The next part is difficult to watch,' Dr. Jones warns.

With a mouthful of pizza, I bite the end off of a hot dog, sauce dripping down my chin. I chew for ten or so seconds and try to swallow. My eyes enlarge and I begin to cough and splutter. The hot dog falls from my hands and I grab the two litre bottle of fizzy pop. My attempt at clearing my airways with the drink are futile as it all just fills up my mouth and gushes down my front. As the bottle sips from my frantic hands, I begin to heave, my body going into defence mode and trying to regurgitate the excess of food in my system. All that happens is that I froth excessively at the mouth, falling to my knees, desperately grabbing at my surroundings looking for something to help me.

I fail.

I crash against the table and fall to the floor.

All sign of movement extinguished inside of ten seconds.

Dr. Jones turns off the clip and turns to me.

'Is it all coming back to you?' he asks me evenly. He gives me time to reflect.

The memories *are* all coming back to me now.

I remember being in a body that I didn't have to care for. A body that obviously didn't do much to care for itself. I wanted to take advantage of that and have a guilt-free release from the years of checking ingredients labels, portioning food, eliminating sugar and fat from my diet, constantly passing up on desserts as friends around me would dive in and titillate their taste buds. I wanted to regress to my days of being a chubby kid who ate whatever he wanted and felt good about it, not worrying whether the definition of my six pack would be diminished.

But I also remember not being able to control myself and never stopping at just a taste.

I wanted to make up for a decade of abstinence.

'I remember...' The words come out of my mouth and it hurts me. '...I couldn't help it...but surely, you can see that this was an accident?'

Dr. Jones takes a deep breath.

'Mr Novo. If you had done this to yourself...to your own body than...yes. An accident would have obviously been declared. But this wasn't your body. You were given the responsibility of the body of Mr Carlos. You misused that body and put it through such a high level of abuse that his stomach ruptured and died, rare as that cause of death is, I'm told. His father has asked for you to be hit with the full force of the law and is threatening to take Soul BnB to court as well. Of course, you will be put on trial first, but our lawyers tell me that you have little chance of escaping from this. It will be the first trial of its kind and you will be made an example of.'

His father.

The smiling proud face in the picture on the wall.

I feel sick.

'Insurance will cover most of the financial damage and legal costs, but that will not protect you from the law and nor will it protect our company from the damage to our image. We both will probably not survive.'

My head drops. My body in all of its muscular perfection comes into my view but it is frozen, unable to move, devoid of energy.

'So I will be sent to jail in America?' I ask.

'Yes.' It is like a gunshot to a dying body. 'However...,' he says tentatively. '...there is one other option.'

'An option?'

'Yes. You see, the body of Mr Carlos is dead, however his consciousness remains alive in our virtual storage, waiting for to be returned to his body. The only problem is, there is no body to return him into...as it currently stands.'

A sliver of hope.

'Can't we get a body?' I clutch at the wisp of a thread. 'There must be people dying every day.'

'There are,' Dr Jones cedes, 'but we have no claim or access to any of those bodies...but *your* body...you can donate that to house Mr Carlos' consciousness and end the law suit. Damage will still be done to our company but we can spin that into something positive.'

My body? The body that I have carved into something beautiful over years of discipline and planning. But what will that mean for me? My own death? I vocalise these fears to Dr. Jones.

'We have an old body that we used in our trial phase that is still in hibernation that can house you.'

'But why can't you give that body to Juan, Mr Carlos, I mean?'

'Oh, we have already tried. But Mr Carlos' father refused. He is understandably furious and wants only your body if he is to accept this route. Punishment of a sort while escaping punishment of another sort. And he has seen images of your body. He appreciates your...maintenance...of it.'

'I think I need to speak to a lawyer. This is all way over my head.'

'Valens. Please listen carefully. This offer is only on the table now. If you don't accept the offer now, then the offer will be rescinded. And you will be kept on remand until your extradition to America for trial goes through. You have seen the footage of your actions yourself. There isn't much...wiggle room here.'

Waking up, I feel drowsy. My mouth is dry. Need to find some water. I lift myself from my seat. There is a mirror by the doorway, full length. Let me take a look at my reflection.

The familiar sight of my face looks back at me.

I look tired and irritated, like a need a shower and a holiday to recover from the exhaustion of all of this mess. Ironic, after this was supposed to be the holiday I didn't need to recover from.

I move closer to my reflection.

Something doesn't seem quite right.

The reflection didn't move in with me.

My movements don't look like they're being matched.

The *me* in the false mirror actually speaks to me. 'Are you Valens Novo?'

'Why, yes. I am,' I reply, confused. *Is this a dream?*

The false me begins to tremble. He tenses his muscles impressively, curves and mounds forming and stretching his fitted blue t-shirt. Suddenly, he lunges at me. Punches me on the side of the head. The force is impressive. The ground comes up to meet me. Or do I go down to meet it?

A scuffle ensues and when I turn back to look, a group of people are holding the false me. He doesn't struggle anymore. The people lead him away, down a corridor and out of sight.

Dr. Jones comes in the room and quickly helps me up off the floor, puts me back onto the chair.

'What's going on doctor? Who was that? Why did *I* hit...*me?*'

'You must still be dazed and confused. He shouldn't have had access to you. I apologise. That was Mr Juan Carlos. We have transferred his consciousness into your original body as agreed. He is finding the situation difficult to deal with. All of a sudden in a new body and in a different country. Psychologists surrounding him, trying to put him at ease. Lots of paperwork to deal with to change photo identifications and documentation. Which we need to do with you also, Mr Novo, by the way. Anyway, it is a lot for him to deal with. You remember what we have done, right?'

The memory catches up with me with a mental slap.

'Oh...yes...I remember now.' I feel sick.

'Good.'

'So...who am I now?'

'You are still Mr Novo, as before.'

'I know that, but whose body do I have. It doesn't feel very...sturdy. Feels like it needs a lot of work.' I don't want to look down at myself. It doesn't feel like I will be pleased.

'Have a look.' Dr. Jones shows me to a real mirror attached to a far wall. As I stand in front of it, I recognise the face instantly.

'Sebastian Graves!'

'The one and the same. The inventor of this technology and founder of this company. Years ago he permanently unloaded his consciousness into the company network and lives in the virtual ever-lasting environment of his own design. He still works with new customers as an adviser. He enjoys it. But he is constantly pushing the boundaries of his technology...from the inside. His body has been on ice ever since. When he heard about what happened, he offered it for your use. He doesn't need it. Hasn't wanted to return to reality since the divorce.'

'I'm...old...balding...and fat.'

'Yes...but also free. Don't forget that part. All charges dropped.'

I examine my receding hairline, jowls hanging from my chin and lack of toned muscle...everywhere.

'Maybe I need one of those psychologists next.'

Dr. Jones puts his arm around me.

'Look, Valens. Your body may be older than you were before, but only by about a decade...or two...or three...but whatever the difference, your mind is still young and fresh. You can work with it, make it your own. Get back to your disciplined self.'

'I guess so...what else can I do? I'll have to explain all of this to everyone who knows me first. Going to be a long month.'

'And don't forget...if you ever feel like a break, you know where to come.'

THE INTERVIEW

'Why are you so nervous?'

'Nervous? Who's nervous?'

'Well...*you.*'

'Why do you say that?'

'I can hear your heart beating. It's like Buddy Rich is doing a solo.

'Buddy Rich?'

'Yeah, Buddy Rich. Only the greatest drummer of all time.'

'Oh.'

'Oh?'

'I've never heard of him.'

'How old are you?'

'Twenty six.'

'Okay, never mind. He is a bit before your time.'

'Guardian, please don't underestimate me because of my age.'

'Oh? Then why should I underestimate you?'

'...you shouldn't.'

'Shouldn't what?'

'Underestimate me.'

'Why not?'

'I'm smarter than I look.'

'And how do you look?'

'Young…some might say immature.'

'I don't think so.'

'Good.'

'Good.'

'Then we can begin?'

'Lets.'

Kira, the young, Asian interviewer gestures towards a cushioned armchair for The Guardian to sit in. He does so with a nod of thanks and his usual grace. Kira takes a seat to the angled left side of him, a small glass coffee table in between them to hold any beverages or snacks for later on. A large plasma screen sits slightly behind the gap between both chairs. Two metres in front of them is a tripod with a digital camera sitting on top, Greg operating it from the rear. Greg has them both in shot and ready to begin their historic interview. Microphones attached and working.

These three are the only ones in the plush London penthouse suite on top of a thirty storey building affording them amazing views across the city. Unfortunately, the camera has its back to the windows of the outermost room that they are filming in, keeping the gorgeous floor to ceiling glass windows entirely out of shot. This is to ensure that the live feed they will be broadcasting cannot be identified for its location and tempt anyone else from tracking them down and interrupting proceedings. You always attract a few opportunistic loonies if you give temptation.

Kira looks at the camera. Greg gives her a thumbs up.

She smiles professionally, nothing external giving away the fact that she is feeling very nervous as The Guardian pointed out not too long ago. There is very little about this interview that would conform to the rules of anything that she has done in the past. She tells herself that if she can just get through the first few minutes without cracking, she could probably settle down fairly easily and ride out the rest of the show without much else affecting her. A lot is riding on this show going perfectly.

Greg the cameraman, and general dogsbody is ready to begin proceedings. He holds up three fingers…two fingers…one…action.

'Hi guys and gals. This is Koffee with Kira and I am your host, Kira Saan.' Her voice undulates pleasantly to the ear in her now famous style. Her professional smile shining through as always. 'Now as you know, today is not going to be a normal show. It is going to be a very special show indeed. A live show. As you can see, we are not in our usual studio. Today we are overlooking the capital from a penthouse suite with a gorgeous view of all of the famous monuments that people flock here to see from across the globe. And the reason that we have pushed the boat out today is because we have won a competition, guys. We have won the absolute mother of competitions. Even Mother Mary would be agreeing with us, apologies to any Christians in the house, no offence intended.'

Kira turns to her right and the camera zooms out to take in the full view of the interviewee.

He is a marvellous sight.

Dressed head to toe in a skin tight, matt-black mesh suit and black calf-high boots, The Guardian strikes an imposing and radiating figure. An emerald 'G' embossed onto his chest plate shimmering in the sunlight, he has an authoritative air about him which makes the atmosphere crackle with electric.

The camera zooms in a little closer to take in his much photographed face; the flowing black locks, solid jaw and well-defined cheek bones, everything you could ask for in a hero, a saviour. He could easily take his place on the catwalks of Paris and New York if he so desired, the concrete six foot plus stature constantly straining at his suit forming muscular curves on every inch of fabric.

The Guardian stares directly into the camera; his eyes squinted reminiscent of the great Clint Eastwood. He gives a tiny nod and a gentle smile which gathers on the right side of his mouth. Soft thuds are heard all over the world as young woman, and some men find their undergarments hitting the deck. Never has a live appearance been more eagerly awaited than this, the viewing figures are off the charts. You can bet that this interview will be replayed and analysed over and over by millions all across the globe. Most for good reasons. Although a few for bad reasons.

Greg zooms out once again to keep both in full view of the camera. This will be the view for the entire show as he busies himself with other behind the scenes duties, including managing the social media accounts which are set to explode very soon. Unfortunately, due to the secretive nature of the interview, Greg has only one set of hands at his disposal, his own.

Kira clears her throat and glances at the iPad held tightly between her hands. It shows her the prompts for the interview, along with any new important information sent through from Greg.

'I would like to introduce a man who needs no introduction. It is The Guardian everyone. Whoo!'

'Thanks Kira, I am glad to be here. Thank you for having me.' The Guardian's voice is a rich deep baritone, more bass than treble, more Barry White than Michael Jackson. His accent however, gives away his east London roots, a smidgen of cockney surfacing with a gently dropped 'h' here and there.

'Please, the honour is all mine. Thank you so

much for giving us this amazing opportunity to be the first to officially interview you since...well...ever.'

The Guardian tips his head.

'Not a problem. I think that now is the right time to come out and answer some of the multitude of questions that people have been asking. Fill in gaps of knowledge about me. So I will do my best to answer anything that you ask as well as I can. Don't be shy to broach on any topic that you or your viewers have been asking.'

'That's very kind of you,' Kira says with a beaming grin, 'before we begin however, I would like to send a huge thank you to Global Express newspaper for holding the competition which allowed us to win this interview with you. I'm curious why you didn't hold your first interview with them, Guardian? You do, it seems, have pretty close links with them.'

'Well Kira, you are correct. I am close with the paper and more specifically, some of the people that work there. But I am also mindful of the future and just how news is being obtained these days. I am a big fan of types of shows such as yours, where the viewers can have direct input and have their voices heard. I thought by offering my personal interview to an online live streamed show, as well as reaching across the planet, it might encourage others to follow the same path as you have Kira. And can I say congratulations on such a fantastic production, I have heard many good things about you.'

'Wow, thank you! Very kind words.' Kira turns back and addresses the camera. 'Viewers, this is a historic occasion, the importance of which I cannot stress enough. We have with us The Guardian! The world's first and only superhero in every sense of the word.' Kira checks her notes very quickly to check where she is, her head is still spinning a little. 'Mr Guardian…is that okay to call you? Mr Guardian? Or what do you prefer?'

'Honestly I am not bothered. But you can drop the *mister*. Just Guardian is fine, I guess. The public named me in the first place. *Guardian* has been thrust upon me, it's not a name that I chose for myself.'

'But it looks like you have readily adopted the name,' Kira waves her hand by The Guardian's chest plate, gesturing towards the shining G logo. I mean, it is built into your suit.'

'Hmm…It felt like a good fit when I read about it. Kind of encapsulates my feelings for why I do what I do.'

'Because you like to guard people?'

'To stand up for those who can't stand up for themselves.'

'I think that's how you obtained the name in the first place, isn't it? To those of our viewers who don't know what I am talking about, we have the clip from the initial time that you were seen in action on camera and the person who coined your name for the very first time. It has long become one of the most viewed online clips in history, but for those who haven't seen it and those who just want to see it again because it's so amazing, here it is. But a warning to younger viewers and those of a sensitive disposition, there is violence that can be difficult to watch.'

Greg uses his extensive panel of controls to switch on a video clip to play on the plasma screen behind them. As Kira and The Guardian both turn to look at the screen, the viewer is given a full screen clip to look at on their feeds.

An amateur shot video springs to life, most likely taken on a smart phone. It is shot from the first floor window of a building looking out onto a cross junction of two intersecting residential streets somewhere deep in east London. The day is calm, sun shining heartily with clear skies, the few stragglers walking around are dressed lightly for the warm weather. All is normal apart from the angry looking teenager standing over an old pensioner who is on the floor and propping himself up on one elbow. The other arm is out-stretched, palm out and limply facing outward to form a feeble barrier between him and the teen.

It is pretty obvious that the man has been attacked by the boy but he isn't looking at his attacker. Instead his face is turned down and he is weakly coughing and blowing a mixture of blood and spit from his mouth, a long strand of liquid reaching to the floor. He looks like he is breathing heavily, all of the energy sapped from his body, doing the best he can to stay conscious and put up a defence.

It doesn't have much effect as the boy easily navigates around his defence and kicks him square in the jaw. Hard.

The old man collapses fully to the floor. Prone and vulnerable.

The boy, dressed in black shorts and a sleeveless t-shirt, stands over his poor victim and screams obscenities at him, stamping on his knees in between syllables. A distant mass of pedestrians is gathering and staring, many with open mouths, but none are intervening. A car stops in the street and honks his horn loudly and repeatedly but to no effect. The driver doesn't take the next step of getting out to help and drives away after a lingering moment.

You can hear the person taking the video clip gasping at the blows raining down on the old man. The footage is becoming shaky as he zooms in a little closer. It doesn't make for easy viewing. Instead of easing up on the old man, the boy is attacking more and more furiously with each passing second.

It doesn't last much longer though.

There is a blur of colour, a flash of movement.

The boy is suddenly and unexpectedly launched

high up into the air and across the road where he hits the rooftop of the building across the street from where he was. From a height of around fifteen metres, he comes crashing down to the ground, his legs crumpled and pointing in odd directions. He isn't moving.

In his previous place stands a hooded figure, it's difficult to see where he came from. It looks like he simply just appeared out of thin air. He is kneeling down by the battered old man, checks up and down his body and within a split second, he scoops up the old man in his arms and flies up into the sky at an incredible speed.

The phone attempts to follow but soon loses him while simultaneously zooming out and pointing around in the sky. The man is gone. The clip is ended with the video-taker shouting and screaming 'oh my God!' over and over again, with someone in the background crying out 'An angel! That was a fucking guardian angel man!'

The video ends and Kira is back in the studio with The Guardian.

'Believe it or not, that's actually the first time that I've seen that clip.' The Guardian shifts in his chair, a little embarrassed with seeing himself on camera. Or could it be the violence that he himself inflicted being caught on camera?

'Really? It is from almost fifteen years ago now.'

'Really? I mean I heard about it and read about it in the papers once they picked up on the story, but I never thought to watch it.'

'You know it took about six months for people to accept and believe it was real. We all thought it was faked, like so much else out there. But when there were more and more reports of you out there and these amazing things that you were doing…well…views of this clip exploded. It has amassed over a billion viewings across the planet.'

'A billion? Wow.'

'Can you tell us about that day?'

'Sure. I was actually up on the rooftops that day. My powers were still quite new to me so I was testing them out. A bit of flying here and there. Then I heard the distinct sound of bone crunching.'

'You could hear that? When the old man had his legs stamped on?'

'Yes. I was about a mile away so I flew over to check it out, all the while I could hear that angry young boy swearing and cussing. I knew something was wrong. I didn't actually want to hurt the boy but when I saw what he did to the old man, I had to get him away and fast.'

'Do you know what actually happened to him?'

'Who? The boy? No. He got off easy in my opinion. I could have ejected him from the atmosphere if I felt like.'

'That did cause a lot of controversy around you in the beginning, but we'll get to that later on. What happened to the old man?'

'He was okay. Very badly beaten but it was mostly things that would heal in time. I still check in on him from time to time, just to make sure he's keeping well. I'm sure the mental distress was far worse than anything physical.'

'It's nice that you even find time to comfort people. I think it's one of things that people love you for, your caring. But what else do you do in your life apart from the super-heroing? How do you unwind after a hard day's work?'

The Guardian visibly relaxes as the generic nature of questioning comes around. He is a natural on camera, but obviously prefers to keep the chat simple.

'Well, I do love to eat. I love food. I have a huge appetite.'

'I bet you do,' Kira laughs easily, a hint of flirtation in her eyes as her straight black hair waves gently, curving around her heart shaped face.

'And I like to try food from every different culture I come across. Believe it or not, but my taste buds are normal, much like yours, so I can appreciate the various flavours of the world. Chinese, Thai, Indian, Mexican, Zulu, I will try anything and everything. But you can't beat a good old cod and crispy chips, sausage-in-batter on the side and some curry sauce for some tang.'

'Nice. So how does your eating situation work exactly? Do you have to eat like us, three times a day? Do you get hungry or thirsty?'

'Not really. I have cravings for the taste of things. But my body doesn't need food for energy, it makes its own energy from everything around me, like the sun or the wind.'

'Wow, okay, so you are like a huge renewable energy plant, no waste, no poop.'

'Hahaha, exactly. No poop.'

'And sleeping or resting?'

'Sure, I do need to recharge every now and again, but more mentally not physically. I like to kick back with a nice Jack and Coke while watching the latest Star Wars movie. But it's more to process the events of the day and to plan what I'm going to do next. I don't sleep but I can close my eyes and mentally drift away.'

'Like mediation?'

'Yeah, exactly like that. Clear my thoughts and I find it refreshes me after a hard day's work.'

'Ah, you mention that you work, I understand that it's a figure of speech but do you get paid? Do you have a boss or answer to anyone?'

'I do have a boss, yes. Many bosses actually. I work for humanity. Mankind. To come to their aid whenever they need me to and whenever I can. My payment is their goodwill and appreciation, so hopefully they can do for someone else what I have done for them. The *pay-it-forward* type scenario. I think that it's the only way that humanity can survive in the long run.'

'Humanity, hmmm.' Kira squints while quickly processing the information she is hearing so that she can springboard to another question.

'But do you count yourself as one of us? Are you...human?'

'Oh absolutely, one hundred percent. I was born just as you or anyone else. I just turned out a little different, that's all.'

'That brings me on to a big question that has been on everyone's lips for a very long time now. Where did you come from? Or how did you become who you are?'

'Well, I can't go into too much detail about family history.' The Guardian sits easily in the chair, not moving much but being fairly expressive with hand motions as he talks and explains. He looks like he has anticipated much of the questioning so far and has thought out replies beforehand. 'But I was born and raised here, in London. My parents both passed away when I was young and I was put through the foster care system.

'I look very different today to the person I was growing up and I ended up not having anyone close to me that I could rely on. I spent many years being kicked from pillar to post until I reached an age where I found myself on the streets and having to fend for myself. I love this city, but damn, it can be harsh when it wants to be. Anyway, I knew that I had to do something, I couldn't spend my entire life just trying to get through till the end of the day, that was no life.

'So I decided to get out of the city. I gathered what few rags I owned and made my way north, hitchhiking where I could, which wasn't too often to be honest. I mean, who would want to pick up a smelly dodgy kid?' The Guardian gives a wry smile but obviously there is emotion lingering just behind it. 'But mostly I was just walking. Through fields and forests, down paths and up hills. I just kept walking. I lived off the land, picking berries and finding fruit which I could hoard. Water was more tricky than the food but I kept a couple of bottles with me and whenever I found a stream I would fill up. After a long, long time, I found myself up near Scotland. I couldn't even tell you how long it took me to get up there on some moors. I remember that it was wet and chilly. Should've expected that at least.

'Then one day, as I was camped for the night, the sky brightened up as if it were daytime. I woke up and walked out into the middle of the field that I was camped on the side of. The source of the light was this huge glowing orb in the sky, getting bigger and bigger. It was hot as well, so much so that I could feel my forehead begin to sweat. Within a few seconds the light and heat was so intense that I tried to get away but the thing crashed into me. Knocked me onto my backside. I was out. Unconscious. But when I woke up, I don't know how long afterwards, I was like this. How you know me today.'

'Guardian, that is crazy. What was that thing that hit you?'

'I don't know. I never found out. And I haven't heard anything about it since. In the air, it looked huge, must've been its brightness. But when it hit me, it felt like the size of a football but with the force of a truck. I don't know,' he shrugs, 'maybe one day I will find out some more information on it but that's all I know right now.'

'And you just woke up with your powers?'

'Yep. I didn't that I had them at first. But I soon came to find out after trying to hop over a stream and landing on my arse about a mile away.'

'Do you think you could give our viewers a quick display of what you can do?'

'Oh, I don't know.'

'Please. I'm sure they are dying to see it up close instead of some grainy YouTube footage.'

'Hmmm…sure. Why not?'

The Guardian looks around for a moment, thinking about what he can do, Kira giddily clapping her hands in delight.

'Guys and gals. Brace yourselves for some magic,' Kira tells the camera and the viewers from around the world.

'Hey Greg, toss me a pencil' A pencil flies into the shot and The Guardian gracefully plucks it out of the air and holds it out in front of him.

He squints his already narrow eyes a little more in concentration and the pencil hovers vertically in the air on its own. It begins to vibrate, gently at first, then vigorously. Soon, the lead inside the pencil slides completely out of its wooden housing, entirely intact. The wooden part drops to the floor and the lead hovers in mid air until it too begins to vibrate. The dark carbon begins to lose its solid structure and turns into a cloud of powder that just hangs in the air.

'Did you know…that the lead found in a pencil is actually carbon arranged in a certain way?'

Kira doesn't say a word. She shakes her head as her mouth remains open in awe at what she is witnessing. 'Well, if that structure were to be arranged in a different way, it would become…'

The cloud of black dust shrinks in size until it becomes a tight little ball, slowly losing its colour until…

'Diamond!' Kira says, her eyes wide open in astonishment as a tiny little diamond hangs in the air, slowly rotating and glinting in the light.

'Go on,' The Guardian prods, 'take it.'

Kira slowly stretches out her delicate fingers and holds the levitating diamond between her thumb and index finger and takes it from the air.

'It's warm.'

'It will be. Great energy is needed to do what I just did. I can control it easily though so it's completely safe. A gift from me to you.'

A loud cough resonates through the air.

'It was my pencil,' Greg shouts out from behind the camera.

'Oh shush, I'll buy you ten pencils,' Kira calls back playfully.

'You'll give me more than that,' Greg replies. Kira looks like she's been shaken out of a trance and remembers where she is.

'Sorry, Guardian. You had me on another world there for a second. That was fantabulous! How the hell do you do that?'

'It's simply manipulating atoms and molecules. Scientists can do the same thing as I can in labs today, but I just do it more efficiently.'

'Guardian, that is truly amazing. And you do it with your mind?'

'Kind of. It's more as if I am reaching into the air with an extension of my body.'

'What do you mean?'

'You know how our hearts beat on their own? It's an involuntary process. But if we want to move our legs or arms, we have to tell our brains to move it and then it moves, it doesn't just happen. It might feel like it does but it is actually our brain that tells our leg to move with many other things happening at lightning speed inside of our body, electrical impulses, muscular fibres contracting, energy being expended and so on. Well, I find that my body doesn't stop at the tips of my fingers, it extends past that into the surrounding space. Some cultures call it an aura, others call it a life force. I'm not sure precisely how it works or how far it extends, but I can tell my brain to control objects within that sphere of control. Are you with me, Kira?'

'Yes I think so. I love all of that stuff, auras and chakras. I just didn't know that you could use them it that way.'

'I'm still learning about it constantly myself. For years I didn't know I could do this. There are probably still things that I haven't discovered about myself. It's like any of us really. Until we try something, we don't know what we can achieve.'

'Definitely true. I would always jump on a chair any time a mouse was in the room. But one day I saw a mouse and I didn't have anyone to grab it for me. So I found out that I could roll up my own newspaper and bash it to death.'

'Yes…well…not exactly what I meant…maybe do something about your mouse in the house problem, Kira, if you're seeing so many of them?'

'Aaaand swiftly moving on, and what a great interview we've had so far,' Kira tells her audience, 'but ever since Koffee with Kira won this momentous interview with The Guardian, we have been inundated with questions that our viewers want us to ask, so that's what we'll do next…*Viewer's Q's*….after these short messages from our sponsors.'

Greg gives the okay signal from behind the

camera to let Kira know that they have switched the feed to the commercials which they were able to sell at high profit to the show. Greg wheels himself out from behind the camera and stops his wheelchair by its side.

'Kira, going great, keep checking your iPad for question prompts. And Mr Guardian, you are doing fantastically, our comments section has erupted with praise for you, people are loving this close up version of you.'

'Thanks Greg...um...sorry about the um...,' The Guardian nods his head to the wheelchair Greg is sitting in, 'let me know if I can do anything for you. I know you're running on a skeleton team because I requested it. I didn't realise that...um...'

'Oh don't you worry Mr Guardian, you don't need to do anything for me, you've done quite enough already. I've got the whole set up back here so I'm good, you guys just keep it up, we've got a minute left.'

'Sure. Will do. Thanks,' The Guardian replies in his deep voice as Greg returns back behind the camera. 'Kira, is Greg okay back there on his own?'

'Who, Greg? Oh sure he's fine. It's his first time with me but he came highly recommended, he is a pro. Really, he can surprise you with what he can do. Now once we go back live, we're going to go to some viewer questions which can get a little thought provoking, but just be your honest open self and you'll be fine.'

'Okay. When you say thought provoking, what do you…'

'Oh the viewers like to delve a little deeper into their idols lives, that's all. And thank you so much for the diamond, it is literally the most amazing thing I've witnessed in my entire life.'

'Oh that's…'

'Okay here we go, get ready.'

Greg holds up his fingers once again. And…they are live once again.

'Welcome back everyone. Carrying on from where we left off before the short break, we have with us The Guardian, yes, *The* Guardian, protector of Earth and diamond maker extraordinaire.' Kira affords herself a little giggle.

'And we have learnt a lot about the mystery behind the man. But now we move on to the part of the show where *you*, the viewers, can get involved too. We have had masses and masses of questions that people have requested that we ask, so we have selected some of the most popular ones. Mr Guardian, are you ready?'

The Guardian chuckles to himself, possibly the first sign of nerves peeking through.

'I'm ready when you are, Kira.' She swishes around on her iPad.

'Right, first up is a question from half of the global population of planet Earth and the most popular question by far. I think you all know what

I am about to ask. What is your relationship status, Guard?'

For the first time during the interview, The Guardian looks uncomfortable. Not a lot but enough. He clears his throat.

'My relationship status? I should have expected this one.'

'*Should have,* meaning someone didn't prepare for this one?'

'Something like that. Okay, wow, right, good, so…I'm a man.'

'Yep.'

'And that means that sometimes I feel attractions to things…'

'Things?'

'…and people. Mostly people. Just like anyone else, I guess. So sometimes, I'm saying, is that there is a mutual feeling with others also which leads me…and them…to be…attracted…you see what I'm saying?'

'Nope.'

'That was bad, right?'

'So bad, dude.'

'Dude?'

'Yep, dude. You have to work your way back up to The Guardian, I'm afraid.'

'Okay, let's just say it's complicated.'

'Alright, now we're getting somewhere, G-Man.'

'G-Man?'

'Not working for ya?'

'Nope.'

'Alright, moving back to it's complicated. What that usually means, from a woman's point of view, is that she has a guy in her life that she likes slash loves, but there is some obstacle in the way of their relationship that is pulling them apart. Or that she has two or three guys to choose from and can't make up her mind but let's leave that alone for a second, and concentrate on the first reason. Now does that strike any resonance with you and your relationship status, at all, Guards?'

'You're good, very very good Kira. It is exactly like the second reason there…no I'm only kidding, it's very similar to the first reason you gave. Yes, there is someone in my life who I care about deeply, but as you can guess, my line of work pits me against people that want to harm me so to keep her out of harm's way we can't fully be together. But at the same time, though we are not completely together, it closes the door for anyone else. It's her or no one, I'm afraid…and let's stick to Guardian.'

'Sure no worries…did you hear that ladies out there? The Guardian is closed for business, the late night kind of business that is. Criminals, you still better watch your backs.'

'Damn straight, crims.' Kira takes a sip of her cool coffee to calm down from her laughter after hearing The Guardian say *crims*.

'Okay, next question is another popular one asked by a lot of viewers. Guardian, what is your role and how far away do you help people from us here in England?'

'That's a good question.' The Guardian firming up as he is back on territory that he feels at ease with. 'Going back to where I came from and the difficult time that I had growing up, I find it hard to stand by and watch others go through similar hardships. And while I realise that it is close to impossible to change a person's mind or attitude for them, I can improve the surrounding environment as best I can for them to operate in, in the hope that a more positive environment can help people generally. So I help the police fight crime, take drugs off the street, stop trafficking of people and so on and so forth. But I also believe that no problem is too small to dismiss. And what I mean by that is that if someone has lost their dog, you may say that that is a small issue. But to that person who has lost their dog, it is like a family member has been lost so their problem to them is huge. And I try to empathise with that, meaning if I can help, I will, whatever it is. Always in the hope that by doing the right thing and taking the good option, I can lead others down the same path.'

'So also being a good role model for others?'

'Yes, exactly.'

'Okay great. And the second part of that

question was how far away do you help people?'

'Oh right, I will go as far as the sky takes me. If I really push myself, I can travel very fast so while I can't be everywhere at the same time, I will not discriminate as to where I help.'

'So you help people in every country?'

'Yes. Anyone that I can help, I will help.'

'Great to hear, Mr Guardian. Right, the next question is from a long time viewer of ours who goes by the name of Little Timmy. This isn't a general question, it is to do with his own life. And it's pretty heartbreaking, I'm going to try and read without welling up. He says he is thirteen years old and has been bullied rather viciously for the best part of a year. It is giving him suicidal thoughts and he doesn't know what to do. He asks, can you help me, Guardian?' Kira lays the tablet on her lap and stares into the camera, speaking directly to Little Timmy if he is watching. 'Aw, Timmy. I am so sorry that this is happening to you. Guardian, can you give our viewer some wise words of advice, please?'

'Timmy. I am very sorry to hear that you are going through this hell at this time of your life. I really want to come and give you a hug and help you through this. And I will do my best to come and pay you a visit, but listen to me carefully, please. You have probably kept this buried deep inside for what feels like a long time by now. I thank you for bringing this out into the open. I will help you Timmy. As soon as I am done here, I will come and pay you a visit and we can sit down with your parents and teachers and deal with this nightmare that you're going through. Okay buddy, you just sit tight.'

'That's amazing of you, Guardian. You have a big heart. I hope you're watching Timmy, you've got The Guardian on your side and he is coming to help you. That is just great, thank you for helping this poor boy.'

'Not a problem, Kira. Sometimes people just need a helping hand, I find.'

'You are not wrong there. Okay because of time constraints we will move onto one more question, though we will definitely follow up with you, Timmy. This question is another popular one. Guardian, do you have any alliances with any country or government and do you operate under any set of rules or laws? Quite an intense one there. Guardian?'

'Yes, it is. Very. Your audience don't mess around, do they?'

'No, they do not.'

The Guardian is silent. Looks down at the ground, contemplating how to answer the question. He would tell the truth, of course. But there are always various ways of telling the truth, some more genteel and forgiving, others brash and full of contention. After a fleeting moment in which a thousand thoughts run through his mind, he looks up once again.

'To be honest, it is an issue which I have tussled with over the years. I have found that the ground is always shifting. New laws are constantly being made or altered and governments who put forward these changes are also changing. We all know that different parties will have different agendas, some of which I can gladly get on board with and others not so much. So nowadays, I try my best to keep out of the way, let those guys do their job and let my own moral compass guide me as best I can. I do liaise with law enforcement agencies in their work though, sharing information with those who are appreciative and in turn I try and do the best job possible. It's not a perfect system but it works.'

Kira thinks on The Guardian's words, processes them quickly.

'Interesting. Now I'm going to play Devil's Advocate for a bit, spice up the conversation for our viewers, I hope you don't mind, Guardian?'

'Not at all, I enjoy verbal sparring when it comes my way.'

'This is just to ask some questions that some viewers may be thinking of right now.'

'Of course, please continue, Kira.'

'Thank you, Guardian. Now, you were raised here in the U.K. so obviously you will follow our laws and processes?'

'Yes, I do, to the best of my ability.'

'When you say to the best of my ability, it sounds a little ambiguous. The law is the law. Either you follow it, or you don't.'

'I do follow the law, but sometimes I will be placed in a situation where I have to extend past it. I make a judgement call. I do it all the time, kind of follow an instinct into what is the right thing to do. Always for good, however.'

'So you follow the law when it suits you?'

'Not when it suits me, but when it is for the best outcome for society or the individuals involved.'

'So for the greater good, you mean?'

'Yes exactly, for the greater good.'

'But at the same time you purport to being a good role model for others. So do you want others to follow you in doing things for the greater good, even if it means working outside or against the law? As *you* sometimes do?'

'No, absolutely not. I mean, I want people to follow my ideals in serving for the best for humanity, but if it comes to a point where a law must be broken to proceed then the law must *not* be broken. The right department, for example the police, must be informed at that point. Most definitely.'

'So do as you say, not as you do?'

'Well, okay. I wouldn't put it as succinctly as that, but okay.'

'But you operate in other countries too? Not

just here in the U.K.?'

'Sure, as I mentioned earlier, I try to patrol all over the world. I have kind of a sixth sense for injustice so if I can, I will help out.'

'That is very admirable. That means you have working communications with all of the various governments of the world?'

'Not exactly…I'm not sure I follow what you mean.'

'Well, you fly all over the world providing your service wherever you go and in every country. You must have visited a lot of them?'

'Yes, actually I have been to every single country on this planet, all one hundred and ninety six of them.'

'One hundred and ninety six? Wow, that is amazing.'

'Thank you, the world is a beautiful place.'

The Guardian feigns modesty in accepting his praise at this feat, a quick change from the unease he was showing seconds ago.

'So you consider Taiwan to be its own independent country?'

'Yes, of course. It is a country, isn't it?'

'Well, that depends on who you speak to. China has a one-China policy where it assumes Taiwan to be part of China. The Taiwanese say the opposite. It is a subject of great…debate.'

'Oh, I wasn't aware. But I have been there regardless.' The unease returns swiftly.

'Anyway, as I was saying, you have been to every country on the planet, so are you in communications with the government of every country? In their good books, shall we say?'

'No…that hasn't been possible as of yet. I am working on it.'

'So you enter countries according to your will, not according to the legal Visa requirements of that country?'

'A Visa? No, I don't apply for a Visa.' The Guardian frowns lightly at this. 'I am The Guardian, after all. I am there to do good and solve a problem, not to indulge in a round of tourism.'

'That means you enter countries illegally all of the time.'

The Guardian sweeps his long locks back with a sweep of the hand and lets out a nervous chuckle.

'Ahem, I think I need my lawyer present.'

'Oh no, please don't think that, it is just conjecture, *shooting the breeze* as the Yanks say.' Kira replies with an inviting smile. 'These are just some of the things that come up in conversation when we all speak about you and the wonderful things you do for us. You know like, what does he eat? Or what does he do for money? Does he date? You are a legend Guardian and we all love you. I guess that we just craze information on that which we love. Does that make sense?'

'Yeah, I guess it does.'

'Great, so let's forget about that whole Visa slash illegal entry topic and speak about these countries around the world that you haven't managed to communicate with yet. If we speak about the barriers, hopefully they will hear about it and reach out to ease relations, benefiting us all in the end, don't you think?'

'Umm…okay sure. Go ahead.'

'These countries around the world with whom you haven't managed to create a dialogue with, is there anything that you would like to say to them, here and now? Live around the world, Guardian?'

'Right now?'

'Yes, go ahead.'

'Alright…um…leaders around the world. To those of you who I haven't been able to contact as of yet, please know that I do wish to get in touch with all of you. Be aware that I do not operate according to any kind of political manifesto. I am not affiliated with any party or country, I do not wage war on behalf of anyone. I only mean to do good for the oppressed and the abused. If we can all work together, we can improve this planet for ourselves and for our children of the future. We have an amazing chance in our hands to make a difference the likes of which have never been possible in the past. Let us grab onto this possibility and change the world. Thank you.'

Kira puts down her tablet and slow claps at the end of the mini speech.

'Awesome Guardian. I think the olive branch that you have offered out is a meaningful symbol of your purity and goodwill. I am sure that once your message reaches those leaders, they will respond with positivity. How should they contact you?'

'Well…they can contact your show here, how would that be? And I can check in with you from time to time and we can go from there.'

'Not a problem, Guardian. Do you hear that leaders of the world? Contact the Koffee with Kira show, mad as that sounds, and we will put you in touch with The Guardian. To forge a better world.'

'Absolutely. Thank you, Kira. That was very kind of you.'

'The pleasure is all mine. Now I am guessing that it is with the leaders of the more eastern countries of the world that there is some reluctance to engage with you?'

'I wouldn't like to class them all in the same group, but you could say that.'

'Is it a language barrier of some sort, do you think?'

'Possibly in the past. I only knew English all of my life and the odd word or two from the larger European countries. But I have learnt to become more proficient in many languages now. About forty.'

'Really? Forty! I didn't know you could

understand so many languages. Is it another of your powers that no one knows about?'

The Guardian reaches into a hidden section around his waist and pulls out a rectangular object which he points towards the camera.

'iPhone application. Invaluable in an emergency.'

Kira rolls her eyes.

'Oh, Guardian. You had me going there.'

'Sorry, but it's true. It is amazing what it can do. I can even converse with a Gujarati fellow if need be.'

'And I am sure Apple will thank you as well for that free product placement.'

'Are you sure it was free?' The Guardian asks quizzically.

'You are full of surprises, aren't you?'

'A regular Matryoshka doll.'

'A what?'

'You know those Russian dolls, where you open one and find a smaller version inside and then you open that one to find another smaller one, and so on.'

'Oh, that's what they're called.'

'Yes.'

'Right. So getting back to the language issue, that is not an issue anymore, because of your app. But there must be a reason why so many countries have closed the door on your services, that is madness, isn't it? I mean, you're a superhero. Who wouldn't want to benefit from your services?'

'I don't think it is that simple. Over the years I have discovered that you never quite know what is going on in someone's mind. There are over seven billion people on this planet and every single one of them is an individual with a unique makeup of genetics, environment, chemistry, life experience etcetera. So each one will think and behave in their own unique way, respond according to their own expectancies. And unfortunately mind reading is not one of my powers. So if I come across a party that is unresponsive or shows suspicion towards me, I don't waste my time trying to figure them out. I go my way and I let them go their way. It's that simple really.'

'But there must be some underlying factor that dictates the way that they view you. If we step back to take a look at you, what do we see? A dark haired, light-eyed Adonis, coming out of England speaking a bit cockney, flying around without permission, and carrying out acts that even God is unable to do. If someone were running a communist dictatorship, they would be a little nervous, wouldn't they?'

'I guess. But they should know that I don't get involved in regime changes. Politics is a murky business and I keep well clear.'

'Even if they are killing their citizens by the truckload? You still wouldn't get involved?'

'I would protect the citizens against harm as

best I can.'

'But isn't that simply dealing with the symptom instead of dealing with the cause?'

'Maybe it is. But it has immediate impact on those I help.'

'Even though it pits you indirectly against those regimes that are trying to harm the people you are saving?'

'Then so be it. Let the chips fall as they may.'

'But you can't reach every humanitarian emergency, can you?'

'Unfortunately not. I am just one man. I can't be in two places at the same time.'

'So how do you choose where to go and who to save? There must be instances where you are aware of simultaneous emergencies in separate places?'

'Yes there have been. Many, in fact, over the years. It is always a heart-wrenching decision to make knowing that I can't help everyone.'

'So you are, in a way, playing God?'

'Oh not at all. I have never claimed to be in any way, shape or form, a God. Nor am I playing at being God. Nothing could be further from the truth.'

'You say that. But to a mother who is on the street watching a child burn to death in a house fire in London, she must feel hurt that you have chosen to abandon citizens of your own country to help, in effect, a foreigner.'

'What can I do? I can't help everyone, can I?'

'But people are relying on you, Guardian.'

'And I am doing my best. I will always do what I can, but people need to help themselves as best they can too.'

'That's an interesting thing for you to say.'

'What?' The Guardian is getting a little testy now.

'That people need to help themselves. Aren't you, by your constant heroics, weakening the weak of society by always pulling them out of trouble?'

'What do you mean, weakening the weak? By helping and supporting, I strengthen people.'

'What it means is that by taking care of the difficulties normally done by normal everyday people, they lose the ability to do or act and that in turn makes them even more reliant on you. Kind of like the father in the family who takes care of every financial aspect of a household, the bills, the tax, the investments, the wages and spending, but if something incapacitates him, the remaining figures in the family are lost, too weak in those aspects to function. By being so controlling, the father has weakened his already weak family in general finance.'

'That is the opposite of what I am trying to do.'

'No I understand that. But take for example, Little Timmy from earlier, you want to help him overcome adversity in his life by becoming the solution instead of empowering him to take control of his own life and problem.'

'I am just trying to be a good person, that's all.'

'But you are contributing to a future where the weak are weaker, while you go around the world breaking numerous laws as you go and completely ignoring the justice system in every country. And on top of that, you want people to look up to you while doing so but ignoring the fact that many look at you as a God and will mimic whatever you do. People pray that you will come and save them from their troubles, but you can't always save them, can you? People die on your watch, don't they?'

'Like I said, I just try and be a good person. I don't let people die on purpose.' The Guardian is closing up now, realising for maybe the first time at all of the negatives that he produces.

'But people *do* die, Guardian. Do their deaths even affect you? The failures of trying to save someone? What do you get from saving a life when many more are losing theirs around the world? How much can you do?'

The Guardian's face changes from the genial expression it was wearing a moment ago and becomes hard, stone-like.

'I think that…this interview…this may have been a mistake.'

But Kira isn't letting up on her line of questioning.

'Why do you really do the things that you do?

Helping people constantly? Are you searching for an approval, a place to fit in the world or the praise of the public? Or do you want to be seen as a God? You must enjoy the feeling of strangers worshipping you in place of their own deities, taking the place of Jesus or Buddha. A God that can show them he *is* a God. A real God, not an invisible one.'

'A God?!? No! Not at all. I have never said that I am anyone's God. That's just crazy and highly offensive to many people Kira, including myself.' The Guardian says incredulously, unable to believe the nasty turn that the interview has taken. He knew he would be facing some tough questions, but this has propelled to another level of attack.

Again Kira simply ignores much of what The Guardian is saying to her. She seems determined to plough through the entire list of questions that she has at hand and ignoring the effects that they may be having on her famous guest.

'But that is exactly what is happening Mr Guardian.' Kira spits the *Mr* sarcastically, the playful twinkle in her eyes now replaced with a deadly concentration, almost hawk-like. 'You are floating down from the heavens to rescue those in need, the sick, tired and hungry. All the while, seemingly invincible. What would you call yourself?'

The Guardian emits a heavy sigh and leans forward on the armchair, clasping his hands together as his head hangs low on his shoulders. With the look of a man zapped of energy, he gets to his feet, his neutral demeanour hiding his true emotions. He begins to remove his microphone.

'Kira, I have to end this interview.' He drops the microphone on the table.

'Guardian, what's wrong? I'm sorry if I get a little carried away,' Kira says, suddenly innocent without looking all that sorry in reality.

'I have to go, thank you for your time.' The Guardian suddenly strides away out of camera shot as Kira frantically ad-libs some unscripted words about the interview.

Just before he reaches the exit, his phone vibrates.

Only one person has his number.

He quickly checks and reads the incoming text message.

Slowly he replaces his phone in its compartment and turns back to look at Kira as she is speaking on camera.

His mood has changed. Face thunderous.

You can see the rage building up inside him.

'Greg. Go to commercial.' The Guardian's voice is low, flat and controlled, barely. There is a menacing beast straining to break free.

'Sorry Guardian, w…w…what was that?' Greg replies stuttering, surprised that The Guardian is speaking to him.

'I said go to commercial…now!' The Guardian

stuns Greg into action with a single look that contains the fury of the Sun.

'Oh…o…okay…I uh…that…just one…and it is…done. W…we are at commercial, Guardian.'

The Guardian points an accusing finger at Kira.

'You!' Kira looks dumbfounded, unable to move at this new anger from The Guardian. The man who she had just broken down with her words minutes ago. The Guardian walks up to her, a heat emanating from his body as his rage struggles to be released. 'You set this whole thing up. You hacked the competition to get this interview with me. Why?'

'I…I…didn't do…'

'Don't LIE TO ME!' The Guardian bellows into Kira's face, her hair flutters backwards from the force. He grabs the front of her suit jacket by the lapels and lifts her up off the ground. Brings her face close to his. 'I was just sent a message by the only person I trust in the entire world. And she tells me that this whole production is a charade. Fake! The competition for my interview was hacked for votes. This is your show. You set me up. Why? Who are you? What do you want?'

'I…I didn't do anything.'

'You're lying. You've embarrassed me and belittled me in front of the entire world. Now tell me what the hell is going on!'

Finally Kira relents. She has never been faced with so much might before, enough to wipe her clean from existence.

'I…I had to…I'm sorry…I had to destroy you. You have too much…power.' Kira shakes with fear as she says it, especially as she can feel the burn of anger directed at her. The Guardian glows red with fury. He remembers all of the destructive things that Kira was saying about him during the interview, making him look like an idiot and someone who is unneeded and unwanted in the world. It makes him lose the one thing that he has kept throughout his life.

His dignity.

He hurls Kira down through the glass coffee table.

Her head smashing through the glass and her body crumpled up into an odd-shaped heap.

The Guardian stands there, his breath fast and heavy.

Have I acted too rashly, he thinks to himself. What the hell is going on? What have I done? Did I just hurt a defenceless woman?

Greg quietly wheels himself out from behind the camera, slowly and deliberately. A layer of reflective sweat is covering his smooth bald head, worried eyes sitting behind his black round glasses.

'Guardian?'

The Guardian doesn't react. He continues to stare at the limp body he has created.

'Guardian,' Greg says a little louder this time, trying to get The Guardian's attention. It works.

He slowly turns his head towards Greg, the anger dissipating from his face, steadily being replaced with shock at what he has done. 'You need to leave, now. Don't worry about Kira, I will look after her. The live stream is still at commercial, no one knows what has gone on here.'

'But...what have I done? It was only an interview...how did I...I should have walked away...'

'Guardian, please. You are bigger than this. I will get help for Kira and end the stream. You have to go...now!'

The Guardian begins to snap out of his daze and shuffles over to Greg, each step feeling as though ten tons of lead is in each boot.

'Thank you Greg, I don't know what I have done to deserve your help, but thank you. Please tell Kira that I am sorry for what I did today and for whatever I have done to her in the past that has made her...hate me so much...I...'

'It's okay, I'm sure whatever it was can all be put in the past. She won't go to the authorities I'm positive, hacking is a crime too. I had no idea, I assure you.'

The Guardian tries to speak but his words choke in his throat, tears filling up in eyes.

'I should take her to the hospital...' The Guardian moves towards Kira's body, but Greg stops him.

'No, please, you have to leave. Don't worry, I

will make sure she is okay. We can't have you in custody which is where you will end up.'

With a final remorseful glance at Kira, he is gone. He floats out onto the balcony and flies up into the sky.

Greg watches The Guardian soar into the sky, almost instantly becoming a small dot and vanishing as he accelerates to an incredible speed.

Quickly he rushes around to the back of the camera where his control console is fitted in a corner of the room. He ends the extended commercial playing on the live stream, and puts up a technical difficulty message, followed by some archived footage from previous shows. After taking care of the viewer's footage, completely ignoring the message board, he rushes to Kira's side. She has cuts to her face and neck from being smashed through the glass table.

Thankfully none of them are deep.

Apart from being knocked unconscious by the force of the impact, she looks just a bit banged up, bruising forming on the right side of her face making her look in worse condition than she actually is. Greg double checks to make sure she is breathing and she is. He sits back in his chair and lets out a huge sigh of relief.

Just as he is about to try and wake Kira up, he sees the tablet resting on Kira's armchair.

He takes hold of it and navigates through a few folders. Plays the fifteen year old clip of The

Guardian saving an old man from a teenage attacker that some chap caught on his smart phone. Watches silently as the teen is flung across the street and ends up in a lump of skin, clothes and fragmented bone.

He pauses the clip at the image of the broken teen.

Stares at it for some time and lets out a puff of air from his nose in disbelief.

Greg was that teenager in the video.

He was beating the old man after finding him walking in the street, without a care in the world. Even though years earlier he had spent much of his time sexually abusing Greg and his younger brother, instead of babysitting them as a neighbour normally would. Seven years had elapsed since Greg had last seen his abuser and his anger wouldn't be contained or stopped once unleashed.

Until, that is, The Guardian swooped in and confined him to a lifetime in a wheelchair.

Kira begins to come around. Moaning and groaning as the pain from her injuries is finally felt. He does his best to help her up out of the rubble and she makes it onto the armchair. Without checking her wounds, she regards Greg through angry eyes.

'Is that the end now? Is it done?'

'Oh yes indeed, Kira. And I must say, you performed admirably.' Greg's voice and tone changing into something proud and confident. 'I could see that you were a little nervous at the start, but you settled into your role nicely. You followed my prompts exceedingly well.' Greg holds up the iPad which Kira was using.

'So you will let my baby go? You promised you would.'

'Yes of course. In fact, he is safe and in the arms of your mother as we speak. They are alone at home and unharmed.' Kira closes her eyes and her head falls back into the headrest, relief drowning her fear like a tidal wave. Finally an end to her personal nightmare is here.

Greg chuckles to himself. He really is a production manager. Being in a wheelchair all of these years had taught him the benefit of working with computers and electronics. Really makes life easier for him. When he heard about the competition to win the interview with the famous Guardian, all it took was a small team of hackers to put Kira's show in the winning spot. They even helped to hack The Guardian's private phone to goad him into returning when he threatened to walk away.

Turning Kira was even easier. A mother would do anything to save her only child, even help to destroy the world's only superhero. Her child and mother were both held hostage by a couple of low level thugs, happy to do anything for a valuable payday. Greg had already messaged them to leave, the job was over.

'So are you happy now?' Kira spits venomously at Greg once the euphoria of knowing her family is safe has passed. 'Have you got what you wanted?'

'Oh yes. Very. I have got exactly what I wanted. It was a lot easier than I thought it would be to be honest with you. We didn't even have to produce any of the negative comments from the message board for him to see. I spent a long time making those.'

'You're sick, you know that?'

'Sick? Who me? Maybe. It would have been fun though, watching him disintegrate as thousands upon thousands called for his head in real time. Anyway, there's always a next time.'

'Next time? You think he won't come for you when he finds out what you've done?'

'Oh, I'm counting on it. But for the time being, I think he'll be too busy dealing with the fallout from what the world has witnessed here today.'

Kira stays silent as Greg wheels himself away from her, towards the front door.

He stops and turns, exaggerating the motions of pretending to remember something that he has forgotten.

'Oh, silly me. I almost forgot.'

'Forgot what?'

'Your viewers, of course. They're stuck watching old re-runs of your amazing show. We can't leave them hanging like that, now can we?'

'What do you mean? You turned off the stream when Guardian came back into the room…right?'

'Yes that is correct. But we were still filming.'

Kira's stomach flips at the knowledge of what Greg is about to do. 'Please Greg, don't.'

'Everyone needs an ending to a story.'

Greg approaches the control console and switches the live feed back on, showing the smashed up set and Kira on the armchair, cut and bruised.

He overlays text on the live image.

Here is what happened earlier.

He presses a final button.

The live stream ends and replays the missing footage of the enraged Guardian, showing everything he did to the poor and defenceless Kira across the globe.

'The world will finally see what The Guardian is capable of.'

THE CASE

The serrated steel knife slices through the old man's chest.

It pierces his heart.

Within seconds the organ stops beating and the body takes its final breath. His arms fall to the side, neck muscles lose their tension and the fragile head rocks to the side. The man has seen many changes over the decades past. Survived through many of life's tests as the aged usually have. Wisdom had grown accustomed to taking residence in the man's weary mind. Until this moment.

The killer remains there for a while longer to make sure that life has definitely been taken. The murder doesn't make him happy. It brings out emotions of sorrow and guilt. Regret however, is far from his mind. This is how it is meant to be. The first step of the mission is almost complete. Just some final setting of the scene remains. Selective tidying.

Now on to the next.

Monday morning in London, the city of great tradition. Rebuilt since the Last Great War of 2047, the gleaming new skyscrapers create a majestic backdrop to the horizon, visible from miles away and acting as beacons for the business centre of the world. Thirty-five years on from the global conflict which engulfed the planet, the latest young batch of adults have re-written rules and laws, broken down walls and borders, and released the people of Earth from the greedy clutches of elite bankers. Equalising wealth and allowing technology to flourish and serve all people, the global populations all have hope and opportunity instead of only the rich lucky few of past generations.

As dawn breaks, thousands of drones take to the sky all over the capital. Seventy years ago, the tasks being carried out by these machines would have been carried out by men in employment, traipsing around town in vans and on bikes, delivering and collecting. Now the technology is here to take over these jobs. As well as hundreds of other menial tasks that our ancestors have had to suffer in the past; collecting waste, cleaning bathrooms, sweeping the roads. Bots have saved humans from many of these poorly paid tasks that were previously undertaken simply for a wage, money to survive to make it through life.

However, whilst taking the jobs from people, they have not taken the money as in the past. By taking control of the money supply and eliminating national debts to the banks, new global government provides everyone with the best that life has to offer and the freedom to pursue the activity of choice, whatever that may be.

It is a good life.

Although, where there is good, there is often also bad.

Over in Cassian's bedroom in east London, he stirs gently, the remnants of a good sleep slowly fading away. The Morphone device wrapped around his forehead from temple to temple monitors brain activity, constantly powered by utilising the movement of the temple's pulse as blood passes through the vein. As it records information, it regularly sends the data to George, the artificial entity who runs the home computer along with the alarm clock which is set for nine am, plus or minus ten minutes.

By utilising effects against all five of the human senses, the alarm wakes Cassian up in the most refreshing way possible. Working in tandem with the information provided by the Morphone, Cassian is analysed for the end of the last deep sleep cycle to ebb away closest to the set alarm time. It can then begin illuminating the room with softly brightening artificial daylight and playing varying pitched sounds, getting louder and louder. The bed begins to vibrate near the lower back with aromatic sprays of liquid fragrance to resemble strawberry and honey being diffused near the head, stimulating taste and smell sensors to wake up the facial nerves and muscles involved.

The time hits ten past nine and Cassian is still fast asleep. The gentle alarm not having worked. The bed flips the side while an ear-piercing klaxon blares loudly, blinding strobe lights flashing like a nightclub rave. Cassian is sent flying from the bed and crashes to the floor, finally awake and rubbing his eyes.

'Bloody hell,' he mumbles. I need to crank up the settings on that alarm, can't keep ending up on the floor like this, he thinks to himself. 'George, I'm up, turn off the god-damn alarm,' he calls out to the home management system.

The room quietens back to its normal state while Cassian rips the Morphone from his face and flings it onto the bed which has resumed its natural horizontal position.

'George,' Cassian calls out again.

A tiny flying drone the size of an apple hovers into the room from its charging station in the hallway. As it approaches Cassian, it scans his retina and in an instant, projects the full man-size hologram of a subservient butler, ready to do its masters bidding.

'Good morning, sir,' George says with a bow.

'Morning, George. I'm going to have a shower. Can you get my usual breakfast ready for me, give me twenty minutes to be down.'

'Are you sure you wouldn't prefer the *special* option, sir?' George asks tenderly, causing Cassian to glance down at his bulging stomach, giving it a gentle pat.

'The usual will be fine, George, I think that sleep burnt off a few pounds. We'll do the healthy option tomorrow.'

'As you wish, sir,' George replies with another bow, disappearing while the central drone flies on to the kitchen.

Cassian struggles to his feet and takes a look in the large wall mirror. It isn't the prettiest of sights. A shaggy-haired, middle-aged man looks back at him, sporting a middle-aged spread and non-designer stubble. A look around his sterile, minimalistic bedroom and he lets out a sigh. He struggles to get out of bed partly because it has become harder to find something to get out of bed for. Maybe he can make something meaningful happen today.

The Morphone rings out with a holocall. Before he can think properly, Cassian answers and he presented with a life-size hologram projection of his old boss, Captain Chilvers, from the local police station.

'Good morning, Cassi...oh God...Jesus Cassian, can you put some clothes on please for

God's sake!' Captain Chilvers cries out as Cassian's naked hologram, scanned by the Morphone, is projected to the Captain's end, in all of nature's intended glory.

'Oh sugar…sorry Captain…' Cassian apologises, quickly diving to the floor, away from the scanning receptacle of the phone.

'Call me as soon as…as you sort yourself out, Cas. This is urgent. Don't dawdle.'

'Yes, sir. I will…sorry,' Cassian replies as the Captain's hologram flickers away, a disgusted look on his face burnt into the air for a second as a ghostly image.

Cassian lifts his hulking mass up off the floor. It hasn't been the best start to the day. Maybe he can freshen up and make up for it. The Captain doesn't call every day, this could be important. Hopefully, he hasn't been scared away by having his eyes attacked by the vision of a hairy slug-like creature.

Cassian steps into the bathroom to take a shower, entering curled and hunched over from the morning bathroom chill. The small white ceramic room has a cubicle in the corner, fully enclosed with a stool inside. As he steps in and seats himself, the unit powers up emitting a warm glow. A touch screen comes to life on the inner side of the door while a voice speaks.

'Please select your programme,' it says in a

seductive feminine voice.

'Full body three, mouth one, facial hair one, skin tone two,' Cassian replies clearly, opting for extra additions to his normal basic wash. Captain Chilvers doesn't appreciate a lack of grooming. He taps at the touch pad to switch on a news channel as jets appear above, below and surrounding his body. A sensor quickly determines his body temperature and the jets shoot out a wash mixture at five degrees above, infra-red sensors guiding them to clean and remove all dirt from Cassian's skin. Water shoots out at differing intensities depending on the area being targeted; the back gets a good pounding massage while some areas lower down get a more…gentle touch. Soon Cassian is nicely warmed up and unravels his body in the comforting heat.

An electric blue hue envelops the cubicle, a UV light on a three minute cycle. As it is powering up, the news channel flashes up with some breaking news. The news presenter today being the three dimensional holo-image of James Earl Jones to lend some gravity to the situation, his famous boom demanding attention.

'The city has been shocked and stunned today after learning from Seven Kings Police Captain Chilvers of the first murder in the London Borough of Redbridge and Dagenham in over two decades. Details are still a little vague on the ground as this is being treated with the utmost seriousness. Only basic information has been provided to us until it is decided what we can be informed of without affecting the case. We have our case reporter at the site with a neighbour who can give us some specifics.'

As the screen cuts to a young woman on the street of the murder, Cassian is told to open his mouth as a squirt of gel is spread inside. The biodegradable single-purpose nanobots contained within the gel go to work destroying any foreign matter and plaque they encounter, leaving behind a harmless minty fresh by-product which is spat out after three minutes. A similar process occurs on his stubble, leaving him as smooth as the day he was born.

A dark-haired twenty-something lady is facing the hovering news camera. In the backdrop, the cordoned police investigation area can be seen with various robots performing a multitude of tasks around Captain Chilvers. He appears to be directing them around like a conductor, although looking slightly confused.

'Thank you, James,' says the enthusiastic reporter, holding a metallic microphone to her mouth, 'we have here Mr Sandy Wicks, a neighbour of the recently deceased Ben Erso, who has apparently been murdered, late last night.' She turns to Mr Wicks. 'Mr Wicks, what can you tell us of this troubling event?'

The obese Mr Wicks, chewing nervously on his

lip, shifts from one leg to the other.

'Well…uh…I heard the commotion going on this morning at about half seven. One of those huge police transport vehicles showed up. I knew something big was going down.'

'Did you know the deceased well?'

'The deceased?…oh, Ben? Well, he kept to himself mostly. Except his godson who used to come around, but no one has seen him in ages. An old boy who liked things done the old fashioned ways. He hated all these bots and tech. But what a lovely fellow. Always stopped to say hello whenever he was taking out the rubbish.'

'Taking out the rubbish? What do you mean?'

'He used to carry out the rubbish bags himself…leave them at the bottom of the road for collection.'

'Wow, that is amazing. I didn't think anyone still did that. Did you witness any strange goings on leading up to the unfortunate crime?'

'No, not really. Although it is a bit weird as to how the police came so quickly. I don't know who would have tipped them off. Ben didn't really get visitors. But what a terrible thing to happen to a nice kind man. We're all really shocked.'

'A terrible shocking event here in Seven Kings, James,' the reporter says, looking back to the camera, 'if we have anything else, we will let you know. But for now, it's back to you in the studio.'

The screen switches back to James Earl Jones

in the studio. You can see his holo-image flickering back on for a split second as he continues his coverage.

Cassian stares open mouthed and shocked at the news. It must be what Captain Chilvers was calling about this morning. He attempts speeding things up in the shower now that he is clean shaven, massaged and fresh mouthed, also a slightly more healthy-looking tan brown than before. Just a few more minutes under the jets of warm water…

'Cassian, I am sure that you have by now heard the news of the murder over in Seven Kings, Ilford,' Captain Chilvers asks Cassian by traditional, non-hologram phone call.

'The old man Erso? Yes, I saw on the news. Mind boggling.'

'I know. Nobody expected it, especially in Ilford of all places, one of the swankiest and safest areas in the entire capital. It is the birthplace of capitalism for humanity, the ethos that the country now lives by, for God's sake. Is nothing sacred anymore?'

'It is madness, Captain.'

'I have to admit Cas, we are baffled on this one. The lack of data, inside and out is leaving me and my bots paralysed of any insight whatsoever. No witnesses, no DNA, no retina scans, no motive, nothing stolen…I mean, where do I go from here?'

'Sounds like the perfect murder,' Cassian suggests.

'That could very well be the case on this one. But, I do know of one man who could possibly solve it. Could *you* consult on this case for me, Cas? Double your rate, no restrictions for the duration?'

Cassian thinks for a moment. The Captain must really be in a bind with this case if he is laying all of his cards on the table already. Be wise not to play around negotiating. A proud man like Chilvers could rescind that in a flash.

'How could I resist, Captain? I'm in,' Cassian replies.

'Great. I will have all of the case notes sent over along with the system access details. Let's touch base this time tomorrow and we'll see where we are. Sound good?'

'Sounds good.'

Cassian sits for a moment to think. More than a moment. He does a lot of sitting and a lot of thinking. He grabs his Morphone and snaps it around his wrist, where it alters to take on the shape of his forearm, automatically taking the correct position to be powered by his wrist pulse. Almost immediately, George hovers into view.

'Sir, your blood analysis is indicating that you need to eat your breakfast soon. Also your white blood cell count is low so we will begin a course of boosters.'

'Sure, sure. Thanks George, I'll be right there,' Cassian replies automatically, his thoughts now on the case of the first murder in the borough in twenty years.

After breakfast, Cassian sits in his favourite armchair in the living room. Multi-functional with life maintaining systems available, slight overkill for a front room in east London.

'George, please arrange the case notes for viewing,' Cassian tells his faithful assistant.

'As you wish, sir,' George replies obediently.

The windows darken as an electric current passes through them, activating photochromic crystals embedded within the glass. The room soon takes on a nightly shade and George begins throwing up life size hovering holograms of case files, screens and other tabs. They slowly rotate around Cassian, glowing various pastel colours, awaiting further instruction. The Morphone around Cassian's wrist projects a functional, virtual keyboard in the air just below his fingers, ready to use.

Cassian cracks his knuckles and loosens up a little. He takes a deep breath and dives in, using hand gestures to navigate his way through the information, analysing data, speed reading through text and getting George to take specific intriguing notes. The sheer scale of information gathered is vast. It looks as though the Captain has taken this case upon his own shoulders, his first murder in his head role. He has used every type of bot at his disposal, even if they wouldn't necessarily normally be employed at this stage of a case. He is not leaving any stone left unturned, sure that the media and the public are watching closely and eagerly. There are case notes pertaining to forensics, in-house and nearby surveillance, victim's known associates, family history, medical records, full inventory, autopsy, crime scene recordings and analysis, financial records, legal instances, legal history and more. Absolutely anything and everything about Mr Erso and his death has been documented in an unneeded level of detail.

The only files which are slightly on the light side are that of motive and crime suspects. In fact, they are empty. The Captain and his team of bots could not come up with a single possible suspect, or any leads to investigate and no clue whatsoever as to why someone would want to murder this lonely old man; that too in a terrifying and brutal manner. Usually crime scene information would give up some DNA, a piece of fabric or a fingerprint. The unhackable home computers found in more than 99% of homes would offer mounds of detection data, video evidence and often report crimes themselves as they were in progress. Violent crimes, thefts or burglaries would turn up mountains of traceable clues on weapons or tools used, though they are all dwindling rapidly as the bots cleaned up most cases. Despite these avenues, Captain Chilvers was at a dead end, possibly from the archaic manner in which Mr Ben Erso has existed. He was a technophobe, shunned all things electronic and advanced. This meant no home computer, no monitoring, no Morphone, no virtual purchases or tracking chip. No electronic storage of home movies, pictures or holoclips. No remote scanned visits by the doctor or a social monitor making sure all was okay.

Nothing.

And without the normal everyday methods of interaction with the system, no links could be made in the normal ways using the standard modern methods.

'George,' Cassian calls out to his butler. He has been working on the case for eight hours straight. He stands, stretching out his arms above his head. 'I need to have a break. Save all of this for now and bring up some *solitude* for me.'

The butler hovers into view, simultaneously normalising the room back to its former state. The windows clear in time for the sunset, the fading amber glow easing its way in.

'Will you be going for a walk as well, sir?' George asks.

'Yes, a stroll will do me good.'

'As you wish, sir,' George says, gliding away out of view. As he does, a round circle outlined in the middle of the floor has its edges illuminated. Cassian takes a stance in the circle and the room transforms to become the Grizedale Forest in the Lake District during a warm summers evening. Woodland forest surrounds him as rays of sunshine break through the trees and strike his face, gently warming. Native birds and animals chirp and call out their cries of individual communication, flying and scurrying around. He is standing on an ancient rocky path which he starts upon. In the distance it leads to a beautiful horizon marking out mountain tops and a river source running down to a calm, blue lake.

As Cassian walks, the circular section of the floor takes on a multi-directional treadmill quality which also moves and tilts, giving the impression that he is where his eyes tell him he is. He breathes deeply, the fresh earthy fragrance of his surroundings calming his mind, the refreshing scenery superbly detailed.

Back in the room, George is sensitively monitoring output from the Morphone around Cassian's wrist, combining the detail of the rendering of the forest with plumes of the coinciding scent while precisely adjusting the terrain beneath his feet. He manages the walk until Cassian's heart-rate elevates to around sixty percent of its maximum and maintains it there, just enough to work his sluggish muscles and send blood pumping to areas not well used, the starting point of fat burning.

For Cassian, this is a welcome break from the avalanche of facts and details that have been attacking his brain cells over the past eight hours. It has been a while since looking at any kind of case with this much inspection. Apart from a few pieces of consultancy for the Captain and some random bits of hired work, the last time would have been when he was actually still employed as a detective with Seven Kings Police Service. There were so many sections and procedures with a lot of paperwork for each case. Everything had to be documented, checked, double-checked and organised. It was keeping detectives in the office longer than out on duty where they could be investigating crime. This was one of the main reasons for the changeover to the automated system of crime investigating. It just needed minimal management and the admin work was all done instantaneously. The technological advances were amazing. Specific bots were created for certain factions of tasks, constantly growing in ability as advancements were made. The revolution had arrived.

It has been a few years now since the change-over. Cassian and his old partner Scarif receiving their marching orders. Although there were a few teething problems along the way, the bots have really streamlined operations, never getting tired and making mistakes, following the law to the letter and never having morality or ethical issues. They just follow their programming. Put aside the early model 'apprehension bots' receiving some beatings that a couple of overly violent suspects had dished out when they first appeared on the streets, they have been very successful. The beatings actually were helpful as they led to an armour upgrade making them near indestructible.

Stepping over a rogue log on the path, Cassian continues through the tranquil environment. The setting is going part way to easing the tension that was building in his mind. However, the more he treks through the forest, the more his thoughts can't help but turn over the case. Something is tugging on threads of doubt, threatening to unravel a mystery about the murder, some aspect being missed by everyone. He puts the uncertainty to one side for the time being, asks his subconscious to work on the issue and see if anything reveals itself.

He is breathing fairly heavily after some time. A trail that a young child could skip down with ease is putting Cassian through his paces. He decides to stop for a moment having reached the edge of a downward path. The massive lake has come into view. Bright sun shining off its even surface providing a picturesque wonderment. One of these days, I'll get out there in person, he thinks. On second thoughts, based on his huffing and puffing after seven minutes, maybe not.

'George,' he calls.

'Yes, sir?' replies George without coming into view.

'Can you get the case notes and go over them with me? I'm sure I'm missing something here.'

'Certainly, sir, although are you sure you don't want to continue enjoying your hike?'

'Hikes are for people that enjoy doing this stuff. For me, this is therapy, and no one enjoys therapy.'

'As you wish, sir,' George concedes, 'where would you like to begin with the notes?'

'Let's go over the basics. Give me the victim's stats.'

'Okay. The victim, Mr Ben Erso. Born twenty second of August, nineteen eighty-nine. An only child to parents Jay and Riya. No siblings. No first or second removed family members, only distant relatives who are not found to have had any contact with Mr Erso. Blood type is O negative; height is five feet and eleven inches. Enjoyed a vegan diet. Lived in Seven Kings since he was twelve. No RFID chip implanted. An atheist since birth and retired thirty-one years ago from a career in politics. No disabilities. Although he seemed to be a poorly sick man, had been suffering from Parkinson's for the past six years.'

'Okay. All fairly normal so far, Parkinson's is quite common in the aged,' Cassian says continuing his walk down the slope towards the lake, the circular floor beneath him tracking his walking speed and tilting downward to imitate the hill. 'Except for the career in politics. Not many people have had a career in politics. And his career was involved with a unique time in our history, was it not?'

'You are correct, sir.'

'Let's see what the Captain turned up in his research. Break it down for me, George.'

'The file notes show that Mr Erso was in the New Liberal Party at the time of the Last Great War, before, during and after,' George says.

'Interesting. What role did he play?'

'Mr Erso was an adviser and consultant to the chairman during the transition. An actual architect of the main plan for change, he came up specifically with the push for automation of basic roles in society. To remedy the loss of jobs, he also planned for the overhaul of the currency debt process, had redirection of excess capital to support the public and was a key player in the society as it is formed today.'

'Wow,' Cassian says dumbfounded, 'how come nobody has heard of him? Or from him in all of these years?'

'Old medical reports show that he regularly had psychiatry visits. The files are confidential.

Possibly Captain Chilvers can gain you access.'

'Hmmm...maybe...okay leave that for now. Describe the crime scene for me.' Cassian tells George as he continues down the path to the lake.

'Mr Erso was found in an old leather armchair, black in colour. He was wearing blue cotton pyjamas, and brown slippers. A generic military knife had pierced his heart, four inches of the blade through the skin. He was found in the living room of his bungalow home which was maintained in a very off-the-grid manner. No phone line or web connections. No home computer, no entertainment centre, no television. In fact, there were no items of consumer goods that were made after the war.' Cassian listens carefully. 'The walls were shelved with a range of books covering many genres. The walk-through kitchen contained a basic sink and electric hob. Electricity supplied through solar panelling and turbines, although an absence of molecular kinetic power.'

Cassian raises an eyebrow at this last point as he did when reading the case notes initially. Molecular kinetic is the standard method of creating power in the modern age. Completely renewable, no pollution, free and available anywhere on earth at any time. It works by harnessing the rapid movement of various gas molecules in the air around us. Gas being the most excitable form of a substance, its natural vibration, movement and energy is captured and converted into electricity. One of the main revolutions to equalise nations around the globe many years ago - the elimination of the reliance on oil. For Mr Erso not to use this form of energy, indicated that he really did yearn for an older time in history.

Cassian stops walking once he has reached the edge of the lake. He kneels down and gazes across the surface. It glistens. Gentle waves rippling to and fro, swishing sounds relaxing to the ear. As he has done many times before, he reaches out and dips his fingers into the water. Unfortunately without his haptic feedback suit, it feels of nothing but air, reminding him that all of this is just an illusion. Maybe Erso was onto something by shunning advanced tech. In his time he would have been shaking off wet fingers right now.

'Okay, George,' Cassian says, standing up and beginning walking along the water's edge, 'can you show me the list of findings from the grid analysis?'

'Bringing it up now, sir.'

'And stop calling me 'sir' all the time.'

'Yes, sir.'

The compiled list from the surface analysis of the crime scene area is brought up to the side of Cassian's eye line. It contains a full sweep of identified particles on and around Mr Erso. A couple of them catching Cassian's eye.

'And the contents of the fridge and cupboards.'

'Not a problem,' George says.

'And the investigation steps taken by the bots. Anything that they have looked into at all.'

Cassian walks on in the virtual environment, scanning the pages floating around his centre of vision. Like the pieces of a puzzle, all of the answers are here somewhere, in some kind of order. It is just a question of joining the dots. But irrationally. Otherwise the bots would have discovered the link long ago.

He stops.

A connection made.

'George, get me out of this thing and get the Captain on the phone.'

'Talk to me Cas,' Captain Chilvers booms, his head projected in front of Cassian from his Morphone, 'you have to give me something on this case. I'm getting my arse walloped from here to Gravesend every hour, on the hour.'

'Captain, I don't have anything solid. But...'

'Oh a *but*, I love that *but*...talk to me.'

'Well it's probably nothing, but I was looking at the grid analysis and something struck me as a bit odd. Now Erso was a very clean man, organised and disciplined. Everything had a place and there was nothing in the bungalow that was waiting to be tidied. Yet, there showed up some foreign bodies on the kitchen table.'

This peaks Captain Chilvers interest, his eyebrow raises.

'Foreign bodies? I didn't notice…'

'Yes, dried cheese pieces, traces of flour, basil, pepperoni and pesto'

'Oh, pesto…' Captain Chilvers says with exaggerated exuberance, '…foreign bodies you say?…Now what the hell is foreign about food…in a kitchen?'

'Bear with me for a moment. Were the bins searched?'

'Yes, scanned, x-rayed and searched as standard. No sign of a murder weapon, no documents that can be used for a lead, just waste. Nothing out of the ordinary.'

'Do you still have the waste bins? Nothing has been thrown out yet?'

'Cas, until this is figured out, we are keeping every strand, every molecule.'

'The bins contents aren't with the files notes that you sent over to me. Can you bring them up now?'

'Yes hold on, they probably were processed a little later after being brought back from the waste disposal area.'

Within moments Captain Chilvers sends over the file which George brings up in front of Cassian.

'There it is. A pizza box, a couple of slices left and disposed of,' Cassian says after scanning the list quickly.

'Yes, your point being? The old man ordered a pizza. We need to be looking for a murderer, not a bloody chef, Cas.'

'Firstly, every area of the old man's house was spotless. That's why the grid analysis didn't bring up much except cleaning compounds and substances, except the food particles that I'm assuming are from the pizza. Yet, the table was not wiped down. Erso would not have left it like that. And the pizza, thrown away with pieces left over and wasted, Erso would not have ordered a medium size just for himself. He knew how hungry he was and would have ordered a small or even kept the leftovers for the next day. But you know what the kicker is?'

Captain Chilvers is feeling some interest now. His eyes wide in expectation.

'Judging by the evidence, the pizza was from the local Italian delivery restaurant, Ragu's and was their Meatalicious with a thick crust in a medium size. Of course, this will need to be verified. I will follow up as soon as we finish here.'

'Is that your idea of a kicker?'

'Oh, that isn't the kicker.'

'So would you mind blessing me with your wisdom, oh great one?' Captain Chilvers says sarcastically.

'Well the pizza eaten was the restaurant's meatiest selection.'

'Yeah, so?'

'Erso...was a vegan.'

Cassian is tasked with urgently chasing up the discrepancy with the greatest of haste. The Captain becoming excited for the first time since this case fell into his lap. With the entire country watching with bated breath, there is an enormous amount of pressure on him to deliver and reassure the public that the nation isn't regressing back to the immoral desensitised violence of the first half of the twenty first century. Nobody wants to return to the times where a murder wouldn't even create a passing comment, let alone place pressure on a police chief to deliver an arrest.

Captain Chilvers was a young boy when the Last Great War began. A war fought between supposedly leading nations of the world. It had led to the deaths of almost three billion people from five continents and close to forty countries. And for what? Lies, smoke and mirrors. Misdirection. People were led one way when behind their backs the true horror was happening.

Once the dust had settled, no one had won, except maybe the architects of war. Those who made it happen and those who promised to make everything better again came out at the end with some positivity in their lives. But humanity felt a shift. It wasn't easy and it wasn't immediate. But it had begun. With so many dead, secrets weren't as protected as they were before and a wave of truth emerged which people rode. People had suffered enough.

The mass manipulation of humanity was laid open, plain to see. New global governance emerged with one core change. Transparency. There was very little that was hidden or confidential or too sensitive to discuss. Everything was on the table and if things needed changing, it was plain to see where the issues were.

It was a historical time of change.

And nobody wanted to return to the times where one hundred of the richest people in the world had more wealth and power as the poorest three billion.

Cassian follows the single slim lead that is evident in the case. He contacts the manager of the restaurant that the pizza was from, the sole branch in the area. After a brief holocall with the manager once his temporary credentials are shown, he learns some information that he relays back to Captain Chilvers straight away.

'What? Say that to me one more time,' Captain Chilvers tells Cassian once he hears the news.

'A pizza was ordered, but the drone that delivered it to Mr Erso, returned with it because it was not accepted. We have the recording showing Mr Erso refuse it on camera in person, saying that he didn't order a pizza and he doesn't want a pizza. The delivery drone returned that back to the restaurant a few minutes later.'

'So where did the pizza come from?'

'Well, after a little more questioning, the same restaurant did have an order for the same pizza to be collected in person. I thought it odd that the staff would remember a single pizza order, but apparently it is hardly ever done anymore. Drone deliveries are the norm these days. Although collecting an order in person isn't unheard of, so I questioned why this particular order stuck out in their minds.'

'And what did they say?'

'The man who collected in person, paid in cash, insisted that his RFID chip was malfunctioning as a payment method and didn't even want to attempt to scan it.'

'Cash? So it doesn't leave a trace. Do you have a description?'

Cassian shares a clip taken from the store in-house video surveillance which shows a slim built, young Caucasian male, dressed all in black, his face obscured with a cap and glasses.

'Great work Cas. We will have him tracked with the street camera footage and find out exactly where he went from there. This could be something good. I'm impressed Cas. You know, you really came through for me on this one. I guess nothing beats good old intuition.'

'It was just a hunch, Captain. Erso was a

member of a very liberal party, hated violence of any kind, especially to the defenceless. And that includes animals. The traces of meat in the kitchen just clicked in my mind and I pulled at the thread.'

'I'm grateful. These bots, the way things are now, it's all doing a good job. And I understand the shift to automation, no bribery or blackmail, no scandals and brutality; they're always on the job. I mean, their success rates can't be argued with. But there isn't always going to be a logical process that they can follow, like in this case.'

'I agree, but I guess they'll improve, like everything else that is still pushing forward.'

'Until that time comes, I'll still be here making decisions. And I have been thinking. I want you back, Cas.'

'Sorry Cap? Back where?'

'Back here on the team. If you'll come back, you lazy sod. We'll find a section for you to run, put those talents to good use.'

'Wow, I mean, that's very kind of you. It's kind of sudden though. Can you give me some time? Wait till this case is wrapped up at least?'

'Sure, why not?' Captain Chilvers says, 'this lead will hopefully keep the vultures off my back for a while. Give me space to do my job. Let me know if you get anything else click in that mind of yours.'

'I will,' Cassian says as the holocall ends.

He sits in his front room, elated at the offer.

Back in the field. It has been missing from his life all of this time. Ever since the force retired his entire section and replaced them with the bots. To be part of society now as it is, there isn't any direction anymore. Money isn't an issue, which was the reason for working in the first place. Everyone is paid by the state whether they work or not. It is a time of abundance and sharing. Financial hardship is long gone, you just do what you love.

Cassian did what he loves; was good at it too. But that role was taken away for the good of society. He could have gone on to do anything that his heart desired. Travelled the world. Wrote a book. Trained as a doctor. There was plenty of time. Time to do anything he wanted except do the one thing he loved. Be a detective. That was taken over by entities with huge storage of information and fast processing times. Bots that never got sick or took a day off, never made a mistake because they were tired and who always did their duty. They didn't scoff and sulk at new rules and procedures, they were just updated or replaced and carried on.

Cassian gets to his feet and pats his ever increasing belly.

'George,' he calls out.

'Yes, sir,' George replies, glowing into view.

'I'm going to take a walk.'

'I will get the simulation ready. Where would you like to venture? The Great Wall of China is always nice for a stroll.'

'Think I will go outside today.'

The next morning Cassian is up before his alarm frightens him into consciousness as it normally does. He is excited, eager to find out if there have been any developments in the case. After showering and getting ready with the help of his faithful equipment, he is hungrily scouring the news channels for any whispers regarding the investigation.

'George, can you bring up the case notes again. See if there is anything else that I've missed,' Cassian tells his faithful helper.

'As you wish.'

Just as the files begin to rotate around the room once again, Captain Cassian holocalls.

'Cassian you gorgeous lad,' he bellows at Cassian exuberantly, his holographic head unexpectedly enlarging at the same time, 'you are a genius. I could just kiss you, lad.'

'What? Why? What's happened? And also, please don't,' Cassian spurts out, the giddiness building up inside like a child at Christmas.

'We've got him. Max Unduli. We followed that lead you gave us from the restaurant and believe it or not, we've got him entering the same road that Erso lived on…while holding that bloody pizza. He's in custody right now speaking with his lawyer and shaking like nervous jelly.'

'Really! Is he admitting to the murder?'

'No, I don't think he will, he's keeping quiet, not saying a word. But we've got plenty of circumstantial to charge him and go to trial. Especially after the scanners found traces of Erso's DNA at his residence. He's got less leg to stand on than a paraplegic.'

'Not really appropriate…for a police captain…I think, sir.'

'I don't give a shit, Cas. I can finally sleep after three days. I might go and abuse one of these bots later for a bit of relaxation…sexually.'

'Um…okay…I don't really want to know about that side of your life, Captain. But how come nothing is in the news? I've been checking the entire network all morning.'

'I'm going to play with these bastards, Cas. They have been riding me since this case broke and it is time for a little fun. Let them think that they've got the upper condescending hand on me, I'll crush them.'

'I'd want to be around for that,' Cassian laughs.

'Oh, but you can be. Have you thought anymore about my offer? Are you coming back?'

'Well about that…I do want to come back, actually I would love to. But I have a condition.'

'Oh go on then, what is it? You've caught me on a good day.'

'I'd want to come back with Scarif, my old partner.'

'Done…anything else, you wily fox?'

'Nothing, Captain,' Cassian says, gleaming with happiness inside, 'thank you so much.'

'Not a problem, Cas, I will see the two of you on Monday. You can tell Scarif. And lose some bloody weight, you hippo.'

'I will do, Captain.'

Cassian ends the holocall, disbelief washing over him at the knowledge that he can get back to the job that he loves. It all seems too good to be true. Too perfect a situation. Sometimes life does offer up instances of perfection for you to savour.

Cassian spends the rest of the day preparing for life back at the police station. Updating himself with new processes and systems, new rules and ways of doing things. There aren't many humans left in the police department, just those who manage the bots and those who maintain them. It seems that Cassian and his old partner will be some of the managers. They'll just have to manage them on the streets.

Later in the evening, a little before Cassian turns into bed, Captain Chilvers holds a press conference regarding the developments of the case. It isn't the most politically correct of affairs, but let's just say that the Captain is probably going to have some sweet dreams tonight.

In bed, Cassian is himself drifting off to sleep, reliving the events of the past few days. On the surface, everything appears to be calm now, but like an iceberg, most of the danger lies beneath the surface. Something has been bugging him for a while and he can't figure out what it is. Yes, old man Erso had an incredible history at a momentous time in human society, but he had ridden under the waves for decades now, always in the sidelines. There couldn't be any surprises there.

The bots missing the link between Erso being a vegan and the meat particles in the kitchen. They were never programmed primarily for murder cases as they are so rare, probably something which just slipped through the net.

The pizza box retrieved from Erso's rubbish. The remaining slices had been thrown away. A normal thing that someone would do if they weren't going to eat them later. But if Erso didn't eat them, then that means the killer ate them, and he must have been very hungry because there were only two slices left. Would he really eat that much while killing someone?

Cassian bolts upright in bed suddenly wide awake.

There are two killers.

Bounding down the stairs in the dark, Cassian yells out to George.

'George, the case notes, quickly.'

But there is no response.

Cassian mumbles under his breath.

'George, for God's sake, now is not the time to run out of power. At least tell me how long you'll be.'

But still nothing.

'I have to do everything around here.' Cassian says to himself walking into the front room, before he gets a huge shock, the fright of his life.

'I wouldn't say everything, Cas,' a voice growls behind him.

Cassian spins around and sees a man sitting in his armchair, dressed all in black. A mean grin on his face, eyebrows arched wickedly.

'Scarif, you idiot. You scared the life out of me. You need to stop doing that. And did you mess with George again?'

Cassian's old partner gets up to give him a hug.

'Yeah, he annoys me anyway. All that *yes sir, no sir* bollocks, does my head in. And you need some better security in this place, you don't know what kind of crazy person could break in.'

Cassian laughs.

'Only nutters from outside the area, but I can handle them.'

'I saw, Mr Nerves of Steel,' Scarif jests.

'Whatever, now sit down we need to talk.'

'As you wish,' Scarif says with a small bow. 'So give me the word from head office, I saw on the news that they finally caught him for the murder.'

'Yep, Chilvers is milking this one like a bulging cow.'

'Ha-ha...I bet he is.'

'And we got our jobs back.'

'Yes!' Scarif yells, punching the air excitedly and leaping into the air as high as his old legs will allow.

'But that's not what I wanted to talk to you about.'

Scarif sits back down and shifts in his seat.

'Okay, sure. What's up, Cas?'

'Did you...eat some of that pizza?'

Scarif gets up from his seat without answering. Cassian follows him with his eyes as he walks around a little before kneeling near the front door. He fiddles around in a power box, flicking switches and pressing buttons until George wakes up with a little melody that is easy on the ears.

'Yes. I had to Cas,' Scarif replies finally getting up from the floor, 'it was the only way that idiot, Max would eat some too. He would've been suspicious that I was up to something if I hadn't.'

'You know that if *I* have worked out that there were two people there that day, then someone else might as well?'

'Hmmm...I know. Guess we'll have to make sure we can work something from the inside once we get there.' A cheeky smile grows onto Scarif's lips.

Cassian regards his long time friend through jaded eyes.

'I'm sorry about your godfather, it must have

been difficult to…well…you know.'

'Yeah…thanks.' Scarif says as his eyes begin to shine with moisture, the smile losing its form. 'It was his idea I know, but it still haunts me. I still can't believe the sacrifice he made for me…and for you.'

'He loved you a lot, mate. More so since your parents passed away. But imagine the guilt that he had felt living in a world that he had helped to create, and hating it more and more every day. Especially when you lost your job to the bots. The plans were rattling around in his mind for years. I understand that he gave up his life for you, but it was more for his own peace of mind. He always thought that the automation had come along too fast and people had become too aimless in life…the complete opposite to his own life experience.'

'I wasn't going to go through with it, you know,' Scarif tells Cassian, as he begins to pace around the room. 'Uncle Ben used to go on about it for a long time. It wasn't even an option for me to go through with this whole stupid idea of taking his life in a way that I would get my job back. Until his Parkinson's diagnosis came about.'

Cassian doesn't say anything. Instead he stands up puts a comforting arm on Scarif's shoulder who responds with an appreciating grimace. Scarif continues.

'It was so hard seeing him struggle so much

over the years. He wouldn't accept any kind of help, you know how proud of a man he was. Most days he would be okay, but when it was bad, it was really bad. I would often find him on the floor and unable to get up. Even the simplest tasks were so difficult sometimes, making a cup of tea became a roulette. Becoming like that must have been soul destroying for him.'

'I know, buddy. Listen, if you didn't go through with his plan, which was to help us as well don't forget, then he would have gone down the assisted suicide route. He'd found out all the details long ago.'

Scarif lets out an anguished cry as all of the emotions surface. He drops to his knees and his head falls to his chest.

'He was so happy when I was there to end his life as he wanted,' Scarif wails through uncontrollable sobs. 'I could see all of his guilt fade away when I stuck the knife in. It was so hard to keep up the act in front of Max.'

Cassian comforts his friend, hand around his shoulder and holding him tight as he lets out some grief. After some time, Scarif calms down and sits back on the chair.

'Where did you find that guy, anyway?' Cassian asks.

'Oh that moron! It's amazing who you can find to do certain things when they haven't got a thing to do in the world.'

'And he won't talk?'

'Him? No, never. He didn't expect to get caught but where he's from, they don't say a word.'

'Are you sure, Scar?' Cassian asks directly.

'Yes. We don't have to worry there. I'll probably get a visit one day, but I'll deal with that when it comes.'

'*We'll* deal with it, together.'

Scarif looks Cassian in the eye and nods in gratitude at the sentiment. They both take a seat once more and sit in silence for a while. Cassian looks at his friend who looks right back at him. After regarding each other for an intense moment, they both smile, and then break out in laughter at the outrageousness of the situation.

It all began once Ben Erso, the godfather of Scarif, was suffering more and more from his disease and was able to apply for euthanasia. He used this fact to pressure his dear godchild into accepting to be part of a ploy which would be unsolvable for the police bots and require a partial return to old fashioned policing, thus gaining his godson and best friend, Cassian, their jobs back, allowing his soul to rest partially in peace at least.

He had planned everything using his old political knowledge of the way things work. Secret meetings with the two ex-policemen filled in any gaps that arose in his plot. Having been instrumental in defeating the banks, changing the global economy and releasing the public from the need to work meaningless jobs simply to eek their way through life, he was unprepared with the rapidity with which automation took over the jobs and left people with no purpose, whether they liked it or not. The big careers were still there but the majority were left with money in the bank but aimless milling around.

Laziness is infectious, once it gets hold of someone, it is hard to shake.

'Scar, I know we haven't spoken since we set this whole deal up and it has all gone pretty well. But if anything does come out, you just keep your mouth shut. It was all my idea. You follow me?'

Scarif shakes his head.

'No Cassian, you only did this for me. I get that you benefited as well, but I got you into this with my emotional blackmail. You didn't give anything to the planning except what you know about Chilvers. This was Ben's set up. You know he even had the idea of the fake pizza delivery then getting Max to gain access to the house by pretending to be a restaurant manager with an apology pizza. I mean, he thought of absolutely everything even the crumbs on the worktop. If anyone goes down for this, it will be me. You just keep *your* mouth shut and say you were just doing the job tasked to you by Chilvers.'

'Well, we'll see what happens if it comes to that. In the meantime, just get your shit together, 'cos we're starting work on Monday'

'Hahaha…yep work on Monday. I think I need to book some time off. I'm knackered.'

THE FOLLOWER

Molly lets out a deep sigh of frustration.

She is sat slouched on the edge of the old cream-coloured bathtub at her grandmother's home. Her worry causing her to bite her nails down to tiny rough stubs.

She just can't understand why people are finding her so boring.

They are switching off in their dozens on an almost daily basis. This was meant to be her direct route to popularity and stardom. To allow her to follow in the footsteps of the hot talent of today, the greats before her and her idol - the true Queen of social media mayhem, Kim Kardashian. Though she is at pension age now, more saggy than plump, that often discussed and dissected path of once being Paris Hilton's chubby friend to becoming a fashion trend-setter of epic proportions has its place in history; being narcissistic and dysfunctional are not obstacles on the journey to rise to the top – they are necessary.

So why is Molly finding it so difficult? She has all of the tools that she needs, but they are not serving their purpose.

She stands and looks at herself in the streaky bathroom mirror. The eyes which look back at her are tired. Lifeless. *Who would want to stare at them all day to try to escape their own lives?* She is meant to entertain, inspire and uplift. Not depress, sadden and create suicidal thoughts involving a jacuzzi and an electric curling iron.

Molly takes a deep breath, adjusts her black headband and lightly slaps her cheeks. Attempts to engage some blood vessels into rising to the surface to inject some life into her pale complexion. She pulls her shoulders back and lifts her chin to an angle that accentuates her cheekbones. The angle makes her look as if she is having a seizure and unwittingly got stuck in that position because the wind changed. Maybe not the best look.

'Molly!' her grandmother calls from the kitchen, 'your breakfast is ready, darling.'

'Coming,' Molly replies.

One last look at her pout-face pose in case it is needed in an emergency situation, checks her ear piece and heads out of the door with a light beep sounding in her ear.

'Hey, Grammy,' Molly gushes over her sweet old grandmother while she receives an encapsulating tight hug, the kind that only a grandmother can give.

'Good morning, my pumpkin,' replies her grandmother, her white curls resting like a fluffy cloud on top of a kind jolly face, 'what can I get for you to eat? You really look like you need a nice, hot meal.'

'Aw, you really think so?' Molly smiles as she looks down and appraises her own slim figure. 'You're so sweet.'

Slightly confused, her grandmother carries on regardless. 'Oh…that's okay my lovely…how about a nice good old English breakfast? The kind I used to make you when you were little?'

Molly's face instantly lights up as the memory fills up her mind with the clarity of a full colour picture.

'Just as you used to make me?'

'Of course, dear. Now you just relax and talk to your poor old granny while I rustle it up. Tell me what you've been up to. You're like a stranger these days,' her grandmother says while shuffling about the kitchen, gathering the ingredients.

'Not much really. I've just finished up at university so just working part time at the opticians while I find a job in my field.'

'*In your field*. Ooh, look at you. That sounds very professional. I'm sure you'll get your dream job soon, love. Any man in your life? Pretty girl like you must have all the young chaps following you around like wet puppies.'

'Not at the moment, Gran,' Molly laughs, unsure how to talk to her grandmother about boys and romance. 'I'm still looking for my Prince Charming.'

At this last comment, Molly's ear piece beeps in her ear indicating that someone has left her account a message. She flips out a rectangular piece of clear perspex which illuminates up as soon as it has scanned her retina. Quickly reading, she speedily taps out a reply and swiftly lays it on the table.

'What's that you're doing? Has your knight found you already?'

'No Gran, I'm just replying to one of my followers.'

'Followers? Is someone stalking you?' Molly laughs hard as her grandmother stares at her with a semi-serious, semi-confused expression. 'What did I say? What's so funny?'

'Gran, I'm on SeeSeeTV,' Molly replies. When she receives a blank stare in return, she feels the need to explain in terms that her Gran can understand. 'It's how I keep in touch with my friends and show them what I'm up to…and I'm set up for broadcasting to everyone else too. Hopefully I'll be discovered one day and be famous.'

'Oh, so it's like Facebook or Twitter? I'm on Facebook. Let me add you as my friend so we can keep in touch a bit better than the occasional visit once a year.'

'Facebook? What's that?' Molly queries.

Her grandmother proceeds to tell Molly all about Facebook and how thirty years ago, it was one of the biggest social media apps in the world. How people all over the world kept in touch, showed off pictures and videos to each other and shared information. Molly found it hysterical learning about how life was back in the early part of the century. People taking hundreds of pictures of nights out, their tanned legs on holiday from the sun-lounger and even their plates of food. Filtering out the best ones, sometimes tweaking the lighting and posting the most appealing shots. Sharing the very best bits and pieces of their lives, hoping that people will *like* or say something nice about it. It was all so contrived, needy and fake. The worst party in the history of parties could be made to look amazing by posting the right six second clip of a few simultaneous 'woo-hoo's'.

The evolution of social media and reality television took place long ago as the newer generations grew tired of being lied to and manipulated constantly. They preferred raw footage, unaltered and real. Facades could be created by anyone with a laptop and a secondary education in computer programming. Need to show off a flat stomach while at the beach? Done. Need to show how great your boyfriend is for arranging a candlelit dinner? Done. Want to proudly display the hundreds of friends you have? Done.

Photoshop can easily change that convex belly into a straight line. Google has millions of images of romantic dinner settings for you to borrow as your own. And for twenty pounds, a Scandinavian IT tech can add hundreds of *'friends'* to your social media account inside of five minutes.

People became sick to death of all the YouTubers, Viners and Instagramers. Fame by deception. None of it was ever completely real. It was all just marketing. The real world, real life, doesn't allow retakes or twenty minutes in complete silence while you can think of the perfect reply to a tweet. Reality is fast, constant and unforgiving. You can't redo real life. Time doesn't turn backwards.

SeeSeeTV was the brainchild of a victim of social media. Or at least her mother, Tanya Wilson was. Tanya divorced her husband way back in 2013 for cheating on her. The split hit her hard like a truck and her life collapsed into a pool of nothingness. It took years of therapy for depression before she worked her way back to the surface of the pit she was drowning in. Nevertheless, she found a group of supportive friends who had helped to carve her a new life. One of independence and pride.

Facebook actually had helped her in this cause.

Allowed her to expand her four walls at home to include socialising with many others at any time of the day. Kept her confidence propped up with acceptance and praise for visuals of her new life and trim physique. She attracted many random friends, all whom she had accepted readily, each one providing an enriching shot of dopamine, that highly sought after, naturally-occurring addictive substance.

Unfortunately, one new friend became one too many. The wrong kind of friend. She was hoodwinked by the fake profile of a man who bamboozled her with romantic affection, the single missing link in her new life. Wooed in a way that she had never experienced by a man with the lifestyle that excited her. At least, that is what his collection of personal photos and videos indicated. She wanted desperately to meet with him before long.

So she did so.

After he raped her at their first meeting at a random hotel, he disappeared, along with his fake profile which he was nothing like in real life. Probably off to entrap some other vulnerable woman. But before he did, he left her a parting gift.

A baby.

That baby grew up to be Jyn Wilson, the creator of SeeSeeTV. Having spent her younger years watching her mother disintegrate with each passing year, while becoming more and more distant as she grew into the facial features of her mother's attacker, Jyn vowed to destroy the culture of interaction that allowed lies to be part of the framework. With her own story being known the world over, she used it to her advantage. Bad news travels the fastest, and her story was one of the worst. Maybe that was a good thing as it gave her new idea an international platform.

That idea was *SeeSeeTV*.

'Gran, you need to get with the program,' Molly tells her grandmother who is serving up a scrumptious breakfast. Fried eggs, bacon, sausage, mushrooms, tomato, all made into the shape of a smiling face, with a triangle of lightly toasted bread as the hat. 'Nobody uses that ancient stuff anymore.'

'I'll try, dear. So what's this latest new thing that you youngsters are using these days?'

'Well…,' Molly begins, while dipping the point of toast into the yellow yolk of one of her fried eggs, 'we're all using SeeSeeTV.'

'CCTV?' Her grandmother is puzzled. 'Isn't that what the government and secret service uses to spy on us?'

'You're so funny Gran. No, it's See See as in *See See*.' Molly puts up rings in front of her eyes with thumbs and index fingers. 'It's basically constant live streaming so all of our friends can see and follow. And I can follow anyone else that uses it. Make comments, send messages, chat. That sort of thing. But it's live, you see. So there's none of these fake poses and setting the scene for pictures. It's all real life, nothing made up. It's constant. Look Gran, let me show you something from Emma's history that's hilarious.'

'Oh, okay.'

Molly proceeds to scroll through her phone until she finds a clip of her best friend Emma, playing a prank on her younger brother, Jack. She had dressed up as the cushions on an arm-chair and waited for him to sit down before jumping out and scaring the soul out of him. The different thing here was that you could see the entire preparation to the prank as well which added to the suspense. It was pretty funny at first, but Jack had gotten so scared that he'd wet himself. Possibly not the best idea to prank a six year old, but she did get loads of views and followers so she reasoned it away in her mind and ignored the negative comments.

Molly's grandmother scrunches up her face as the understanding of the app seeps its way into her brain. The sharing of lives had become so intrinsic to the younger generations that it is now a part of life. Only the best bits aren't shared anymore. *All* of the bits are. Whether they are fun and exciting, or dull and mundane. People just want to have access to everything and make up their own minds as to what they like and don't like.

'Isn't that a bit dangerous, Molly?'

'Dangerous? Not really Gran. You do need to go through a full identity check these days to have social media accounts. I think it was because of what happed to the Prime Minister's daughter ages ago.'

'Who? Theresa?'

'Uh-huh. There was that massive story about how she got cat-fished by someone pretending to be someone else to get some juicy gossip on the PM. So the law was created to make all of these accounts properly vetted and registered. Judges are handing out long prison sentences and life bans from even *browsing* online. You can't just make up ten different personalities now and go out and con people.'

'Hmmm. Like the good old days,' her grandmother laughs, 'well, you just be careful young lady. There may be laws protecting you, but just remember that when you put yourself out there, you're putting yourself in harm's way. So be responsible, my child.'

'Oh, don't worry Gran, I know what I'm doing.'

'That's what I'm worried about.'

After spending some more time in the bathroom, the only place where the SeeSeeTV app is programmed not to function, Molly feels rejuvenated. Among other things, she has a few nice comments about her encounter with her grandmother. Especially the cute plate of food that was made for her. They are all from a couple of friends who are probably at home lounging around without much to do except hold their phone inches from their unblinking eyes. There is also a message from a stranger named Chris. He'd said that he 'wouldn't mind being your prince charming'.

A bit of flirting always gets Molly's juices flowing, seeing as there is so little of it these days. She makes sure that her headband is positioned correctly, the location of her SeeSeeTV cam, and begins her way out the front door having told her grandmother.

Once she is on the bus heading in to the local town shopping district, she pulls out her phone and checks out what a few people are up to. As she opens up the app, she has picture-in-picture on her screen. The main screen showing the video of the people she is browsing, and the smaller in-picture shows her own feed as it browses other feeds. When people came across these feeds of users browsing other users, they either switch to someone else's feed or scroll through their historical videos which save up to six months worth of data in the cloud. Although occasionally, some people enjoy indulging in seeing feeds of people viewing other people's feeds...viewing other people's feeds.

It can get very complicated and chain-like.

Molly isn't one of those weirdos. She likes to keep it simple. But random.

Just one feed at a time is more than enough for her. Though she can channel-hop like a mad person, skimming through people's accounts on a secondly basis until a tiny slither of interest piques her attention. Maybe someone is playing a competitive game of Pictionary. Like anyone actually does that in real life. Or maybe a couple are arguing about whose turn it is to take the dog for walk. It's usually the guy's turn. Rarely but wonderfully, a person would be among friends in the aftermath of a devastatingly funny moment, the kind that sends uncontrollable laughter around the room, eyes watering and hands on stomachs. Snot sliding out of a nostril is reality gold.

The problem is that most of the SeeSeeTVers don't live lives that are a laugh a minute; constantly exciting and experiencing adrenaline pumping instances. These mad moments don't occur as often as people make out that they do. Have you known a person who can rattle off story after story of the craziest moment that they have ever witnessed? Yet in all of the hours and hours that you are in their company not one memorable event happens. Funny that.

There was once a popular revolutionary television program called Big Brother. The premise was simple. A group of *'interesting'* members of the public were plucked from the throngs of applicants. The chosen were then all thrust together, living in a large house while wearing microphones twenty four hours a day and covered with cameras. The public voting for one person to leave each week until one remaining house-mate won the show. Given tasks, restrictions, and things to do, the producers would then broadcast a thirty minute episode every evening of the best bits from the day.

These daily programs were great.

Any moment of interest was edited into a short clip and played back to back with others with full comedic narration. Jokes, kisses, arguments, controversies. They were all edited and clumped together to make it seem as though the last day's action in the house was non-stop, rip-roaring action. Two house-mates smooching underneath the covers, another guy illegally colluding with another to conspire and cheat, someone trying to escape while another is depressed and in need of a psychiatrist.

The show was amazing fun.

Until you realised that at any time of the day, you could watch the live stream of the cameras for the house. And all you saw was a group of people sitting around in a house. It made you discover that the show wasn't interesting because the people involved were anything special. It was because the show and contestants were edited to look that way. Small tiny moments blown up out of all proportion and into exciting segments. Yet it didn't still didn't deter viewers from watching. In fact, the notion of constant sharing became more and more popular as time went on. More and more different types of media involved, methods varied and topics covered.

A major player in the streaming industry was gaming. As in watching other players play games. Those channels would get thousands of viewers, sharing, liking and making comments. Vicarious gaming. Unreal. But it was very popular. As did many other types of channels.

SeeSeeTV took advantage of this variety and organised everything together and in one place. Through their website you could access all of your normal friend's streams. On top of that, you could browse millions of streams through their subject matter. Sports players, dancers, you could log into all of their live feeds. If it took your fancy, you could even watch someone as they sat and fished. You could probably find someone watching paint dry if you tried.

Molly reaches her destination before long and she hops off the bus and makes her way through the park. The day is bright and calm. Many families out in the sun taking advantage of the picturesque beauty. Couples strolling hand in hand. Most streaming live, sharing the scene.

As usual Molly cuts through here on the way to the shopping centre. Today she is meeting a friend of hers, Emma, for a little retail therapy. They often do this and wait for the comments flood in. Trying on and posing in stylish dresses and outfits. Testing new makeup and getting their hair done in new funky ways. Always having a lot of fun together.

They meet up near the lake in the middle of the park. Hugging excitedly and adjusting their cams straight after, giggling. A pair of old men on a bench nearby watching closely.

'Hey girl, you are looking fantastic,' Emma says smiling, looking her friend up and down while holding her hands.

'Not as sexy as you are, Em,' Molly gives an exaggerated wink.

Now that they are together, they instantly become conscious of how they look, their posture and expressions, as they will both be broadcast close up whenever the other looks at them. They make sure that they use tried and tested poses from in front of the bathroom mirror while they are on camera. Always doing their best to get in good light and at the right angle in other cams. You never know when someone may come across your channel.

A spurt of blood explodes from Emma's head and splatters into Molly's face, sending Emma crashing to the ground with a thump.

Molly stands, frozen in the moment, unsure of what the hell was going on.

From the corner of her eye, she can see the old men on the bench struggle to their feet, shouting at her. She can't make out what it is that they are saying but their eyes are wide. Wide with fear and worry.

Molly looks ahead and sees a large man bounding towards her. He is dressed in summery clothes yet has his face covered. She has no idea what to do. Her friend is on the floor next to her, completely unconscious with her forehead split above the left eyebrow, blood already pumping out and beginning to form a rich red pool around the offending weapon, a sharp piece of stone. The attacker is now just metres away. Thick set muscles stretching and rippling beneath the tight clothing, he is here with purpose.

'Run!' the voices behind her are saying. The words of one of the old men finally getting translated by her lagging brain, probably still in shock.

Her legs turn to carry her body far, far away. Away from harm. Her brain fully engaged in the flight reaction. Staying and fighting isn't even an option.

The attacker must have another weapon on his person, something deadly to use against her just as he had used against Emma's head. Everything in her body is commanding her to get away from this danger. She is set to go.

But Molly drops to the ground. Covers Emma's limp body with her own as protection. Leaving her friend in her unconscious state would leave her open for more vicious attacks with no defence. No way to raise her hands in front of her face to ward off deadly blows. Running away and leaving her could well be the death of her friend.

So she stays.

A second later she feels a terrible pain.

Then she blacks out.

When Molly comes around, she isn't in the park anymore. She finds herself in a bed, but not her own.

The intravenous drip attached to her arm and sterile smell in the air kind of give it away pretty quickly. She is in hospital.

As she looks around the room, she sees her family around her looking very concerned but happy that she is awake.

'Hey there sweetie,' her mother coos gently. A diminutive woman with a kind face. She sits on the bed caressing Molly's face, careful to avoid the bandages. 'How are you feeling there?'

Molly tries to sit up but a searing pain seizes her side completely, immobilising any type of movement.

'Ugh...okay,' she gasps.

'Oh, that's okay, honey. Don't move, just rest okay.'

'Sure…what the hell is going on, mum?' she asks as she sinks back into the bed.

Her mother's face darkens at the question, anger obviously bubbling beneath the surface. Her father steps in to take over answering the question after sensing the level of emotion in her mother. There must have already been some outbursts.

'My poor baby,' he says softly, stepping closer and holding Molly's hand, 'now I don't want you to get too stressed. You have been through a major ordeal.'

'Daddy,' Molly says, pleading as tears well up in her eyes. 'Please tell me what happened. Is Emma okay? Where is she?'

Molly's mother and father both share a glance. A certain sign that something isn't quite right. Everything isn't okay.

'She *will* be, my love,' her father says finally. 'Emma is in a bad way, but stable. The doctors are very confident that she will fully recover…in time.'

Molly lets out a sigh which ends in a few painful sobs. As much from hearing about Emma as from the hurt of her own injuries.

'Don't cry, Mol,' her father says, cuddling her as best as he can, 'it will all be okay.'

'What happened, dad?' Molly asks once again. 'Please.'

After receiving a barely perceptible nod from

her mother, her father explains everything that they know so far.

The kick that Molly received while buffering her friend against the attacker was powerful. It had the full force of a well-built adult man behind it. So powerful in fact that three ribs had fractured and an extra one broken. The shock to her system was so great that she blacked out instantly. But it didn't stop her from taking another kick which broke her arm and then a final stamp on the leg.

The old men who had had been trying to warn her had actually ended up saving her and Emma from further harm. They ran at the attacker with their walking sticks. He didn't stay to fight. Apparently he drew the line at beating up old age pensioners. Whereas women were fair game.

'Emma had made some people very mad recently,' her father says, telling Molly what he knows. 'There was some feed that she streamed showing her scaring her little brother so much that he urinated from the fear and shock. She burst out laughing when he did and it seems that someone has taken exception to her behaviour. Taken revenge on her brother's behalf. She'd been getting hateful messages from a number of people since the video so the police are doing their investigations. But it is just up in the air right now, nothing has been confirmed. Just have to wait and see what their officers turn up.'

'What?' Molly says incredulously. 'Because of a

joke, someone tried to kill her? That's...that's just sick.'

'Yes, it is sick. Disgusting. But...if you weren't there to protect her, she may very well be dead right now. Who knows what kind of blows she would have taken without you taking them instead. It was very brave of you, Molly. Most people would have run away.'

'I...I did want to run...I...,' Molly stutters, vocalising her thoughts when she saw the attacker.

'Sshh...it's okay, my love. Next time you'd better run,' her mother soothes. 'I can't imagine what would have...would...'

Her mother can't complete the words. The thought of losing her daughter is too much to take.

After a few hours interspersed with silent moments of mother, father and daughter crying with one another, they leave Molly to rest in peace for the evening, promising to return early the next morning. The doctors have said that they would most likely discharge her tomorrow after a final few tests in the morning.

Before he leaves however, her father gives Molly her phone.

'Here you are, love. Now listen...before you look at the footage, and I know that you will, just remember that you are safe and the police will track this disgusting psychopath down. Take him off the streets before he does any more hurt and damage. And don't worry about Emma, she is awake and talking. Just a matter of time until she's up and about, okay petal.'

'Thanks dad,' Molly says as he is leaving the room.' Oh…have you seen my headband?'

Her dad smiles at her and points just above her shoulder. The headband with the SeeSeeTV cam embedded discretely into it was resting on a small shelf behind her. 'It's been on the whole time. Your mother knew you would've wanted it there.' He leaves the room with a knowing smile.

Excitedly but cautiously, Molly checks her feed and sees thousands of more followers have joined her account as well as many more who have viewed her live and recent footage, especially everything that has happened since she just came around. The comments are continuously spilling over onto new pages, more flowing through every second. It appears that her recent heroics have made her a star. Not a star in the way she preferred, but one nonetheless. People who have watched the clips are showering praise upon Molly, sympathy for Emma and their attacker is being universally condemned.

As Molly flicks through the clips in her feeds history, she sees how brutal the initial attack really was. When the stone made contact with Emma's forehead, her entire skull snapped 45 degrees to the side before she collapsed. Molly winces when she sees it. But it was strangely enticing, it didn't turn her off. She feels compelled to watch it.

There are also connecting feeds of the attack from other people in the park. Most of which are further away from the action then everyone would have liked. Much of the footage is distant and a little blurry. Molly and Emma's own clips are extremely shaky and are more of the concrete than anything else.

However, there is a great clip of the entire attack from a SeeSeeTV feed growing in popularity.

One of the old men who had been trying to help Molly had his own SeeSeeTV live stream, with the cam embedded in his walking stick. It gives a full, uncut view of the entire attack, start to finish. It caught the whole event. It is brutal to watch.

'Oh my God' Molly exclaims as she sees the footage. To watch while she and a dear friend are being violated with such ferocity and anger is shown in such clarity, the emotions are jarring and raw. Tears fill her eyes and she before long, Molly breaks down in tears. Easing the covers off, she edges towards the bathroom for some privacy, her SeeSeeTV cam still streaming as she shuffles away.

The toilet lid comes down and she sits with tears still streaming down her face.

Her phone lets out a beep.

Privacy mode has been activated.

The small cubicle has an open plan layout,

shower and wash basin on the far side away from Molly. The nightgown that she is wearing is thin. It takes in a lot of the cold from the seat, makes her shiver a little. Molly doesn't really notice though. Along with the physical pain and the emotions she is feeling right now, a bit of coldness can't really make much of an impact. Too many other things have precedence.

Her shoulders shake uncontrollably, her hands covering her face. The events of the day are all running through her mind and it has become all too overwhelming. The hate against Emma for a silly clip. Being depressed about the popularity on her own feed. Not to mention the horrific image burned into her mind of the attack. Seeing her blood covered friend. Prone, unconscious and vulnerable.

Then realising that the entire world has binged on the footage for their own entertainment. Sharing and forwarding, commenting and putting forth comments and criticisms.

Molly's head tips back as she let out a hearty laugh.

Tears still cascading down her face.

Tears of joy.

She can't have asked for anything else to go better.

The plan has been executed perfectly.

'...is that my knight in shining armour?' Molly

asks down her phone, still in the bathroom.

'It's me, babe. How are you feeling?'

'I'm in a lot of pain, but I'll survive. You didn't have to kick me so hard.'

'I'm so sorry Molz, I wasn't even aiming for you half the time. I was after that bullying friend of yours, I kind of went a bit insane. And I wanted it to look realistic.'

'Realistic? You achieved that quite well, I think. My feed has been going absolutely mental, people love me. They think I'm a hero,' Molly says down the phone.

'You are a hero, to me you are at least. When I saw your friend…with all of that blood everywhere…and on you…I've just been so worried about you. I've been watching your feed religiously and I have to admit, you're a star. I was gripped. Couldn't take my eyes off you.' He says taking a long pause, hoping his words sunk in. Finally he continues. 'So anyway, how is that evil soul-sucking maggot of a friend of yours?'

'You smashed her face in with a brick and beat her while she was unconscious like you were stamping out a cigarette. How do you think she is?'

'That bad, huh?' he replies without the slightest iota of remorse in his voice.

'Yeah, but she'll pull through. She's awake already.'

Another pause.

'Do you feel bad?'

'I do now, but I was so mad at her after she played that prank on me, I felt humiliated. People made fun of me and I really hated her for a while. So many people switched off my feed. Not before cussing me out though.'

'You know that I didn't switch off. I'll always be your follower. By the way, I think we did a public service. Did you see how much hate she got for making her own little brother piss himself and then sit there laughing like crazy. Someone would have got her eventually.'

'Yeah, maybe. But I'm still her friend even if she did make my life hell for a while. She didn't actually mean it that way. That's just her twisted sense of humour.'

'Let's see how funny *she* finds it now.'

Molly finds her thoughts drifting back to the time a few months back when Emma played the armchair trick on her. She didn't urinate her knickers like Emma's brother did. But she screamed so loud and uncontrollably that she became viral footage. As expected, Emma burst out laughing and couldn't stop even when Molly shrunk into a heap and began hyperventilating. It just added to the ratings.

The ghost of the memory and the subsequent hammering Molly received from friends and strangers alike gave a steeliness to her will. For all of the sorrow she feels at the plot against her friend, her best friend, the recollection of how she felt in the aftermath of the viral prank was too strong. The jokes, the ridicule, the anxiety and depression. It was all too much. She feels vindicated now.

'My dad told me that the cops have made the connection with her feed and the prank. They're looking into anyone who left her any threats or severe abuse. You didn't join in, did you?' Molly asks once she has shaken away the phase of reminiscence.

'Almost, but no. I only saw the prank clip from the link on your feed. They won't find me. And even if they do, it's all on me. Don't worry about anything okay.'

'Okay.'

'Now get back to your bed. You've got to keep your strength up. You've got a show to put on.'

THE IMPLANT

Hospitals.

Strange places.

I actually love them now, but I used to hate them when I was a nipper.

I can still remember my first visit to the hospital.

It happened because of an accident I had over at West Ham Park with my older brother and his friend. They were on this gigantic see-saw in the playground area and they just rode it for forever. I'm serious, it was probably three or four minutes, maybe even *five*. That is a complete piss-take to a six year, especially one as spoilt as I was. Up and down, up and down, up and down. I was calling for a turn for an eternity. They simply wouldn't stop, the pair of pre-teen sadists. Completely ignored me and my yells for justice. Society had its rules to help the vulnerable and needy, yet I found myself thrown on the scrap heap, abandoned, and discarded like a used ice lolly stick. I mean, who the hell would want a used ice lolly stick? No one, that's who. And I lived through that disgrace to tell the tale.

Fury filled up inside of me when they refused to give me a go on the see-saw. A fury hath the world never seen and would not be seen again until the next six year old was wronged (which happened to be later that same minute when another little child, Maddy, was told to stop sticking her finger in her brother's nose...but that's another epic tale). With the cry of a Spartan warrior ready to defeat an invading Persian soldier by kicking him into a bottomless pit, I ran with zeal and fervour to take my place on the seat of the see-saw.

My throne.

My destiny.

I picked myself up off the floor about three seconds later. It took me a moment to figure out where I was and what had just happened to me. There was commotion and shouting all around. Hands grabbing at me and voices shouting. It was a while before the shock dissipated and I realised what the hell had just happened. In my infinite toddler wisdom, I had decided that the best way to unseat my older brother from the prize of the see-saw seat was to stand directly underneath it while my brother was on the 'up-phase'. The skill of foresight was unfortunately not available to me at that tender age. I couldn't fully appreciate the gravity of the 'down-phase' of the see-saw while gawping up at it from below.

The edge of the seat smashed into me just above the left eye and whacked me horizontal. There wasn't much I could do or say when it happened. First I was on my feet, then I was on my arse. There wasn't an in-between. As soon as I put my hand up to my eye and I saw the dripping blood (with my other eye, of course), I lost it. I was crying and screaming as I ran over to my grandmother who was happily perched on a bench enjoying the sun and eating some salted pistachios.

Thinking back, I'm glad I didn't give her a heart attack by running at her full speed like a zombie monster from the beyond, blood squirting everywhere. Would've needed double the ambulance space with her weak ticker.

I can't remember much else from that episode apart from my parents rushing to the park to accompany all of us to the hospital. To be honest, I think they came just to have a free ride in the ambulance. It was pretty exciting when they put the siren on. It wasn't anything urgent, the driver just got fed up sitting in traffic like standing in the buffet queue with John Goodman in front of you while he steadily clears the place out as you wait politely.

The next thing I realised as I drifted in and out of consciousness was waking up in the surgery room.

'Hello, young Kewan,' a doctor said to me,

smiling down. My family were standing beside him and looking at me with worried expressions. I was six years old by that time so it would have taken ages to replace me, if something serious had happened. And all of that lost investment? Down the shitter. But they needn't have been stressed. I was going to pull through.

The doctor told me as much in his soothing manner, 'You've had a bit of a knock, young man. We've put some stitches in, but you're going to be perfectly fine. After a couple of more tests you can go home with your mum and dad here. Sound good?'

I nodded as the doctor left and my family flocked around me. I discovered early on that my family were the type to always be there for you when things were going bad. If things were good, no one gave a toss. But you can't have it all, I guess.

Once the niceties were over and my mother thanked God about seventy-nine times, my brother was threatened with violence once he got home. I say threatened, but it was actually a promise as the great Steven Segal once said, because it was purely a matter of privacy before it happened.

While the mental torture was taking place in hushed tones in the corner of the room, I had time to reflect in my young mind on the place where I was. Lying on the table, groggy and with a banging headache, the sterile smell in the atmosphere really made an impression on me. Not only at that point, but also as I was being wheeled around the hospital for the x-ray and other tests. The odour of sterility was meant to indicate the absence of bacteria and micro-organisms. Absence of the unclean, all that is pure. Although somehow, the zest of the unpolluted and uncontaminated that permeated throughout the building had ironically infected all of the people within.

You could hear hushed tones of conversation as you passed strangers in the corridor not wanting you to hear about the severity of their piles. See visitors with the joy sucked out of them as they search for the morgue to identify a body which had the potential of making them rich through inheritance, yet dare not crack a smile. Angry mothers attempting to keep their unruly children under control by berating them with whispers and suggestive facial expressions. Waiting areas where patients refuse to make eye contact with one another, instead re-reading the same page in a decade old magazine over and over while listening out for their name to be mispronounced when being called out. Nurses all over the place checking clipboards and humming and ahhing, pretending that they actually have a smidgen of feeling towards the lump with bad breath in the gurney whose bed-pan they'll have to clean in five minutes.

Even though I was a pretty slow kid at the time who didn't really understand anything of the world, the nuances of the hospital environment had made an impression on me. Sickness and death. disease and injury. Sadness and devastation. This was no place for a young boy to be. I had to get away from here and away from all of this seriousness and negativity, back to the sunny streets from whence I came, playing marbles on drain covers and looking for ways to toughen massive conkers.

I hated the hospital.

I wanted to get away and stay far, far away.

Unfortunately, it did not work.

Maybe by creating such an adamant proclamation in my mind against the hospital, my subconscious had inadvertently used the topic as a target to focus on, because over the years I had become somewhat of a regular visitor. So regular in fact, that in the same vein as the hostage who ends up loving their captor after a period of close association, I too had developed love for my mental and physical captor who reins me in with such persistence and consistence. My very own instance of Stockholm Syndrome had formed and that which turned me off in the past, now turned me on with such vigour I could not dream of escaping.

Alas, it is the reason that I am here again today,

in the clutches of the hospital.

The guard who is stood in the doorway of the waiting room that I am in is a hulking beast of a man. Staring through me with his dead, lifeless black beady eyes. I wonder if he is beginning to feel hungry. If maybe saliva is collecting in his mouth as he thinks of the tastiest cut of flesh he can rip from my body without getting into too much trouble. He looks like a leg man. Someone who enjoys the tenderness of the muscle as it works hard and fills with the blood of the man sprinting away from him for dear life, only to realise that he has been running in his imagination while his limb is torn from its usual resting place.

I like my limbs so I try to avoid any sort of communication or action pointed in his general direction. This includes keeping my floating dead skin cells from venturing anywhere in his vicinity less he detects my body is ripe for the picking.

I am breathing out of the side of my mouth and keeping my eyes glued to the pamphlet I am holding, informing me that bacterial vaginosis can easily be detected by observing an unusually strong fishy smell being emitted from the region in question. Important information that I file away for later usage.

My doctor suddenly pops his shiny balding head through the doorway. Actually he has to squeeze it through a tiny gap between the guard's two bulging calves, but nevertheless, his arrival is a welcome break from acclimatising to life mirroring a gazelle held captive by a fully grown Chinese tiger.

'Mr Tan, how are you feeling today?' he asks me with unusual glee.

'Hmmm, yes, I uh...I'm eager to get this over with now,' I reply.

'I understand. Don't worry, we will be taking you through very shortly. We are just making sure that all of the paperwork is in order. I'm sure you realise that these situations are fairly rare for us here.'

'Yes...sure...sorry, doctor.'

And with that, he carefully extracts his head from between the guard's legs with a pop, making me assume that the shininess was due to some kind of lubricant he has spread for just this kind of task. It could also be the reason for the baldness, but that is just a hypothesis which I am fairly unwilling to investigate, so let's move on.

Seeing his shiny yet unmarked scalp informs me that Dr Cousins had not indulged in the surgery which has defined my own life. The sight causes an invisible string to yank my hand up and caress the top of my own egg-shaped head. Beneath the crow's nest of hair that I am sporting, my fingers delve down and touch the multitude of small maggot-shaped scars dotted all over my scalp. They feel odd yet familiar at the same time. As if I sat down in my favourite armchair but someone had adjusted the backrest by a few degrees.

These scars on my scalp are the site of the surgery that I have undergone over the years. Surgery that was meant to improve me, create and form someone new and wonderful, irresistible to all who were fortunate enough to be graced with my presence. Unfortunately, that wasn't the exact reality that ended up being forged. It never is though. All we are promised never does materialise exactly as advertised, does it?

You want to get rid of those wrinkles? Well, after a round of Botox, never be able to display another facial expression for as long as you live; the death of your child will be met with the same placidity as choosing whether to buy the small box of chicken popcorn from KFC or the medium size.

Would you like to sport a perfectly formed pair of abs and pectorals? No worries, just remember that when you're showing off at the beach in Corfu, your chicken legs and praying mantis arms are not going to form the incredible synergy with the rest of your body as you had hoped, and remember to never challenge anyone to a push-up competition. Even that seven year old with multiple sclerosis who ties one arm around his back is going to show you up.

Body enhancement has been the bane of my life. That one destructive process that defines you, without which you feel not much of anything.

I can remember back to a time before all of the alterations. It wasn't a great time for me.

The path that led me to where I am today has been fraught with obstacles.

...   ...

Visually I was pretty much a normal young adult. Five-foot nine, slim with the altogether forgettable features of an average Londoner who you pass waiting at a bus stop as his soul is slowly being sucked out of him by life in the fast lane in the Capital.

I had just finished acquiring three years worth of debt by completing a degree at Kingston university in media studies; so much debt in fact that it was equivalent to the lifetime earnings of a million of the poorest in the world. However, I had the Student Loan Company telling me that I wouldn't need to pay anything back until I earned over a certain amount and that the interest was so low I'd hardly notice. I reasoned that by making the minimum payments from my current retail job and adding back their low interest rate, I could quite easily pass the debt on in my will to any foetuses which have grown bearing the DNA signature of their father. My life prospects looked superb.

Twenty-two years old, a head full of knowledge

of how the media corporations can rule the world, while enjoying a life-cremating job arranging stock at John Lewis and an unmatched shyness that was crippling my chances of being anything close to the kind of person I saw myself being. Life was not an enjoyable venue for me to exists in. Everything I did was wrought with anxiety and stress. How I would be perceived and what people were thinking of me were questions that dictated what I did and how I said it. Add to that my complete inability to understand simple human interaction and how to hold a normal conversation and you can see that it was obvious that life was about as enjoyable as trying to keep your balance on your bum cheeks while naked and sitting on a pineapple.

I could remember the day when I began *the change*.

After yet another rush hour bus journey into London for work which had me firmly wedged in the underarm of London's sweatiest female over the weight of eighteen stone, I began a tube trip which was even worse. A wet Monday morning on the way to work is depressing at the best of times. But when you are squashed like a public stress ball on the central line from Leytonstone into Tottenham Court Road too far away from a pole to hold on to and attempting to ride the train bumps and jerks like a surfer, it took a lot out of me. Trying not to overly touch someone using pure leg power with feet barely an inch apart is murderous on the calves, especially with a centre of gravity somewhere as high as my chin. I wasn't the sort who could nonchalantly barge strangers without a care. It did, however, seem that every other person who used the tube didn't mind knocking me around as if I were Rihanna on a date with Chris Brown.

Even once I reached the surface onto Oxford Street, the most famous shopping street in all of Europe, I was tested to the precipice of agitation and madness. A test which I duly lost without much of a fight.

For some reason that morning, the street was packed with shoppers. So much so that everyone on both sides were walking at the pace of Stephen Hawking, just before the wheelchair that is. I was getting pretty late for work. But the situation in hand required actual interaction with real people if I wanted to wade past them so I just held my position as best as I could, shuffling along behind an annoying woman with an umbrella held just low enough to burst eyeballs if I stepped a centimetre too close.

As I reached just past the junction at Regent Street, I could feel someone fumbling around behind me a lot closer than was socially acceptable. Something wasn't right. I am very aware of any uncomfortable surroundings, yet this awareness manifested in an emotional reaction which froze my body from taking any normal physical action (such as turning around). I did this by rapidly scrolling through scenarios mentally which somehow all ended up with me being beaten to a pulp whatever vein of response I took.

I was not fond of being beaten to a pulp.

For the record, I am still not fond of being beaten to a pulp.

My record bag that hung behind me jiggled up and down for a brief few seconds, than nothing. It was over. As I continued edging on down the street towards John Lewis, someone bumped past my shoulder and began pushing in front of me, creating his own path through the masses. I was eager for the umbrella lady to at least scratch his cornea but his reflexes were too deft. He shimmied through the throng, disappearing with ease, but not before turning his head back to face me and show me *my own wallet* that was now in his possession. With an evil Joker-esque grin, he was gone.

Any normal person would have connected the dots and realised that they had just been robbed by the cheeky arsehole showing them their wallet, not exactly a Dan Brown level mystery to unravel when he showed me my own property. But my mind did that playing-out-all-scenarios thing and came to the conclusion that the best case result would be me catching the thief, attempting to reclaim my property and ending up with a few tasty slaps for the trouble. So I just carried on as if nothing had even happened.

Someone next to me even told me that they thought I had just been robbed but I laughed it off like the gormless village idiot. My pores began sweating profusely. I was glad of the rain for once, but cursing my spineless behaviour inwardly. *Why was I so flaccid all of the time?* I couldn't take it anymore. If it wasn't staying obediently in line while getting late for work, I was getting robbed and accepting it had happened, or agreeing to stay late at work while others shot off a few minutes early or letting others brazenly push in front of me while I want to order a chicken burger meal at Dixy's or a hundred other things.

I had become a doormat. Existing for the sole purpose of being stepped on and having shit wiped off on me before others went on ahead of me. It wasn't a happy state of being but the issue I was faced with was more of a mental barrier than physical obstruction. I wasn't a tiny person that could be ignored or pushed to the wayside. It was more the fact that I was the quiet, shy fellow standing at the edge of the group who stands next to no one and could be ignored as easily as you can ignore a phone call by switching it to silent mode.

My eyes had begun to well up.

I wasn't usually a crier despite being so soft, but this was a little too much for me to take. As soon as I found an alleyway leading away from the main street, I ducked down it and found myself walking and crying in the morning rain. I cursed myself for being such a sap and replayed the morning's events in my head where I instead altered my actions to that of an Arnold Schwarzenegger character; any one of his characters except the one he played in Junior. That one got pregnant. Let's not speak of that too much.

That was a normal reaction of mine. Not living in the moment but going over things in my head after the fact and then living in the past, hoping, praying and insisting that the next time would be different.

But they never were different. Things were always exactly the same.

They say that the mind is the hardest thing to change.

I was testament to the truth of that statement.

Apart from turning water into wine, that is. That change is pretty hard.

And changing from Apple to any other brand in the entire universe. Hard also.

But the mind thing is still very hard.

Hours later that morning, I was still wondering around the back streets of London. Funnily enough, I didn't have a single missed call from work, they'd probably not even noticed my absence.

I was in a daze, walking around aimlessly trying to gather thoughts together in my mind but with little joy. I felt angry, but not sure at whom. I was upset, but not sure why. I wanted to change, but not sure what. Even Bruce Jenner couldn't have competed with the confusion I was feeling. Procrastination, confusion and indecision had decided to visit my brain for a cup of tea and stick around like a plume of expelled arse gas. I hadn't the foggiest at what I was meant to do. I couldn't carry on muddling through life, taking the hits when they came and manoeuvring constantly to avoid others. There had to be more of a meaning to it all then this.

Ending up in Soho somewhere, I was walking past some questionable looking establishments and the occasional scantily clad woman in a doorway cooing and beckoning me over. All I could do was cross the road every time I wanted to avoid them. As I approached a corner, I looked around and saw a black mini cab indicating to turn in, so I waited for him to go even though I had plenty of time to cross. Without a nod or thanks, the mini cab swerved into the road and splashed a great big puddle all over me, drenching me head to foot. I'd thought that the day couldn't have gotten any worse. I was sorely wrong.

As I stood there, water dripping off me, I saw a sign, a poster stuck to the blacked out window of a boarded up shop.

It read:

Be The Person You Always Wanted To Be

Beneath that it wrote:

The Next Step In Body Surgery
Intelligence Improvements, Character Changes,
Emotional Enhancements
Come and see us for a free quote
The Life Engineering Company

There was some tiny text underneath all of that, something about '*at own risk*' but I didn't read too much into that. The alliteration was off-putting enough, but I was gripped. *Was this actually possible?* I knew that you could design your baby before you conceived, but essentially changing the genetics of an adult, that wasn't actually possible, was it?

The poster showed an address which was only in the next street, so for the first time in my life I made an impulsive decision and went to find out what it was all about. After all, being me wasn't all that I thought it would be when I was in primary school getting A's in maths and brilliant parent's evening reports.

It was time to become some other fucker. Any other fucker.

To be honest, once I had traversed the hobo trying to steal my shoe and the Armani suited pimp attempting to recruit me to his raft of gigolo staff by offering me a chase of his dragon on the way to the LEC, I had lost some of my faith in what I would find at my destination. That was all before a small dog-sized rat with what appeared to be sunglasses and a bowler hat overtook me on the stairwell as I climbed to the second floor where the company was located.

But I was pleasantly surprised. As soon as I was buzzed in, I was met with a small oriental lady sat behind a glass desk amidst a setting of brilliant white, all completely spotless.

'Good day, sir. Welcome to The Life Engineering Company. How may we be of assistance?' Her voice was like nectar to my ears, as smooth and comforting as a double Southern Comfort and lemonade.

'Oh…I ah…um…well, I just saw your…thingy on a wall…and…' Words were failing me once again continuing the trend that life had established long ago. I gave up.

'It is quite alright. My name is Tina. Come and take a seat. I am sure that we can be of great help to you.' She came and guided me to a seat, putting me at ease with a strategically placed arm around the small of my back. 'Now young man, let me explain to you exactly what we do here before your head explodes. Here at The Life Engineering Company, our founder, Dr John Cousins, has discovered a revolutionary type of surgery which pushes the boundary of science as we know it.'

I was intrigued.

She continued.

'In the field of body enhancement, surgeons have focused mainly on superficial aspects of the body, most of which you have probably heard of many times before. Breast augmentation, nose re-shaping, Botox, fillers, face-lifts, muscular implants, liposuction, hair transplants, bone restructuring, and many others.' I nodded in agreement, I had heard of these before. 'These surgeries have been around and improved on for many decades now and they all still retain their place in enhancing patient's bodies to produce a higher level of esteem and comfort.

'However, the area of the brain has remained largely untouched in the field of enhancement. Although much work has been carried out in mapping its physiology and functions, surgery of the brain has been largely maintained to repairing abnormalities which cede normal function and negatively impact the life of the affected. For example, severe epilepsy, nerve damage, abscesses, blot clots and so on. Are you with me so far?'

'Oh...yes...indeed...it does kind of...um...sound very...um...interesting, I guess.'

I was thinking about joking that I was just looking for directions to the nearest bus stop but sensibly decided it may not be appropriate.

'Good. Now Dr Cousins has spent much of his career in medicine researching the limbic system of the brain, which as you may know is responsible for managing human emotion and thus behaviour, which is determined somewhat by our emotions and also for other complex related issues. What he has discovered was initially based on rectifying damage to this area and how to repair broken nodes. However in understanding more and more, he has discovered how to alter a person's emotional range and responses, thus altering their behaviour. With the interesting observance being that once a person's behaviour is duly altered, the consequences of their new actions in various situations also changes. If successful, the results can be stark in their positivity.'

She paused, allowing me to respond. But I had just been hit with a truck load of possibility so hard in the face that my great grandchild just had a concussion and had to take a week off school. All I could do was sit there with my mouth open and facial muscles attempting to form a smile. It was difficult.

'Look, Mr...?'

'Um...Tan...Kewan Tan.'

'Mr Tan. I realise that this is a lot to take in and sounds all very wonderful, but there are risks involved as this is an actual surgical procedure. Adding that this is a new branch of science, there may be risks that materialise that we are not even aware of yet.'

The talk of risks and things going wrong triggered the pessimist in me and it brought me to me senses a little.

'Right, sure. I understand. That makes sense. So what kind of risks are you aware of?'

'Throughout Dr Cousins tests and trials, the risks of side-effects that could be displayed are swelling, bleeding, headaches, dizziness, incontinence, light sensitivity, memory loss, stroke, heart failure, paralysis, nerve damage and death.'

'Oh, nothing too serious then, is that all?'

'Oh I left out partial loss of taste and smell sensation. Must remember those.'

'Yes, of course. Can't forget those important ones when you remembered all of the little ones.' Tina smiled at me, missing the sarcasm. 'So did you find these side effects on humans?'

'Oh no, those were all on animal trails while the surgery was being perfected.' A sense of relief flooded into me. 'We haven't had any actual human patients yet.' And there went the relief.

'You haven't had any human patients yet?'

'No, you are the first person to walk through the door to tell the truth. We just opened today.'

That explained the fully detailed selling spiel Tina so patiently and carefully explained to me. She had probably been practising for the past two hours.

'Okay, thanks.' I said getting to my feet. 'But no thanks. I would like to live past today if that's alright with you.'

Tina's friendly demeanour didn't change a bit.

'Mr Tan. There haven't been any patients here yet…but we have had a human test subject in our trial phase. Can I show you a video of their experience?'

The curiosity in me peaked. Watching a video couldn't hurt, so I agreed. Tina swivelled her thirty inch Mac monitor around and played a file, full screen.

A bespectacled young woman filled up the shot as she sat on a chair slightly hunched over with her hands in her lap. Although a shock of hair covered a lot of her face, she looked vaguely familiar but I couldn't place her. A voice behind the camera spoke to her.

'Can you tell me how you are feeling today?'

'Yes…sh…sh…sure…I'm f..f..f…ugh…' The lady in the video shook her head in frustration as the words she wanted to say wouldn't leave her lips, the large fringe covering most of her forehead swaying whenever she shook her head.

'It's okay, take your time.' The interviewer tried to calm her down so she could answer the question. It was an uphill task as within sixty seconds, the young lady grew red in the face and close to tears. Tina stopped the clip and played another one with the same lady. This time her face seemed brighter and more alive, her posture much straighter with an absence of fringe.

As it clicked in my mind, I lifted a finger and turned to Tina who shooshed me quiet. 'Keep watching, Mr Tan.'

'So, how are you doing today?' the interviewer behind the camera asked.

'Actually, I am feeling really good.' The young lady didn't miss a beat, and although very softly spoken and considered, her words flowed normally. 'I managed to deposit some cash in my account at the bank with the cashier, usually I go to the automated machines. It was tough and there was an uncomfortable silence for while, at least with me, but I got through it.'

'That is very positive to hear. Getting used to conversing will take time, but the more you practice, the easier it will become. I'm very proud of you.' The young lady shifted in her seat not knowing where to look, obviously not used to any sort of praise. She didn't reply, instead gave a half smile which disappeared quickly.

The video disappeared as Tina played yet another video clip of the same young lady. However, this time the camera was angled from the top corner of a room full of trendy looking youngsters, all milling around with each other in small groups, some incessant noise playing in the background that I recognised as Madonna from the geriatric years and a barman at the rear was handing out drinks in plastic cups.

After a couple of seconds, the same young lady came into view. It took me a moment to recognise her because she looked completely different from both previous clips. Her glasses were gone (probably switched to contact lenses), her hair was styled on top of her head in a sexy bun and she gripped the room's attention by strutting in wearing a slinky black dress complete with high heels. I couldn't hear much over Madonna's warble that was beyond computer-altering help but what I saw was fascinating. The shy, stuttering lady from previous videos was gliding around the room introducing herself to the various groups who almost instantly all burst into laughter before she left them with handshakes, hugs and cheek kisses. Once her whirlwind trip around the room was done, she did the impossible.

She danced to Madonna's car crash of a song. But that wasn't the only impossible thing that she did. She threw her shapes down in the middle of the room, by herself. Inside all of seven seconds, she had three quarters of the room doing the ugly with her, all cackling with laughter and in great spirits.

Tina switched off the video and we looked at each other.

Tina was the young lady in the video.

My mind was blown.

Not in the way that some ungainly sap auditions on the X Factor and surprises everyone by belting out a Michael Jackson classic as if the master himself were there in person, but in the way that some six and a half foot gigantean, fresh from a tour of Iraq where he had just added seventy kills under his belt had decided to attack me for an early morning workout and I wake up next to his pounded lifeless body after discovering I had turned into The Hulk and Hulk-Smashed him three or four hundred times in the facial region. Trousers obviously ripped but let's not get into that just yet.

My mind was that blown.

'That is insane,' I splurged.

'Yes. Very.'

'I mean, how long did it take you to go from original you to new you?'

'The duration between the three clips that you just saw was two weeks.'

'Two weeks? Where do I sign up?'

Tina smiled at me, reassuringly placed her hand on my knee and looked me in the eye.

'Let's go over some of the details, shall we?'

The following Monday morning, I was leaving John Lewis after quitting my job by storming into the floor manager's office and slapping my letter of resignation down on his desk while he was midway through a McDonalds sausage and egg McMuffin. It felt amazing to unshackle my soul, even though my manager's look of utter befuddlement while I did so meant that he hadn't the foggiest who I was. Not to worry, the letter would've explained it all. He would soon have realised that I was one of his staff and had been for the past two years.

I was on a new path of discovery. Life had taken on new meaning and I was embracing the change, enjoying it as an eagle brought up amongst pigs one day unveiled the secret of his abilities and could fly high in the sky instead of wallowing around in shit all of his life. I couldn't believe that people actually felt like this every day. Now I had joined them in being a partaker in life and not being a spectator from the safety and disassociation of the armchair at home. The initial unshackling of my soul.

Once more I joined a slow moving throng of people on the pavement of Oxford Street as I made my way to the train station. However, this time I wasn't about to let the speed of others slow me down. With graceful manoeuvres and firm yet polite 'excuse me's', I easily navigated my way at triple the speed of everyone else. Before long I was at the entrance of the station, about to totter down the stairs but something caught my eye.

Or should I have said, *someone*?

It was that pickpocket thief from the previous week who had robbed me so brashly and dismissed any risk I posed of defending myself by flaunting his ill-gotten bounty in my face. I turned and followed him through the on-coming crowd, never taking my eye off him as I twisted and turned majestically through the traffic. All that was needed was a ball at my feet and I could've been Lionel Messi…well…a ball and millions of Euro's in tax-evaded money, but that's not what I was getting at.

My shadowing went on for around six or seven minutes and eventually after turning into a narrow side street, I was a few unobstructed feet behind him. His street-sense probably kicked in because he stopped and turned with an angry frown etched onto his face. The frown soon morphed into recognition and then giddiness as he remembered our encounter from before and my complete lack of action at his liberty taking.

'You!' His right hand slipped into his sports jacket pocket and emerged dressed more fancily than was necessary wearing a knuckle-duster. I surmised at this point that I had not thought this all the way through. Though this rapscallion wasn't very tall, certainly smaller than I was, he had a stocky build and a neck as thick as my twenty stone grandmother, though I'm sure not as flabby. As he lumbered intently towards me, a brief glimpse of the previous me fought its way to the surface of my brain.

RUN! Get the hell out of here you stale fart of a three legged goat! My old conscious prompted me rather insultingly. It had a point though; a knuckle-duster to the head was not the outcome I was searching for and that was the most likely occurrence.

But as I bent my knees, ready to sprint away faster than Hilary Clinton from a lie detector test, a new voice came to the fore.

Kewan, stand your ground! You are strong, confident and powerful. You can overcome this situation, never having to give in to bullying aggression ever again. Stand your ground!

My new subconscious was proud and defiant. Never again would it let me scurry to avoid confrontation, never again would it let me become paralysed with fear over action. Belief in self poured through every vein, every nerve, every cell in my body until I stood fast, clenching my fists and puffing my chest. I smirked as this lowly thug approached me.

This was my time.

Having my nose broken had hurt less than I had previously expected that it would. Sure it stung upon impact where the thug's knuckle-duster crumpled the cartilage into a sponge and the severe inflammation meant that I had to breathe through my nose or risk blood from pouring back down my throat. But all in all, it wasn't too bad. Smashing the back of my head into the concrete floor and having my head stamped on was worse, especially after finding out that two of my molars were chipped and dislodged, and would require a costly visit to my local dentists, who I'm sure thrive on their patients having these kinds of escapades. Must keep the tills ringing over.

Nevertheless, now that it was all over and I had been helped up by kind bystanders after there was nothing left to film on their smart phones except me lying dazed on the floor, I was feeling pretty damn good about myself. For the first time in my life, I refused to cower to an immoral and unjust foe, and I had done so while not trembling with fear but strutting with the kind of confidence and decisiveness when you know right is on your side.

The feeling was intoxicating. Making the definite decision within milliseconds of standing my ground came as natural to me as breathing or picking my nose and rolling it into a tiny ball to be flicked into the plant pot in the corner of my living room. And when I did so, I was actually optimistic and confident about my chances to best my opponent who surely had evolved from a pit-bull and not the sensible monkey as the rest of humanity.

Amazing.

Never had I been so glad to try something new in my entire existence. The tape of Tina's transformation had certainly gotten my interest peaked, but that was just stage one. Once Dr Cousins arrived to meet with me later that same day, came an avalanche of information regarding the details of the surgery, physical tests I had to undergo as well as psychological evaluations and legal agreements. The cost was something I am still trying to get my head around but I figure that I have plenty of time for that seeing as I will still be paying for this surgery once money is deemed obsolete and dinosaurs return to reclaim the Earth.

All of the particulars took around three full days of visits to the clinic during which time I had taken sick leave from work, though no one seemed to understand why a stranger was calling to take time off work. It suited me as I didn't have to worry about calling in everyday trying to describe the liquidity of my stool and potential accidents I may have if I came in to work.

The surgery was set for the Friday at a local hospital to me, King George Hospital, and was carried out under general anaesthetic. From what I understood about the procedure, tiny incisions were made through the skull into both the pre-frontal cortex and the amygdala, into which Dr Cousins had embedded nano-devices to regulate certain emotional responses with fluctuating electrical impulses depending on hormone and stimulation level at the time. It was an ingenious concept as the devices used the existing electrical signals from the brain to maintain its power levels, hence never needing replacing.

Dr Cousins had programmed the devices with certain instructions based on the alterations that I had requested the surgery do, namely change my shyness into confidence, and alter my procrastination into a more optimistic decisiveness.

Rather basic changes I had thought.

I didn't want to completely change myself and end up at risk of one of the huge list of side effects that Tina had mentioned to me. Also Dr Cousins recommended that I choose the most negative aspect of myself that I wanted to improve and stick to that.

The recovery was pretty rapid, only a couple of stitches per incision and a headache that felt like I had drunk a whole bottle of Aftershock the night before, but I was home in my rented flat by Saturday morning. It only took the weekend to feel fully recovered, I guess most of the recovery were my new thoughts insisting that I was fine. A very strange feeling suddenly having a new narration going on in my head. At first it felt like there was another voice in there. But soon, I recognised the voice as my own, the old voice sitting quietly in the corner as it always did when someone strong and dominant came along.

It was this new voice that told me to pack my job in.

This new voice was the *new me*.

One month later and I was flying higher than Ozzy Osbourne on a magic mushroom session. I was looking great, had a new job as junior assistant in a news room and said hello to five out of my six neighbours for the first time in my life after living there for years. Jamie, my closest friend from college who had drifted away after becoming fed up with my constant excuses when inviting me out was also back in my life after I reached out to him one bright day.

These positive emotions had elevated my attitude into a realm of positivity and awesomeness. Instead of thinking about doing things and wishing I had carried out imaginary reactions to situations where I did nothing in reality, I was proactive. Operating as a normal human being was fun.

'I can't believe how much you've changed,' Jamie told me while sipping on a pint of Fosters on one day out at the local, 'I would see you like this maybe once a year back in the day.'

'Really?' I was more surprised about the upbeat version of myself appearing once a year instead of the depressed version existing for the other three hundred and sixty four days (three hundred and sixty five in a leap year).

'Really dude. I mean, don't get me wrong, you've always been a top guy but you were just so worried all the time. About what people think, what you should say, how you should act. But every once in a while, when you were completely at ease, I saw this great cool guy come out. And that's who you are now. The cool guy.'

'Wow.' Jamie had never told me he observed all of this stuff about me in the past. It shocked me that he analysed me so deeply. But it also felt comforting that he did. 'That's really good of you to say, Jamie. I appreciate it.'

Jamie lifted up his pint glass in my direction and I responded by clinking my glass of whisky and coke with his.

'I missed you, man.'

'I missed you too, it only took a few holes in the head to get me to call you.'

'Hey, you know how many times I called you and invited you out to places. I'd always get an excuse.'

'I know, I know.'

'That's if got through to you at all, usually it would just be answer machine and then a text reply if I was lucky. And I know you saw my call, your phone is part of your goddamn anatomy.' We both laughed knowing it was completely true, but it got me thinking.

'You say that I'm not a new person, Jay?'

'Right.' Jamie threw up a dry roasted peanut in the air and tried to catch it in his mouth. The bartender gave him a dirty look as it bounced off his buck tooth and flipped behind the bar.

'But I'm just more of the positive mood Kewan, instead of the negative mood Kewan?'

'Um…yeah, I guess so.' Jamie lifted a hand to the bartender in apology. 'I've seen this version of you before, just not very often.'

'So that means these things in my head just enhance bits of what was already there and suppress other bits. My worrying for example.'

'Yeah. And your talking. You used to sit and listen to me, now it's the other way around. That was one of the things that I actually liked about you.' We both sat back and chuckled in our stools beside the bar, drinking and taking in the scene. I felt good there. I used to prefer a table in the furthest, least populated corner of the pub on the odd occasion that I would be pulled out of my pit at home. Why someone would want to sit up at the bar never made any sense to me, constant hustle and bustle, the chatter and noise and the threat of beer spillage by small-handed tipsy revellers.

But that was exactly the attraction of the seat upfront, the action and liveliness. From this angle, the closed-off booths around the pub looked boring and cut-off, apart from the one with a naughty couple getting up to borderline illegal activity; that one looked fun.

To the right of me a good looking couple approached and ordered drinks.

'Alright mate?' I greeted as I caught the man's eye.

'Good thanks fella, you?'

'A drink and some nuts, I'm good.'

He gave me a friendly smile, paid for their

drinks and headed off to the bathroom. Jamie's open mouthed stare as I turned back to face him made me worry that he's just had a stroke.

'Fuckin' hell, Kewan, what was that? Having a chat with a stranger without sweating and stuttering? What have they done to you?' My worry disappeared as Jamie was just being patronising, or so I thought.

'Shut up, you nonce. I'm not five.' He held me with a serious expression as I laughed him off.

'Please. I'm being serious, mate. You would almost refuse to speak to strangers before, as if you *were* five. Try and chat to his missus.' He whispered, flickering his eyes in her direction while she waited.

Instead of engaging my brain in formulating every excuse under the sun as to why I couldn't possibly do that, I turned towards the woman. As I did, her angular features struck me, long eye lashes fluttering away and eyes as piercing blue as Obi Wan's lightsaber gazing around. That is very blue, by the way.

'Nice guy, your boyfriend.' She smiled as she looked at me.

'Oh, he's not my boyfriend.' She paused as she waited for me to respond. My brain searched for a witty, funny reply. All it could find were empty cupboards, dusty with cobwebs. No wit ever lived here. 'There's a bunch of us old mates meeting here. Catch up, you know.'

'Well. Have a good one.'

'You too.'

As I turned back around on my stool, Jamie looked as if he was having a stroke for real this time.

'What the fuck?'

'What?'

'What? What do you mean, what? What the fuck, man?'

'Okay, you've lost me.'

Jamie waited in exasperation until the man returned from the toilet and the pair left with their drinks, the lady glanced lingeringly at me before she left.

Jamie punched me hard in the arm. I'd forgotten how violent he was.

'Since when do you chat to random girls in pubs?'

'I don't know, since today I guess.' He snapped his head back in a cry of laughter. This time a double punch to the arm. He was magnitudes more happy than I was, though I was pretty excited about it. But something was nagging at me.

'You could totally have pulled her dude. Did you see the way she looked at you before she left? You've got the balls man, big hairy balls. Soldier of fortune, mercenary for hire, one-arm push-up balls man.'

'Hahaha, alright Jay, it was probably because you're here too. Gave me some moral support, it was your idea.'

'No way. You went straight in there, no fear. You are something else now. I'm gonna call you *Universal Soldier* from now on.'

'But you know what, I went blank when I was talking to her.'

'What do you mean, blank? You were talking.'

'No, I was trying to think of something clever or cheeky to say to her. I didn't have anything. I could talk, but boring talk is all.'

'Aw, you're too hard on yourself. I think you did awesome. We need to go out tonight. It looks like I've found my ultimate wingman.' I shook the worry from my mind at his suggestion and downed my drink as Jamie did his.

'Okay, yeah, let's go out.'

A week later, I was back at the surgery with Dr Cousins.

'How about excess pus leakage from your tear ducts?'

'Uh…no, doctor.' I was sure that pus leaking from my eyes wasn't on the list of possible side effects from this surgery I had undergone.

'Okay good. Bloody stool?'

'What? Bloody stool? No Doctor.' That was definitely not one that I was warned about. I am sure that I would have remembered being warned that my stool may be accompanied with blood, the life force of my body.

'Okay.' Dr. Cousins seemed oblivious to my distress. 'Any appearance of warts in or around the genitalia area?'

I managed to choke on my own spit. 'No, none that I have observed. Dr Cousins, I am pretty sure that Nurse Tina didn't warn me of these things that could go wrong.'

'These are new ones,' Nurse Tina said as her head popped around the door frame.

'Yes, thank you, Tina,' Dr Cousins said, taking it entirely in his stride. Tina intercepting patient visits seemed to be a regular occurrence. 'As Nurse has just so kindly pointed out from the adjacent room, these are new side effects that we have recorded. Perfectly normal for new ones to pop up as this is a very new treatment. However, do not be alarmed, these recordings have been made from observing gerbils which have undergone similar a procedure as you have. None of our human patients have developed anything untoward.'

'Other patients being…?'

'Well, there is you…of course…'

'Of course.'

'And Nurse Tina so far. And you both have shown only positive responses to the surgery.'

'So according to our huge control group, everything is fine.'

'Yes.'

'But the gerbils…not so much?'

'Right. Although the male gerbils have been showing signs of rampant sexual activity which always is a positive when transferred over to the human population. Very desirable trait, I'm sure you are glad to hear.'

Dr Cousins had managed to placate my concerns about as much as when Jordon told the British public she was a great singer going in to the audition to represent our great nation at the Eurovision Song Contest. Unfortunately for television blooper shows, she didn't make it.

I was at the surgery after my eventful outing with Jamie for a standard check-up, to make sure that I hadn't grown wings or developed sadistic tendencies that would put Jimmy Savile to shame. As I had expected, everything was proceeding as planned.

But I wasn't completely happy.

There was something making me decidedly unhappy.

As the questioning of side effects was rounded up with whether I had experienced feelings that I wanted to dress up and live my life as a sexually deviant gerbil, I was able to convey my concerns to the good doctor. He listened intently, as I'm sure Nurse Tina was also doing through the paper thin walls, letting me explain myself fully and encouraging me whenever I felt a little lost in my words.

As I was speaking, I felt a foolish explaining

that while I was amazingly happy with the change that had taken place, not only in my mind but also with the resulting change in my life, it wasn't enough. Sure I had a new found positivity and optimism. Along with confidence to make and act out decisions that previously would have paralysed me with fear of soiling my under garments and crying like a steroid taking world famous cycler losing his multi-million dollar sponsorship deals.

The issue was, that when I did get to where I wanted to go or to speak to whoever I wanted to speak with, I didn't really know what to do or what to say. Sounds confusing, I know. The best way I can describe it is if I was finally getting my own talk show on national television and it turned out I was doing a new version of the Jeremy Kyle Show and spending all day having to shout at chavs and read out results of DNA tests to discover whether the chap on the sofa did actually have intercourse with a goat or if it was only oral.

You'd want to be in the realm of Oprah, Jay Leno or our own legend, Killroy, talking about the real issues and with heart-breaking stories, not watching Jeremy hide behind his seven foot bodyguard as somebody goes for him for calling them a twat.

And that was the position that I found myself in. Whereas before the surgery I had kept to myself, now I was mixing in circles which expected riveting conversation and wit and humour and a cheeky bit of flirting. All I could do was laugh at the banter coming my way and open a discussion about American foreign policy and the benefits of eating lemon zest. It felt like I was deflating the atmosphere slowly but surely wherever I went.

I didn't fully comprehend what was happening until the night out with Jamie the week before. We hit Leicester Square with a rampage, picking up fellow party-goers out for good time and watching them fall away like lemmings as they couldn't keep up. We were having a raucous time. And while I was amidst the thick of it, buying shots ten at a time, dancing like an electrocuted grasshopper and directing the masses as we went bar to bar, I wasn't the life and soul of the party. I was barely a small toe pulse of the party.

I was missing the charisma, the charm, the pizzazz.

A night can get awfully lonely, awfully quick when person after person turns away from you within two minutes of conversation and you know that your breath smells of roses, it's really the soggy conversational cardboard spewing out of your mouth that is the problem.

When I had finished unloading on Dr Cousins, he paused, letting my words penetrate and take real meaning.

I waited patiently but expectantly.

'Kewan, I understand what you have told me

and what you are experiencing. The process that you have undergone is revolutionary. A world's first, or in your case, second. The altering of an emotional range which has been developed over the course of your entire life is an immense mechanism that takes time to alter and more importantly, adjust to. You will be feeling things that you have never felt before and in ways that you never thought possible. In reality, by recalling our numerous conversations, you have undergone instances that previously were only imaginary thoughts of yours. Daydreams, if you will. Now, they are being played out by you in real life. Please do not underestimate, that is an epic feat. But as far as you have come, your journey of learning and discovering is beginning again. You must give yourself time and patience to acclimatise to this new existence.'

I nodded as Dr Cousins was speaking to make it appear as though I knew what the hell he was talking about.

I didn't.

I got the gist of the content.

Blah, blah…takes time…blah, blah…I'm just trying to deal with your complaint to make you go away…blah, blah.

That wasn't going to help me. Just waiting to see what happens.

My life was important. Damn important. More important than some caution because of safety rules regulations. Doctors always have some avenue that they can venture down, I just had to push until he broke.

'Dr Cousins, listen, I get it. I get it completely. Already you have pushed the boat out on me and I'm a walking, talking, living, breathing success story for your surgery. You don't want to spoil the result by trying to go further with me with the chance of boils growing in my anal passage. Or some other crazy side effect happening. But I believe in you Doc, all the way, okay. You are my hero and I am really in a bind at the moment. Waiting six to twelve months for the possibility of me to adapt and change is going to drive me insane, maybe even *give* me side effects because of all the stress I'll be going through. Now I'm not laying on any emotional blackmail on you. At all. I just want to say that if there is anything you can do to help me, please don't worry about being cautious. I am more than up for it. I believe in you, Doc.'

My heart was pumping fast after that little impromptu speech for the good doctor. I had stood up sometime while speaking so I sat back down as Dr Cousins regarded me silently over the tops of his glasses. With the yellowy glow of the sun shining in through the window, bouncing off his shiny bald head, he reminded me of Kevin the Minion. I thought it wise to stifle my erupting guffaw.

'Kewan. Wow.' Dr Cousins leaned back in his chair finally. 'A speech like that before the surgery would have been nigh on impossible. But now? I am very impressed. The directness, the strong-minded resolve, the empathetic emotion. You truly have come on leaps and bounds.' He was standing now. 'Look son, there is an option to take to help you.'

'Please Doc. I will do anything you want.'

'Easy Kewan. Take it easy. It isn't that simple. There is a major obstacle in the way before something can even be attempted.'

'Obstacle? What do you mean?'

'The changes that we have already made have dealt with enhancing and altering with the existing structure and operation of your brain. The shyness that you previously experienced and to some extent the procrastination and pessimism had deep roots in your emotional fear. So the implants that we used controlled the fear response and corresponding hormonal and electrical systems that are activated, mainly to reduce the levels of cortisol that would previously flood your body. This controlled your fear emotions, thus reducing the intense feelings of that you were concerned about.'

'The shyness…pessimism…that stuff'

'Right. Exactly. But what you are talking about now is a completely separate range of emotions and corresponding behaviour that you want to change or instil in yourself.'

'But it can be done, can't it doctor?'

Dr Cousins mouth opened as he was about to reply.

But no sound came out.

He looked as if he had been frozen in time.

That thought was quickly dispelled however when I spied Nurse Tina's ear poke into view around the door frame, obviously straining to hear what was being said. I forced a cough out of my lungs and time resumed its normal course.

Dr Cousins looked at me and smiled.

'Did you see what you just did there?'

'What I did? What do you mean? You're the one who was playing musical statues'

'No, before that. When you asked me but it can be done, can't it doctor?'

'Yes. I did say that, but you've lost me. I haven't got a clue what you mean.'

'It felt normal for you to say the sentence, it came out very quickly, very naturally and without much thought. But if we analyse the way you said it and the words that you actually used, they give us huge insight into your brain and how it is functioning.'

'How so?'

'Well for a start, the sentence was encouraging, optimistic, and hopeful of a positive outcome. You didn't ask if it *could* be done, rather you said *can* be. And although you submitted to my expertise by asking me. The closed question that you asked which required only a yes or no answer, based on our conversation today, you knew that it was a possibility and that the answer would be yes, which is exactly what I was going to say. Yes, it can be done. But to ask a question in such a manner where you are not the expert requires a factor of expectancy or confidence in the outcome. And your lack of hesitancy in asking, especially in the format that you did, was firm and decided, almost forceful. Very impressive indeed, Kewan.'

'Okay.' I wanted to give a more intellectual answer but again the doctor was hard to follow at times. I just went with it.

'You see, before your treatment, this is exactly the kind of answer that you would have been completely unable to give. To be honest, I think that you would have left the office already by now when I had told you to give yourself a few months to settle in. But here you are, fighting your corner for what you want. It shows that you may possibly be ready.'

My ears perked up quicker than a ten year old with seven nicotine patches stuck on his arm. This was the kind of talk that I was looking for.

'Yes, doctor. I am. I am very ready.' I almost fell forwards out of my chair because I was leaning forwards so far, mentally stretching for the carrot dangling in front of my eyes.

'You may be. We have follow-on tests to determine medically if you are ready. But as I was saying before, these issues that you are having are not the same as the issues that were present when you first came to us. In your original surgery, we worked within the existing structure. However, what you are telling me now are problems not only with your emotional behaviour, rather more to do with your characteristics and personality. These two areas are governed in part by your emotional range. Although, more than what your brain *does*, what your brain *knows* is more of the issue. Are you following?'

'Not really.'

'Let me explain in another way. I am a pretty talkative person myself, especially when it comes to my field of learning and vocation. If there were a group of medical professionals discussing anything, I would feel quite comfortable and would be able to join in the conversation easily, contributing here or there. But, if you placed my in a group full of Sri Lankan comedians, all telling jokes based on their cultures and experiences, you would find that I would be quiet as a mouse, because I wouldn't know how to tell a joke for one, but also I have no knowledge of their culture and origins so I wouldn't be able to contribute. I would be the exact same person, but behaving differently based on the context of situation.'

'I get what you are saying. That my issues of

not being able to mix with other people have more to do with my dullness as an individual than an emotional restriction.'

'Yes...I mean not that you are dull. I find you to be very personable and polite. But you need knowledge and experience to know how to converse in certain situations. For example, you often find that a child raised in a large family with very talkative parents and siblings also becomes talkative and less inhibited because they have been brought up conversing with many different people about many different topics, often in quite an outspoken way if they wanted to be heard.'

'I know exactly what you mean.' The comment brought flashes of my own childhood into my mind where I was often alone and raised by very quiet parents, my older brother preferring his own friend's company to mine. Although my parents were loving and supportive, but my dad's idea of hilarity was finding Trevor Macdonald sporting a slightly skewed tie while presenting the News at Ten and my mum's sense of adventure limited to trying a pack of ginger nut biscuits instead of the usual digestive for tea. That change in teatime accompaniment was the source of the greatest fight I witnessed my parents ever having. I say fight, it was more of a lingering disagreement.

'So you're saying the problem is *me*,' I conclude from the doctor's words.

'Yes.'

'Right.'

'But that isn't to say that there isn't anything we could do.'

The next few days were a whirlwind of tests, examinations and evaluations. Dr Cousins put me through the paces along with Nurse Tina who I found out was called Nurse Tina Cousins. Seemed that the good doctor was very taken with the new Tina and went in for a little further examination.

Going through another round of surgery, this time being the actual first to undertake it, wasn't as bad as I thought that it would be. In fact, I was eager to go through with it. I couldn't wait. Wherever Dr Cousins wanted to scale back the project, I wanted more and pushed for the latest ideas to be tested on me. As soon as I discovered that my previous deficiencies were eliminated, I searched for anything and everything about myself that I didn't like and persuaded Dr Cousins to improve it or get rid of it.

The new techniques he put me through involved a new type of nano-device, one that housed a powerful computing system that would regulate communication between the various areas of the brain which were used in memories, retention and recalling.

I then underwent a stringent psychological process which made me learn about all of the things that I wanted improved in myself, to be witty and charismatic, happy and magnetic, all around a super-pumped version of myself.

As all of this was happening, the nano-devices were placing these new memories in my long-term memory and cementing them with a natural boost of chemicals to enhance each one, the happy chemicals of the brain: dopamine, seratonin, oxytocin and endorphins.

By the time the entire process was over, I was a completely new man. Able to stop the most random person in the street and have them laughing and in the palm of my hand within sixty seconds, the new devices in my brain eliminating any sort of fear and unease, and then immediately accessing actions, gestures and words for me to completely ingratiate myself with someone. A touch on the arm. A friendly smile. Whispering a naughty joke, the old biddies loved that one.

The next time there was a night out with my colleagues from work was a riotous affair. Completely different from the night out with Jamie when I couldn't hold a conversation longer than a toilet break. Seven of us were attacking the pubs of London one after the other trying to finish the Circle Line game where you start at Liverpool Street and find a pub to have a drink in. Then you jump on the Circle Line on the underground and travel one stop before getting off and finding another pub to have a drink. And you carry on through all of the stops on the Circle

Line until you return back at Liverpool Street. You could walk between stops if it was close enough, or crawl if that was all that was possible.

There are twenty seven stops on the Circle Line pub crawl.

Many have attempted.

No one has made it all of the way around.

I think some us are still unconscious on the train going round and round London.

We did give it a good go though. We decided to go anti-clockwise on the line because we thought it would be funny for some inane reason. Seven lads, all suited and booted, looking the part of idiots thinking that they have come up with a good plan. We did Liverpool Street, Moorgate, and Barbican pretty easily. All drinking pints of Stella except one Guinness drinker who thought it made him a man to sip on the black stuff, as he called it.

Farringdon got a little testy. It was a Friday night so there were other people letting off steam after their work weeks. With that and being a lovely night in the middle of summer, the streets were heaving. There were a couple of lightweights in the group and the forth pint was getting close to the limit. We were at The Castle on Cow Cross Street, an ideal local pub right near the station so that we could easily fall back inside when we were done.

Me and my manager from work, Don, were leading the group. He was an old boy, used to these kinds of nights out but you could see with his huffing that time had not been kind to him. Halfway through his pint, a shiny sheen of sweat had appeared on his forehead which made me a little concerned so I grabbed him and took him outside.

'I need a quick word, boss,' I told him so no one would suspect anything was wrong.

As soon as the cool air of the night hit him, Don became woozy on his unsteady feet.

'Bloody hell, Kewan. I'm getting my arse kicked tonight, fella.' Don lent against the outside wall of the pub, his face turning the shade of sickly green that makes your own stomach flip over.

'Hey. You listen to me boss, you're a champion. You're gonna take a couple of minutes and then we're gonna smash this town to bits. Nothing can stand in your way.'

'Cheers lad. You're a good guy.' Don gave me a couple of friendly taps on the cheek, mafia style, except his eyes were watering too much for him to be part of the underground elite. He held up a finger indicating that he needed a second.

As he lifted his head back up after emptying his guts all over the floor, he smiled at me. 'I'm alright now, let's do this.'

I would have believed him as well if a long, stringy piece of phlegm wasn't dangling from his bottom lip and extending all of the way to the half-digested piece of tomato on the floor. The tomato was part of the vomit that Don had just sprayed out of his mouth, exorcist-style, if that wasn't clear.

'Do not move a muscle,' I said to Don after searching my pockets for a tissue which didn't materialise. 'I'll be right back.'

I had to find something, anything to clean up Don. And quickly too. So I grabbed a magazine from a shelf just inside the main entrance and made my way back outside. The rest of the group were gesturing messages to me using exaggerated hand movements pointing to their wrists and mouthing expletives and leaving instructions. I replied with a complicated mix of palm out front (wait a minute), pointing to me and back to them (I'm coming back), solid point to them and palm out front (you lot stay there), v sign with watch point and point to them (I'll be back in two minutes) and wide scary eyes (do as I fucking say).

The group of five tipsy lads stared back at me with confused looks so I decided to traverse the three metres of distance over to them and explain to them in actual words that I was returning in two minutes, they were to stay there.

Skinny Bob who worked in the admin department assumed the look of someone who was trying to figure out the square root of three to five decimal places as I spoke. I decided to leave him with the others who would hopefully help him as I returned outside to Don and his new tentacled growth.

But as I stepped outside into the cool fresh air, I was taken aback by the sight that greeted me. Don had taken a new lying-down position on the ground with his back to the pub front wall. But the reason for my shock was the person standing over him and rifling through his pockets.

There were a few bystanders staring at what was going on but with no intention whatsoever to get involved probably because the guy doing the law-breaking was not the kind of person that you'd want to get into a confrontation with.

As he stood up holding Don's wallet in his hand, his full form became scarily apparent. It took me what felt like three days to scan this guy from foot to head. I almost ran out of available head tilt to reach the top of his scalp. This guy was a man mountain. I would've needed hiking boots, an oxygen tank and an ice pick just to reach the top of his body. It wasn't only height he had, he had width as well. Muscular width not fatty bulgy width. His shoulders were so straight and broad that builders would use him as a set level for a new bridge over the English Channel. This was no ordinary criminal.

His bald head slightly confused me. It was absent of hair, yet resembled a mahogany golf ball, with so many dips and craters that I'm sure he would be aerodynamically superb if fired out of a cannon. Providing one large enough could be found to house him in the chamber. Normal heads do not come with these odd concave portions. Normal heads come with a smooth even surface that goes from front to back, only the bone of the skull providing a range of curvature. The most likely way to gain these dips in the surface of the skull is to have them applied by kinetic force and baseball bat or some other easy to hold swingable object, like a frozen leg of lamb. It seemed that this fellow with the sticky fingers was not unfamiliar with the rough and tumble of life, especially with a jaw obviously moulded in the hellfire of the netherworld.

Despite the growing number of spectators, the giant piece of muscle took his time checking each and every one of Don's pockets for some more goodies that he could steal along with the wallet. He was most likely after a phone. After the wallet and phone, there isn't much else that the average unconscious man keeps upon his person apart from jewellery and his house keys, and Don wasn't a jewellery kind of person. He found it too flash to flaunt shiny bits of metal to project a higher level of attractiveness, he preferred to do that with a jiggly layer of back fat and increasing the number of chins that he had on display. He took a kick to the stomach for this as the mugger stood up putting away his stolen booty.

'Oi!' The kick to my friend's body jolted me out of the strange trance I was in. Non-violent theft was one thing, but to strike an unarmed and defenceless person was shitty. As past events had shown fairly conclusively, physical violence was not part of my attributes even though receiving it was something that I had experience in. The giant turned and looked at me. Ogreish features eliminating any chance of hope that I would be able to reason with him. I wasn't even able to look at him without knowing I would be having nightmares for the next week of Mondays. His eyes were close together, closer than they should have been for any mammal evolved past primate status, topped with the uni-brow of a Cyclops. But it was the manic grin that was etched onto his face that really made an impression on me. Coupled with a pair of barely there thin lips, parted and showing off a set of gold teeth, most probably made from items stolen from the good people of London and melted down, wedding rings, bracelets, studs from genitalia, it was doubtful that this man was bothered as long as it was valuable.

At my cry, he turned towards me.

'Come and have a go, mate.'

His voice was low and threatening. More threatening than a loud shout could ever have been. His tone was deep, full of bass, but dug itself into my eardrum. A normal viewer would have thought it quite non-aggressive but to my eyes his body of mass and muscle tensed up, readying for explosive action.

I wasn't the fighting type. I was about as dangerous as a slice of grilled mushroom and a soggy newspaper. The most that I had hurt another living creature was when I was five years old and battled our neighbour's cat by spraying him with water from my Super-Soaker 500. I still have the scar above my left eyebrow where he jumped me to the ground and swiped at me before turning and urinating on my shoes. It taught me a valuable lesson.

Do not start a fight with anything or anyone.

But I was different now.

The things which held me back before were all gone. The fear of being hurt. The assumption that I would come off worse. The dillydallying while I wondered what my next move would be.

Without hesitation I took a few quick steps towards my opponent.

His eyes gave him away. They widened with surprise at my action. I knew I had caught him off guard.

My mind and body worked in tandem as I quickly calculated my best route to success.

I went old-school.

I swung my leg as hard as I could at his scrotum area as if I was Tony Adams clearing the ball for Arsenal. Accuracy wasn't even in the equation. It was all about how far I could boot the ball away from its initial position.

I'm sure I did Tony proud as this beast had a

lump in his throat and cried out loud.

As swiftly as I could, I jammed the edge of the rolled up magazine I held in my hand far into his open mouth with my left hand and punched the end with my right. Half of its A4 size disappeared into his mouth and he crumpled to the concrete, the back of his head cracking like an egg. His eyes rolled back in their sockets. They had seen the devil and were afraid to look any more.

He was writhing on the floor with a little too much energy than I'd liked so I grabbed a pen from my inside jacket pocket and stuck it just below his Adam's apple. It pierced the skin with an audible pop, blood spraying into my face.

Music to my ears.

He was down and out.

There were loud sounds around me, a woman screaming, men shouting.

I turned to see the rest of our group tumble out of the pub, shock and confusion etched onto their faces at what had just transpired.

Calmly I reached to pick up Don's wallet which was on the floor next to the victim of my beating. Checked to make sure nothing had been taken. But as I did, I heard a voice, loud and commanding, before strong arms grabbed me from behind.

'Don't move. You're nicked.'

It was true what they say about any publicity

being good publicity. Well, at least in the case of Dr Cousins new surgery it was.

When I was on trial for murder, the media went absolutely mad.

It turned out that I had killed a member of the Brixton Balaclavas, a henchman of one of the bosses of the gang famous for carrying out armed robberies.

When the papers discovered what I had done and the treatment that had empowered me to do so, I was front page news up and down the country. Especially when videos of my previous self were leaked, a shy, fearful individual who got stressed answering a few interview questions. Nobody could believe that I was capable of felling Greg 'Jacknife' Jones, mob enforcer and all round bad-guy. Until, that is they saw the CCTV footage of me killing him in ten seconds and with three moves.

After I had pleaded not-guilty to murder, the subsequent trial was electrifying, judge and jury spun every which way in their opinions. My lawyer's closing defending statement to the jury was especially interesting, a ruffled looking sixty year old by the name of Jerry Richards. He had an Einstein-like persona, frazzled white hair, distinct glasses and unkempt attire. But like Einstein, he was also fiercely intelligent. I was glad to be defended by such a character.

That day, the gallery was packed tighter than a

parliamentary orgy after Election Day.

But the silence was sublime.

'Men and woman of the jury. We have reached this point, the end of the trial, after many weeks of evidence and analysis. I appreciate that you must be eager to find the conclusion so I will be as brief as possible. My client, Mr Kewan Tan, is on trial for the murder of Mr Greg Jones. We have heard much of the character of the deceased, as well as his occupation so I will not dwell on those topics. We have heard much about the circumstances which brought Mr Jones and the defendant together on that fateful evening, so it does not require rehashing. Many witnesses have come forward to give their accounts of that night, before, during and after the incident which saw Mr Jones expire from this existence. All accounts reflect an accurate picture for all of you to examine and interpret together later when you retire to discuss your decision.

'What I want to impress upon you before you do, is the testimony given to this court by Dr John Cousins, founder and creator of The Life Engineering Company. The surgeon responsible for the mental alterations undertaken by the defendant. However, I must clearly state that this is not a buck-passing exercise to absolve my client of guilt. No ma'am. This is an analysis of a procedure which uses technology the likes of which have never been seen before on this planet.

'Dr Cousins has been kind enough to share with this court, with the defendant's agreement of course, confidential material gathered during the various rounds of surgery on Mr Tan, most importantly the video interviews conducted to determine Mr Tan's suitability for the surgery, amongst others from later dates. I want you all to think back to those initial videos of Mr Tan before the surgery. He was a painfully shy, unsure individual, completely scared of the world and hesitant at every step. He was also a very kind, emotional and gentle soul, I am sure you would all agree.

'The man that fought Mr Jones in the altercation was entirely the opposite. Impulsive, brave bordering on stupid, confident, determined and ruthless. This man was not Mr Kewan Tan. The man on trial today is not Mr Kewan Tan. This man is unrecognisable to his parents, his friends and anyone that knew him prior to the surgery. Mr Kewan Tan would not have sought out any kind of confrontation with any persons, his first thought would have been to go to the aid of his manager and friend, Mr Donald Thwait.

'So who is this person on trial today, if not Mr Tan? I hear you ask. This man, my client, is a product of a revolutionary yet inadequately tested technology. A technology which altered the workings of his brain. You see, Mr Tan had found life to be an uncompromising and tough place. A place where the likes of him were stepped on, pushed about and used quite liberally. A person who found the smallest interaction with society to be akin to you or I climbing a mountain. A simple trip to the doctors or even the hairdressers, took momentous planning and preparation, for if something unexpected had occurred, he would fall apart.

'Nobody can blame him for going through with the surgery and no one can blame Dr Cousins for providing a service which was intended for good. However the facts are that without these cerebral implants, we would not be here today.

'I understand that my words sound as if I am after full acquittal for the man before you today. No. That is not my intention. A man has lost his life. Whatever kind of man he was is irrelevant. Whatever the circumstances of the incident were, while not irrelevant, are not as important as the fact that Mr Jones is no longer with us due to a violent reaction.

'What I am asking of you today is to understand that you have in your hands, the ability to pass a historic decision. To progress our species further ahead in civility in the same way that those men and women of yesterday one day decided to stop capital punishment, or to make slavery illegal. You have the chance to set in motion an act which will progress our tired old method of punishment and imprisonment. A progression to benefit all people in our nation.

'With the allowance of the honourable judge presiding today, I can inform you that Mr Kewan Tan has signed a Power of Attorney, giving this court full rights, if you choose to do so, to send Mr Tan for a further surgery to remove all implants that he has received and revert him back to the man who would never have committed this act of violence which led ultimately to a man's death.

'Please think and discuss this matter carefully. This is an option of the ultimate and guaranteed rehabilitation, to produce a character who is known to be as law abiding as any one of us. The alternative being sending a man to prison for a long time with no control over what kind of person will be released back into society, whatever his age. Thank you.'

What an uproar this speech produced across the country. The last time a topic created this much controversy, Bill Clinton was trying to keep a straight face lying to the people of America while Monica Lewinsky was still dry-cleaning his DNA out of her suit jacket. Massive debate began everywhere, even as the jury were locked away to produce their verdict.

Should a court be able to send a person for surgery, even with their permission? Was it fair to allow a person accused of murder an avenue to escape normal punishment? How diminished was the responsibility of someone after brain surgery? How was it different from normal cosmetic surgery and the personality changes effected after a botched boob-job? Should it be up to an inexperienced jury to make this momentous decision or passed over to a higher court?

The questions and angles of the issue were endless. Each newspaper, radio station and news channel had their own position on the issue. It seemed through polls that the public were all for the removal surgery and rehabilitation rather than sole punishment, mainly due to the long list of crimes that Mr Jones was accused of while in the employment of the Brixton Balaclavas. Actually the list of crimes extended to before his membership with the notorious gang and made for quite uncomfortable reading. The spearing of a shop owner in the face with a trident being one of the more aggressively noted crimes. Though his family was crying foul justice from the rooftops, most people were shouting them down fairly conclusively.

However, the jury didn't see it all the same way as the public. Some, but not all.

When the judge was given their verdict after two days of anguished deliberation, even he raised a quizzical eyebrow before speaking.

'Mr Tan. Of the crime of first degree murder, the jury has found you...not guilty. Of the crime of second degree murder, the jury has found you...not guilty. Of the crime of voluntary manslaughter due to diminished responsibility, the jury has found you...guilty. The sentence that you will serve is a custodial sentence of seven years, minimum of three to be served in full, with the strict condition that you return to surgery at the earliest convenience and have all brain implants removed. Upon recovery you are to be placed in a mental institute to carry out your sentence, however you will be under the close supervision of a psychiatrist who will report whether you are able to return back into society at the end of your time served.'

Voluntary manslaughter.

Diminished responsibility.

Removal of the implants.

The jury accepted that I wasn't myself.

But had sentenced me in a way that I could only be released as no one other than myself.

...   ...

So here I am in the hospital where I am to have my surgery.

The guard in the doorway staring at me so intently that he must recognise me or have heard of my past actions. Which is why he is projecting his violent thoughts to me via the subtle medium of expression. Subtle for him, I mean. To me he looks like Jack Nicholson under the instruction to overact in a scene where he sticks his head through a gap in a door.

'Okay, Big John, I'm done. Let's get the hell out of here,' a voice in the hallway calls out.

'Sure thing, boss,' the guard in front of me replies with an unusually soft and high pitched voice. Throwing me a last look of daggers, he turns and heads out into the hall where I catch a glimpse of someone I vaguely recognise…I think it is…no…it couldn't be.

Dr Cousins ambles into the waiting room jotting something on a clipboard as I am reaching for a name in my head.

'So, Mr Tan,' he says after finishing the last of his notes.

'Oh, Kewan, please doctor.'

Dr Cousins laughs heartily. 'Okay sure. I guess we've been through enough together. So. Are you completely aware of what you are here for today?'

'Yes doctor.'

'And you are ready to go ahead?'

'Absolutely. I can't wait.'

'Now just to reiterate the procedure that we are carrying out today. We are re-implanting all of the devices that were taken out by order of the court…is it…Six years ago?'

'Seven actually doctor.' shouts a familiar voice, followed by a familiar yet slightly older looking Tina who pops her head around the corner.

Ever the eavesdropper.

'Thank you, nurse.'

'You're welcome!' she yells again, disappearing in a flash.

'Right then. We are taking care of exactly the same sections, the shyness, pessimism, chronic fear, and adding the characteristics that we removed.'

'Yes.'

Dr Cousins looks at me, creases his brow. 'Are you completely sure, Kewan? You remember what happened last time, don't you?'

'Doctor, I can't carry on living life as this person when I know someone so much better is out there. Since the removal, I have been...uh...I can't explain how much...'

'It's okay, I understand. I have seen many a patient since you last came to us. And I must thank you, as unfortunate as your case was, it sent hundreds of patients to us. We have been backlogged for much of the past decade now.'

'That's great to hear, doctor. I'm pleased for you.'

'And because of that, anything we do for you is on the house. No arguments.'

'Wow...I don't know what...I mean...wow.'

'Enough of that, let's go, shall we?' I follow Dr Cousins as he takes me into his surgery room.

I'm glad that he is treating me for free.

Today is just the beginning.

Printed in Great Britain
by Amazon